THE
FIND

THE
FIND

?

ANNA M HOLMES

The Book Guild Ltd

First published in Great Britain in 2022 by
The Book Guild Ltd
Unit E2 Airfield Business Park,
Harrison Road, Market Harborough,
Leicestershire. LE16 7UL
Tel: 0116 2792299
www.bookguild.co.uk
Email: info@bookguild.co.uk
Twitter: @bookguild

Typeset in 11pt Adobe Jenson Pro

Printed and bound in the UK by TJ Books Ltd, Padstow, Cornwall

ISBN 978 1915352 316

British Library Cataloguing in Publication Data.
A catalogue record for this book is available from the British Library.

For Hubert Kwisthout, whose idea this was

Contents

PART ONE

The Ballybere Man

1	The Bog	3
2	The Reveal	5
3	The Archaeologist	10
4	The Body	22
5	The Journalist	33
6	The Keeper	40
7	The Kingship and Sacrifice Theory	47
8	The Director	59
9	The Ancestor	68
10	The Chair	75

PART TWO

The Truth Seekers

11	The Weight of Blame	83
12	The Civic Angles	94
13	The Ways of Seeing	102
14	The Ripples	116

15	The Harassers	125
16	The Fallout	134
17	The Pathologist	142
18	The Tale	150
19	The Pathologist	152
20	The Fallout	159
21	The Harassers	167
22	The Ripples	175
23	The Ways of Seeing	183
24	The Civic Angles	191
25	The Weight of Blame	198

PART THREE

The Upsurge

26	The Chair	209
27	The Ancestor	217
28	The Director	229
29	The Kingship and Sacrifice Theory	238
30	The Keeper	250
31	The Journalist	257
32	The Body	266
33	The Archaeologist	273
34	The Reveal	283
35	The Bog	296

| *Author's Note and Acknowledgements* | 303 |

PART ONE

The Ballybere Man

.

1

The Bog

THE BOG IS A THING OF FRAGILE BEAUTY. IN SUMMER, brittle-stemmed heathers tipped with delicate flowers clump amidst sedge grasses, lime green springy lichens and sphagnum mosses. Meadow pipits and skylarks feed on insects. Butterflies suck nectar from tiny wildflowers. In autumn, birders might be seen, binoculars raised, looking out along the Shannon Estuary watching flocks of migrating terns or geese, and – as seasons become chillier – whooper swans.

In distant times the ocean (since named after the Greek god Atlas, personified by qualities of endurance) slowly receded. Briny mires filled shallow depressions. Rain fed this fenland of mossy hummocks and hollows. Sparse birches and alders surrounded dark brackish pools. Aquatic grasses and mosses took root, thrived, died, decayed.

Peat formed. Layer upon layer. Pools became shallower, disappeared.

Time passed at Ballybere bog.

A winter wren lands on a stone wall next to a stile, flies to a clump of brown bracken dried and flattened by the season. In the dim February dawn, it sings a cautious song, shakes droplets of rain off feathers, looks about for something nourishing. At the sound of a heavy diesel engine kicking into life, the bird takes flight.

Down the slope, beyond this protected area, the crew starts work.

2

The Reveal

JOE CASSIDY STEPS THROUGH THE DOOR – HASN'T removed his jacket or hat – when he hears, 'Can you grab that?'

Here is the first demand for the day: the phone ringing and Betty, whose job it is to answer it, yacking on her mobile. He mimes a drinking action. She, still talking, walks four paces and flicks on the kettle: 'Get away! Bastard! You shouldn't put up with that…' It's her daughter she's talking to, by the sounds of it.

He answers the office phone: 'Cassidy's.'

'Joe!' Pat's voice. 'Been trying to get hold of you—'

'Ah.' He touches his jacket pocket, annoyed with himself. 'Must've left it—'

'Never mind, never mind. You'd best get down here.'

'What's up?' He glances at the wall clock: not yet eight thirty, and here's a fresh demand.

'Not sure to be honest. That's the thing. Maybe it's nothing, but you'd best get over. We've come to a standstill.' There's an edge to his foreman's voice.

'Not another accident?' His heart contracts. That fella had taken quite a tumble last week, and there's been talk of slack safety regs.

'No, no, nothing like... Look, get on over, that's all I can say.'

'Pat, for feck sake, spit it out. What's—?' But Pat's gone.

Joe watches Betty stirring Nescafe in a chipped mug – two sugars, a dollop of milk – talking non-stop about last night's domestics. He sometimes wonders why he hired her, and each time that thought crosses his mind the answer flies straight back. She's untouchable. That's the thing about family firms and the Cassidys tends to be clannish. He downs his coffee and is back out the door without having spoken a word to his sister-in-law.

Cassidy Construction's office is in an industrial street, next to Kelly Brothers used car dealers, along the road from the petrol station and pub, still, just, in the livelier part of Ballybere, up from the once-busy fishing port. This is a dozy town, even in summer. Tourists might do the Ring of Kerry, drive to Dingle, maybe, or fly into Shannon and head east to Limerick. Not many make it out west to this part of County Clare.

In his battered van, Joe sets off to what locals refer to, without irony, as the quiet end of town. Beyond here is where the council has sold a chunk of land to developers, and Cassidy Construction is subcontracted to do the groundwork. A so-called retail park is planned, though God only knows where they think the footfall will come from. No one he knows has cash to splash. Still, it isn't his business to care about the sums adding up. His job is to get the site drained, cleared, and levelled.

The town is petering out. He drives past the chippy, a laundrette, a grocery store. Ahead he sees diggers and dump truck standing idle, his men having a smoke. Asbestos? Pat would've said; in any case there's nothing hazardous here... Is there?

This had been a raised bog, sloping down towards the coast. The upper part, a haven for botany and botanists, is protected. Down here it is unloved. Not long ago, tinkers left horses to graze at the margin, young folk came to make out away from the gaze of interfering oldies, and youths with dirt bikes tore up the sods. It takes a massive leap to imagine a thriving shopping centre.

'Joe! You took your time.' Pat is tugging at the door handle before he has switched off the engine. 'I had to take away the lads' phones – didn't want them taking photos or gabbing.'

'Feck sake, Pat. You're making me nervous. Sounds like you found a body or something.'

'That's it! That's it exactly. We—'

'Ah, sweet Jesus!'

'Y'can't see much of it, and what we can see is kinda squished, like.' Pat is gabbling faster than usual. 'Ye can spy a bit of leg. Leastways that's what we think it is. And ye know how these bodies look—'

'Can't say I do.'

'No, me neither. Not up close, but on the telly. Ye'll have seen them on the telly.'

'One or two,' he concedes.

Pat leads him past scooped-up metal – a car carcass and old bikes – and on beyond the piled-up rocks from an ancient wall destined for recycling. Elsewhere they've heaped organic waste: so much gorse and spindly bushes. Judging by the neat mounds of peat they are progressing nicely, digging down and levelling the site.

Others have fallen in behind him and Pat.

'It was me that spotted it.' One of the younger lads raises a hand. 'I was just having a fag, like, waiting for Pat to level off that bit. Out of the corner of me eye I thought I spotted somethin'. So here's me leapin' in front of the feckin' digger, scoop raised…' he lifts his arms, claw hands ready to pounce, '…Like in the movies, me—'

'All right. All right.' Joe waves him away.

'There.' Pat points two metres ahead of where the heavy bulldozer scoop rests harmlessly on the ground.

Joe peers, stepping closer, not sure he can see anything. Then within the dark fibrous peaty soil he spots an equally peaty bit emerging. Not big, but different in texture. He steps closer, squelching through the mire hoping his old, cracked work boots keep his socks dry. Later, he will remember how at this moment he had been concerned about starting his working day with wet feet.

'Mind how you go.' Pat holds his arm. 'Don't get too close. Might be a crime scene.'

The lads huddle behind, wittering about knee-capped men and bullets through the head.

He turns on them. 'For Christ's sake, get a grip!' The Troubles are decades past, but every so often a body is recovered. He might worry about that up north, but not here. Ballybere's a peaceful kind of place. A dead-end kind of place. But not *that* kind of dead.

'Still,' Pat says. 'It could be a murder. Y'never know.'

'If it really is a body.' Joe frowns, twisting his head left, then right, not convinced. 'I'll get a wee bit closer. It may be nothing.'

Ignoring Pat's appeal that they should maybe call the Garda, he squats. He is arm's length from this thing, can see where the digger has cut through whatever it is.

'Don't you think it looks like a leg?' the finder of the object asks. 'Pat wouldn't let us touch it.'

Joe's mind churns. If it is a murder victim, recently buried, the police will be closing the site down for a short while. Or

8

God forbid – Joe crosses himself – if it is one of those bog bodies that sometimes turn up, he can kiss goodbye to this contract – at least to any cash flowing in for the coming weeks, even months. Bloody officials will be all over the place. *If* this is a body – and he isn't agreeing to that just yet – he'd prefer it to be a recently deceased poor sod rather than an anciently deceased poor sod. His company will withstand the hit better.

'Don't you think, Joe?'

He looks at the lad wearing a beanie, his nose glowing red in the chill morning. All of them, his gang of men, waiting to be told what to do.

For a moment he wishes the damned lad fancying himself a Hollywood hard man hadn't performed his amateur dramatics in front of the raised scoop, and that Pat's fella in the cab had gone ahead and taken another slice off the peat. Maybe then no one would have noticed until too late. A grunt of amusement escapes as he imagines a sweet little granny opening a bag of garden compost and discovering a toe, or worse.

He stands. 'Pat, call the station, will ye? Best let them know.'

'Right you are.'

He squints at this thing – this disruption – protruding from the ground, wondering how long it will be before he can get his men back to work.

3

The Archaeologist

CARRIE O'NEILL IS SETTLING BACK BEHIND HER COMPUTER after a lunch break, when Liam appears at her door: 'Carrie.'

Her boss, Keeper of Irish Antiquities, is invariably cheerful. Now his bearded pudgy face with round glasses perched on his upturned nose looks more moony than ever, a broad smile stretched across it.

'Put your coat back on. Just had a call from Rachel... Limerick Rachel not Cork Rachael,' he adds hastily.

'Is she okay?'

Carrie is a close friend of Professor Rachel Muloney the pathologist, but isn't a great fan of the other Rachael from University College Cork, who had applied for the same assistant keeper position and had been resentful when 'a frigging Kiwi', as she'd been heard to say, had been appointed.

'Yes, yes, Rachel's fine. Wrap up whatever you're doing. Rachel was called out by the Garda. Human remains have been found in a bog near Ballybere—'

'Where?'

'A small fishing port, Shannon Estuary. Rachel's had a look and says it's one for us.'

On Liam's phone she scrolls through images the pathologist has sent: soggy brown peat; a bit of what looks like bone; workmen standing around in the drizzly day. Not much to see but enough to be tempting.

'Wow. You think...?' What she's thinking is whether there will be a complete body.

'I'd love to go over myself, I'm curious, but I've got a fundraiser dinner tonight. No way can I get out of that. You're on your own. Anyway, this is your turf, not mine.'

Liam is the most generous boss ever. Her beaming face shows what she thinks of this opportunity.

'You'll supervise. Rachel's moving heaven and earth to get things sorted: equipment, permissions and so on. Organising a crew to do the digging and getting a truck ready.'

'Boy, how's that all happened so quickly?'

'The authorities, and the contractor, want the thing gone. Let's see what you bring back.' He rubs his hands. 'And take your wellies, it'll be chucking it down over there.'

'I keep spares in the car.' Countryside walks have taught her that much about this new home of hers.

She grabs her scarf – one of Nan's many hand-knitted affairs. This one, a Christmas present from way back, is a bobbled purple and green combo she had loathed as a teenager but has grown to love. A bit of home. It's hideous, but its distinctive characteristics provide a talking point, even an ice-breaker on first dates. She wraps the monstrosity around her neck and heads out of the museum for the nearby tram that will stop at Ranelagh. Pack, tank the car, then off.

She had fallen on her feet when landing a coveted research role with the Bog Bodies Research Project at the National Museum of Ireland. Her doctoral research at University

College Dublin had been a good fit. Then, some months ago, she had been appointed to one of the assistant keeper posts in the Irish Antiquities Division.

Coming to Ireland had been the best decision ever. *Thanks, Dad, for the Irish passport.* She had spent several summers volunteering with one excavation or another. Being on her knees, trowel, or brush in hand, had connected her to the soil and rocks and the long history of the land, while each advance in technology opened undreamt-of avenues for investigating the past.

It is dark when Carrie arrives at the Ballybere find site. What should have taken three hours took nearly four with slow traffic and roadworks. She spots Rachel, keeping warm in her car, head bent over her phone, soft curls falling over her face. Hearing her tap the window Rachel's face lights up. She is of out the car in seconds, saying, 'Hello, stranger, how're you doing?' before enfolding Carrie in a firm embrace.

A year earlier Rachel had taken pity on 'a Christmas orphan' insisting Carrie join her own family for the festive season. Rachel, fourteen years older, made it clear her door was always open. And Carrie had made the most of this home from home.

'So, tell me, tell me,' Carrie urges.

'I exposed enough of the leg to satisfy myself we're looking at something ancient,' Rachel says. 'It's all covered over again, of course, tightly packed.'

'Great.' Air must be kept out to stop decay setting in.

'And, Carrie,' Rachel grins, 'the feet are missing, but there's a good chance the rest of the body is intact.'

Carrie's eyes pop. 'All right!'

'This way.' Rachel takes her by the elbow.

Before they've gone far, two male police officers stroll towards them and fall into step. She learns they'll be guarding the site overnight. Word has got out and the media and locals have begun nosing around. They chat for a minute, then Carrie holds up her hand. 'It's okay, no need to come.' The uniformed men warn them not to trip then withdraw to where their car is parked.

Beams of torch light play along trodden turf where others have been traipsing. Gumboots – wellies – are a must. Step by step they squelch nearer. 'There.' Rachel spotlights the stretched-out tarpaulin.

Carrie loosens a cord securing a corner of the tarp and peers underneath. Her flashlight plays on the ground beneath. She stoops and touches a piece of claggy peat, feeling its texture. Her fingers itch, and she reaches out again. Rachel's laughter startles her.

'It's not going anywhere. It will be waiting for us in the morning. I don't know about you but I'm ready for a bite to eat. Come on now.'

She grins, patting the peat firmly in place then Rachel passes her a bucket half full of water. Scooping out handfuls she sprinkles it over the peat as caringly as she has watched Nan watering seedlings in her glasshouse.

With the tarpaulin carefully secured, she mutters, 'Till tomorrow.'

At daybreak she is back, getting a feel for the environs, thinking about logistics. Soon more vehicles arrive: Rachel, trailed by cars dropping off volunteers, and a trades van is pulling up. She hurries to the designated car park well away from where they'll be working. Young adults pile out – archaeology students from University of Limerick that Rachel has organised – all kitted out in waterproofs and wellies.

'Hi, guys. Welcome!' Her gesture takes in the muddy construction site, heavily rutted from bulldozer treads and truck tyres, a portable toilet off to the side. It looks unpromising. And yet… 'I'm Carrie O'Neill, thanks for coming to help. We really appreciate it.' She eyes one woman wearing a light showerproof jacket and short insubstantial wellies, wondering if she'll last the day. Time will tell. As project leader she will be guiding this group, ensuring they follow instructions and the excavation is carried out professionally, but she also wants them to remember today as a fun day. 'Hope you've plenty of food and hot drinks with you. Best leave it all in the van – in fact anything that needs to stay dry.' Her eyes are on the back of the van, where doors are being opened. 'Okay, let's get this stuff over there.'

She points to where she wants the wheelbarrows, spades, buckets, measuring rods, planks and other equipment taken.

On previous digs she and other archaeologists worked carefully with trowels, stiff bristle brushes, and smaller soft-bristled ones. Those digs might last weeks or months. Then they had been dealing with hard surfaces – stones or bones. This is different. Here they are dealing with waterlogged squidgy peat and an equally waterlogged mummified corpse. She aims to extract the find in one day.

As the tarp is peeled back, she leans forward, inhaling the rich peaty smell. A shiver touches her skin – excitement, but also the dampness of an Irish winter seeping into her bones. Here it is nothing like the dry sharp winters of her childhood, but she's not complaining. This wet climate is perfect for preserving bodies: raised peat bogs particularly, with organic acids in decaying plants mummifying human remains.

It will be a blessing if they find this body intact. She looks at the bulldozer parked off to the side. Unlike the old days of peat-cutting by hand using spades, a heavy industrial scoop like this one usually causes damage before anyone notices an irregularity. And this had been a bog-standard – *forgive the pun*, she thinks – clearance job on a bog-standard construction project. No workman would be expecting to encounter such a thing. A pity the feet have been ripped off, but the rest of the body might be intact. She can barely contain her curiosity, but this must wait. Today they will dig broad trenches around the find, then lift a block out without disturbing what is within.

Methodically they measure, record with notebooks and cameras, take soil monoliths extracting cores of peat from either side of where the body lies.

Beyond the taped-off cordon, curious faces watch for a while before moving on: two police on duty, a journalist – she thinks – taking photos, an older couple walking their dog. The construction boss she has been introduced to has been back and forth, now here he is again clutching a woollen hat in both hands.

She rests her elbows on her spade. 'Mr Cassidy, you look like you're at a funeral.'

'If you say so, Doctor O'Neill—'

'Carrie, please.'

'Right you are, and I'll answer to Joe. But it's not so much this one's funeral I'm thinking of ' – he stares at where they're digging – 'as much as my own. I want to put my men back to work.'

'We can't rush these things.'

She hides a grin; poor Joe, but she is luxuriating in this discovery and recovery. Up till now the bodies she has worked on have been freeze-dried and compromised in one way or another. She has examined preserved Irish bog bodies, well-known ones on display at her museum, and others they have in storage. And she's made numerous trips to museums in Denmark, Germany, and Holland, but other academics and scientists have breathed over those bodies. This one is *hers*. By some miracle of fate, she is coordinating this extraction and she intends to savour every moment. She doesn't like to remind Joe that if this turns out to be from the medieval period, or, rarer still, an Iron Age body, and they find artefacts of interest, then it will be tools down for Cassidy Construction and the whole retail park development for some time.

She squints at Joe. 'Are you sure your men have dug down two metres? Are we that far?'

Joe nods. 'Pat reckons so.' He raises an arm, as if imagining how the land had sloped before they got to work levelling the site. 'I'd say that two metres has to be right.'

Her eyes follow his to a tempting mound of peat waiting to be loaded onto dump trucks bound for the processing factory. She's thinking about those missing feet.

'You think we might dig in there?'

'Are you tryin' to close my business down altogether? Someone from the National Museum gets buried in a pile of this shite while looking for bits of body. No, Doctor O'Neill – Carrie – ye can't go searchin'!'

Joe is muttering something as he stalks off.

Two metres below current ground level. Old, but how old? This may prove to be a previously unknown site associated with early Celtic activity. And the body they are digging out could be part of some sort of ritual: a sacrificial victim or a warrior laid out. *Wow.* She looks at Joe's retreating back. Archaeologists and historians will be all over this site like a bad rash.

'Carrie!' Her attention is drawn to where Rachel has her arm linked through the elbow of a young freckly faced guy peering from under his rain jacket hood. 'Cillian wants a scoop – the story variety.'

The new arrival holds a notepad and phone and has a digital camera slung around his neck. 'Cillian Muloney, *Limerick Leader*… My aunt, Rachel.'

Rachel grins. 'We Muloneys get the best jobs out west, digging up the dirt... Listen, we need better control.' She heads to where the local police are ineffectually turning away curious locals, leaving Carrie to get acquainted with the regional reporter.

'This is big news for us,' Cillian says. 'Spare a minute for me?'

'Sure.' She doesn't really have time, but interruptions are inevitable.

'Makes a change from covering court cases – stabbings and burglaries and so on.' He holds out his phone. 'I've got Joe Cassidy's angle and Auntie Rach has told me some. What can you add?' He presses record.

'Right now, you know as much as I do.'

'But it's *potentially* exciting, isn't it?'

'Oh yes! Rachel has declared it ancient, but we just don't know *how* ancient. So, watch this space! I suggest you keep yourself in your aunt's good books. She wants to keep abreast of things once we've taken the body away. Today, I'd say focus on recording us excavating. Not much more of a story yet, except poor Joe Cassidy's fretting about wasted time.'

RTÉ arrives next and the TV interviewer fixates on the fact Carrie isn't from these parts. The journalist wants to make a thing of it, saying, 'Surely we have our own experts?' so Carrie defers to Rachel, who can be relied on to soften things. Rachel's good at that, her lilting voice so different from Carrie's flat Kiwi tones. But fair play to Rachel, who defers back for confirmation. 'Don't you agree, *Doctor* O'Neill?' And Carrie nods, adds some detail, and passes back to '*Professor* Muloney'. The two of them carry on a double act, enjoying the game. She hopes that Liam, or the museum's senior management, won't share the TV journalist's narrow-minded view. She raises her booted foot to rest on the step of the spade and adds her weight. This project is hers.

The trenches deepen.

Later, her ears prick up hearing an *Irish Examiner* reporter interviewing Joe.

'Mr Cassidy, I understand the council were warned about this. I recall there was some controversy about anything being built here at all.'

She watches Joe shift uneasily from foot to foot. 'Ah, well. Ye'd best ask someone from the council. All I know is that there was some talk. Old stories – ghosts and goblins, that sort of thing – and a few of the locals made a fuss. That's why there was a hold-up before we got started.'

So! Carrie's heart quickens. What might this mean?

After a quick lunch they work on. Near where they might expect to locate a head, she carefully probes the peat, Rachel at her side. Feeling resistance, she stops. She and Rachel share a look. *Yes!* 'Hey, guys!' she calls her muddied volunteers to a halt. 'We have the head, I'm sure of it!' This news is greeted by celebratory leaps in the air, high-fives, and whoops. Immediately she re-packs sodden peat in the hole she has created.

It takes the rest of day to carefully dig drains around the peat-enclosed body then slide a wooden plank underneath. Swathed in water-soaked foam and wrapped in heavy plastic, their secure parcel is ready to be removed like a soft block of marble in a quarry. Back at the museum she and her team will be the sculptors revealing the form within, just as Michelangelo revealed his David. Fanciful, perhaps, but it is sort of like that.

It takes heft to lift. The whole team working together then she forms part of a weird funeral procession straining to carry their precious parcel on to a waiting flat-top truck. It is to be taken to Dublin while she stays with her team of volunteers to continue excavating the site. Liam has promised, 'word of honour', their conservation team won't start work on the body till she is back.

Cillian nudges her. 'This would make a great story, wouldn't it? "Truck hijacked with block of peat and body inside." Something for our local court hearings.'

'Please!' Carrie holds up her hands in mock alarm. But it *is* an alarming thought. Word is out that a body has been found and there are idiots out there who might chance it. The truck sets off, red tail lights glowing in the dark on an otherwise deserted road. She can hardly wait to get back to Dublin herself. How much of the body have they got?

'Carrie, are you coming with me?' Rachel touches her sleeve. 'Dan's cooking. He's expecting you.'

Carrie hesitates. If she accepts the offer of dinner and an overnight stay with Rachel and her family, she will need to start early to get back on site tomorrow. She hadn't slept much last night anticipating the dig. Nor the night before. She needs to get a grip on mid-week pub nights. These Irish are a social bunch, and so is she. Easy to say, 'Yep, why not?' to another round. On coming to live in Dublin she'd been surprised how many still went in for liquid lunches. She drew the line at that.

'Thank Dan and say hi to the others for me. I'll stick with where I'm staying. It's close.' She hugs Rachel, promising to speak tomorrow.

At her old Toyota she peels off her filthy jacket, heels off her wellies and bangs them together to remove clumps of muck, and throws them into the boot. After a shower and change she will make use of the guesthouse WiFi, planning to catch her parents before milking time.

Remembering how nervous she had been leaving New Zealand, aged twenty-two, makes her smile. Seven years later she is still on her Overseas Experience – her OE – without any plans to go 'home'. She had been bowled over by the richness of Ireland's past – history and folklore – and now with this find, she will be here for some time yet.

'Hi, dear!' Dad's voice comes through loud and clear. 'What's cooking? Wait... I'll put you on speaker.'

'Is that Caroline?' Mum in the background. Dad switches to visual and there they are: weather-wrinkled faces, wearing open-zipped fleece jackets, shorts, feet enclosed in woollen socks ready to thrust into gumboots outside the back door where the dog bowls will be.

'Hey, guess what? I'm hoping I've a new fella in my life.' She leaves a dramatic pause. 'In which case he might even make the news out there.'

'How come? A film star or something? Or is it because some fella's willing to hook up with you? Didn't know that was newsworthy?'

'Yeah, ha ha, Dad.'

'Caroline? What is it?' Mum's voice is crisp. She wants to know her news yet wants to get on with her day. Carrie knows this tone and sees a crease forming between her eyes.

'I've been excavating a bog body. Ta dah!' A grin splits her face.

She tells them what's been happening, says to look up the location, promises to keep them informed, then before long asks, 'And how's Nan?' Nan deals with email but has a mental block about being able to talk 'for free' on internet platforms. Nan is fine, she learns.

'Carrie. Send photos through when you've something to show us.'

'Will do!'

'Before you go...' Dad walks out to the deck and whistles.

On seeing brilliant blue sky, she says, 'Ah, beaut day.'

At another whistle there is a sound of barks and skittering claws. Moments later Blue's lolling tongue fills the screen, and she is screaming, 'Who's a beautiful boy! Missing my boy!' leaping up and down, setting Blue off, barking madly. Blue is the best trained border collie ever. Seeing them all she feels a powerful tug at her heart.

Carrie has one foot in the land where she was born and bred and the other in the land of her ancestors where she lives now. Analysis of ancient bones, teeth and mummified skin testify that people have travelled across continents from time immemorial. Some of her distant forebears, O'Neills from centuries earlier, had certainly done so. For sure, some will have sailed to settle America to escape famine or a myriad of hardships, and as Australia and New Zealand sought to populate their lands, white English-speaking migrants were welcomed. Her great-grandfather emigrated to Otago tempted by opportunities to farm on a scale impossible in Ireland. And now she has journeyed back, travelling from southern seas to the north.

Past and present shape the contours of who she is.

4

The Body

THE BODY, ENCASED IN PEAT, RESTS WITHIN A SHALLOW tray on a table in their prep room.

Carrie slips a plastic apron over her head, ties it around her waist and wiggles her fingers into latex gloves. She, along with technicians from their conservation team, are ready. And Liam, who is determined not to miss this chance to get his hands grubby. Time to unpack this squidgy gift the bog has given them and find out what they have. The radiographs they have taken look promising, but through the dense peat the body lacks clarity.

She is at the modern red-brick conservation block near the imposing stone formality of the Collins Barracks where museum director Mike Curtis has his office. He is here now, observing them start, and will be 'popping over from time to time'.

Revealing the body is to be live streamed via the museum's website. 'A unique opportunity for us to involve the public,' Mike had insisted. 'Everyone in the Learning Department's been cramming.'

Carrie smiles. Earlier she had been waylaid by a panicking member of that team preparing to field questions from the public – 'in real time!' the woman had squeaked. 'Google,' Carrie advised. 'Have your phone handy. You'll be fine.'

Mike is always a step ahead of everyone else where publicity is concerned. Not long before Carrie joined the museum, Mike had been appointed director. He had come from a major art gallery in England – an architectural prizewinner, all light, sharp angles and sleek lines – to their solid stone edifices from a previous era. Mike is a moderniser, a man with big ideas.

Carrie clocks Mike draping a trendy linen suit in a plastic cover over a chair at the edge of the room in case the suit he is wearing becomes smeared – as it is bound to if he gets close. The media have been promised regular updates and he 'just might have to do an interview for the evening news,' he says. Judging by his hair, fashionably thick on top and close at the sides, he has found time for a trim. And his square-framed glasses, one of many pairs, contrast with Liam's wonky metal frames, his only ones.

A cameraman fiddles with the angle of a videocam he has fixed to a tall tripod for a wide-angle shot, then he slings a stills camera around his neck and picks up a portable camcorder. 'I'm good to go.'

She bounces on the balls of her feet, impatient to get started.

'A Team Museum photo, before we start. Shall we?' Mike, always so urbane, beckons them closer. They bunch up around the table that holds the soon-to-be-excavated find and grin towards the camera. Then the cameraman gets a close shot of the solid-looking glistening lump of peat. Carrie's thoughts shift to friends and family in New Zealand. She must remember to post something on social media with a link to the museum's live streaming, saying, 'Hey, check this out!' Some might look, then repost images and tag her. 'Yeah, publicity's good.'

'Publicity's *very* good.' Liam's eyes suggest cogs in his mind are whirling. They are all ambitious for their revered institution.

To the watching world, Mike introduces Team Museum and the peaty pile, explaining briefly where and how it was found.

First the upper body, starting at the head end.

With a wooden spatula, Carrie begins easing away the loose packing peat, then with fingers, and a smaller spatula, picks away at the claggy peat close to the body. Samples of this stratified peat are zipped into plastic bags and labelled. These will tell stories of the immediate environment – pollens, seeds, beetles – and the peat will be carbon-dated.

Beneath her hands a patch of waterlogged leathery skin appears. 'We have got a head here!' Delicately she scoops away peat until the left side of a skull is exposed. There's a distinct odour now, something that has been absent from preserved bog bodies she has examined. She inhales the musty smell. This flesh has not experienced air, for however long. Flakes of peaty fibres are caught in the creases of an ear. Her pulse races. *Beautiful!* The camera operator moves in for a close shot.

She explores further, delicately scraping, allowing a lab assistant to spray distilled water to clean and hydrate, using a dental vacuum extractor to suck up excess water. At a cheek, she feels threads of gingery beard hair starting up from pores of skin.

'It's a boy! Or rather, a mature male as he has a beard.' Laughing, she touches his forehead. 'We name you Ballybere Man.'

They repeat, 'Ballybere Man,' and raise imaginary glasses to toast the new arrival. Previously it had been agreed that this find would take the name of the town followed by Man, Woman, Girl, or Boy depending on sex and age.

She works steadily, only occasionally straightening, easing her back. Across from her a colleague is cleaning Ballybere Man's matted muddied hair.

So often these bog bodies are incomplete or crushed, needing all the skill of interpreters and model makers to recreate drawings and lifelike models of what they would have looked like. Only then might museum visitors feel they are meeting a real man, or woman, or child. This one is different. His skull is slightly squished and distorted by the weight of peat building up over the centuries – that is to be expected – but other than that, he is remarkably well preserved. She stands back admiring the revealed head. *Awesome.* It needs little imagination to see the man he had been, with shoulder-length flaming hair, splayed out in felted-up soggy bunches looking like Rastafarian dreadlocks.

Liam explains to the online watching public: 'His skin's this colour, rather like a chestnut, because of the acids in the peat. And his hair is this brilliant orange because of the chemicals in sphagnum moss. He didn't look like this when he was alive.'

Mike speaks softly close to her ear: 'We've a winner here.'

Is Mike already planning how Ballybere Man might be displayed, imagining what this might mean for the museum. And behind thick lenses Liam's eyes are owl-like, glasses sliding down his nose. Research grants. No doubt this is going through his mind. And hers. Which of the international collaborative interdisciplinary research funds might offer the best option? She foresees weeks and weeks of work ahead putting partnerships and applications together. Already emails are flooding in with requests from academics and scientists around the world, keen to be kept in the loop.

A sterile plastic sample bag is opened for her. Carrie snips a single strand of orange hair, drops it in, speaking to camera as she works.

Carrie lowers her face mask. 'You'd be surprised how much we'll learn from this tiny sample.' She keeps her voice bright, imagining she is describing something to one person – Nan, she decides – rather than the invisible amorphous masses who are tuned in. 'This precious hair will be sent to University College Cork. They've got special testing equipment we don't have here.' The sample bag is zipped tight and labelled. 'You know, our bones, teeth and hair all have stories to tell.' She gives a wide, toothy grin. 'My teeth enamel will show I grew up far away in South Island, New Zealand, whereas this' – she flicks her tied-back hair with the back of a hand – 'holds its own story. It will tell us I've been living in Dublin in recent years.'

By the look of Mike's face, he is clearly loving being here, and is in no rush to leave. 'Amazing,' he says. 'So if we get a good sample of this fellow's teeth enamel, it will tell us where he was born?'

'Yes,' Liam joins in. 'As Doctor O'Neill said, this hair sample will give us a month-by-month record leading to his death. If he lived near Ballybere, we'll know, or if he travelled from elsewhere in Ireland – maybe even thirty miles away – we'll learn that too. It's called Strontium Isotope Analysis. The teeth enamel will tell us the kind of diet he had as a child, and you can use hair to look at recent diet. Investigating the carbon and nitrogen isotope ratios allows us to reconstruct past and present diet.' Liam nudges his glasses up his nose and continues in the kind of tone Carrie imagines he used when lecturing. 'It's a remarkable thing that we can track so much about a person's environment from tiny samples because the amount of strontium found in the geology differs in each part of the world. It is highly specific. You might be surprised how localised—'

'Super. Fascinating.' Mike butts in. 'I wonder if we might get a close-up of the sample. And let's get a close-up of the head.'

'A moment.' She wants her man looking his best.

With a soft-bristled brush, she delicately cleans strands of peat caught in the creases of his mouth. These lips might not be able to talk, but his body will speak to her. She will learn about him as surely as a portrait artist might study a subject sitting the far side of an easel.

Soon Mike leaves, saying he'll drop by tomorrow.

Carrie picks up her spatula and continues.

An outline of a shoulder: sloping, narrower now the framework of shoulder girdle has been compressed. Upper chest: slightly caved. With deliberate movements Carrie chips away sticky gloop from under an armpit; a gentle hiss of water passes close to her ear as a lab assistant sprays the newly exposed skin. Gently she rubs the burnished surface and brings her face low, fingers going back and forth across a small patch of skin over his ribs. With an index finger she follows tiny grooves in the skin under the posterior still hidden in a bed of peat.

'Liam. I'm not sure if I'm feeling folds in the skin or if these are welts. There are small ridges.'

'Let's see.' Liam walks around to her side and brings a magnifying glass close. 'Difficult to say. This will have to wait till we turn him over.'

She glances at the clock and shares a look with a conservator. They have worked for their allotted three hours, and it is time to cover Ballybere Man in clingfilm and return him to his purpose-built coffin cooler.

Liam stands – arched back, elbows out, portly stomach stretching the plastic apron – and faces the camera. 'We're going to leave it here for today and look forward to welcoming you tomorrow. Doctor O'Neill and I are heading to our office to look at your questions.' He glances wearily at her.

'Can't wait!' She bounces up and down. 'We've got a number of secondary schools with us this afternoon. Remember, we want to receive your artwork. I want to print out some to decorate my office.'

She will be staying late, releasing Liam. His life is complicated, and he will be needed at home.

The following day Carrie excavates nooks and crannies in the creases of an elbow, between the ulna and radius, then works around a wrist, cameras recording and relaying their progress to the wider world.

'Liam. There's a lesion here.' Water squirts away sticky peat. 'Yes, see, the edges… the skin's been pierced.' Together they examine the cleaned leathery skin. There is a hole in the gap where the small wrist bones meet the radius and ulna, the forearm bones. Not a massive gash, but a trauma caused by something sharp. She glances at Liam. 'Peri-mortem?'

'Carrie?' She has been so absorbed she hasn't noticed Mike has joined them. He indicates the ever-present camera. 'Would you care to explain?'

'Of course.' She straightens and removes her mask. She and Liam tend to forget the watching public and their co-workers in the Learning Department who are busy demystifying, explaining jargon and answering questions popping up on the screen from the watching audience.

'The thing is, some bog bodies show they've been injured – maybe broken bones – but the bones have had time to heal before death. Ante-mortem. Others show violent things have taken place about the time of death. Peri-mortem. Take Grauballe Man, a body unearthed in Denmark. He'd taken a real bashing. His skull had been fractured and one of his leg bones.'

'Nasty!' Mike is feeding her.

'And some bodies show defence wounds. There's a gash on one of Oldcroghan Man's arms – we have him in our museum here – where he had warded off a knife attack.' She raises an arm, elbow bent. 'But his assailant scored a hit on his chest. Again, peri-mortem.'

'So,' Carrie continues, 'is this wound we see here a cause of death, or has the skin been pierced after death—?'

'Post-mortem,' Mike jumps in. 'I've seen enough police procedural TV series to know what those are.'

'Absolutely.' Liam joins the conversation. 'And you know, many of these bodies were mutilated at the time of death, or just after.'

'And some wounds are most certainly post-mortem.' Carrie touches the wrist wound. 'A stake might have caused this.'

'Stakes! Sounds like vampire territory!' Mike chuckles and faces the camera. Carrie wonders how much other work the museum's director is doing as he spends so many hours with them enjoying his role 'being Joe Public', as he puts it. It hasn't passed her by that more and more he is asking *her* to be the one to explain something. Liam isn't great on camera – she had watched yesterday's recordings, her suspicions confirmed. He, an older tubby male, came across as being ponderous, fusty and professor-ish, whereas she, young and female – and yes, she'd watched herself too – came across as breezy and fresh-faced. That morning, Carrie had found herself taking more interest in her grooming – washing and blow-drying her shoulder-length hair before tying it back, so it was practical but attractive. And while she usually spent one minute doing her face before heading out the door, having watched herself on screen she had decided a bit more eyeshadow and mascara wouldn't go amiss. Hypocrite! Hadn't she inwardly scoffed at Mike's little vanities, and now here she was doing the same.

Within a short time, Liam, working on the far side of the body, has reached the other wrist. 'Ah, good. As I suspected, a wound here too.' He invites Carrie to his side.

'A stake is the likely explanation,' she bends over with a magnifying glass, 'but I can't see remnants of wood or twisted willows, and the entry wound's quite small.'

She stands back, allowing the camera in for a close shot. 'Sometimes withies – very tough narrow hazel or willow branches – were twisted tightly together and used to secure bodies by piercing wrists or ankles. Or elbows. Oldcroghan Man had braided hazel withies forced between the muscles of his upper arms to pin him down. It's possible that there had been something binding Ballybere Man's chest or across his neck, secured either side, but the fabric has since rotted, leaving no evidence.'

'Ooh.' Mike flinches. 'Sounds nasty, but he would have been dead by then, poor chap.'

'Yes. This might be the case here.' Liam gestures to the yet-to-be uncovered parts of the body. 'We might find evidence of stakes being used under his knees. Imagine, if a body wasn't secured in his watery grave some poor wretch would have the fright of their lives seeing it pop up!'

The cameraman gets the giggles then Liam continues. 'But there are other possibilities, as Carrie explained the other day. This trauma might not be post-mortem. Might not be caused by a stake hammered through to secure a dead man. It's possible this was a violent ante-mortem injury—'

'Before death, I believe,' Mike clarifies.

'But that would be unusual,' Liam says.

Unusual, yes. Keep investigating…

Using a small wooden probe, she begins examining a hand and fingers. 'See how smooth the edges of the nails are, and around the nail bed. We often find these bog bodies have been men of status, not doing manual labour. This seems to be the case here.'

Through a magnifying glass Carrie examines the whorls

on a fingertip, as clear now as they had been when this man lived. She and the team 'ooh' and 'aah', before enabling the camera operator to get close-ups, then Mike excuses himself.

Later, she delicately cleans tanned, spongy, leathery skin around the indent of a navel where the umbilical cord connected to his mother in the womb. Tender feelings tug. She pulls away, surprised. She is a scientist. Stupid to allow these flights of fancy to take hold. While continuing to clean the abdomen, she pauses. There is a small incision to the side of the navel. Her fingers trace the clean edge of the cut. *Unusual.* They note it, record it, then move on.

At his groin now, withered genitals exposed: penis and scrotum shrunken and wrinkled. Nothing is left to the imagination. She sucks her teeth, hoping no school kid artist sends her a charcoal drawing of these private parts. Whatever fabric might have covered this body has long since rotted away. Not a stitch of wool or linen has survived. The cameras mercilessly record the evidence laid bare on the slab.

Next morning, on the tram to Collins Barracks, Carrie flicks through online media stories. The tabloids focus on a celebrity footballer sex scandal, a domestic murder, racing results, controversy over viewer votes on a popular TV show. She searches the *Irish Times* and finds it has an article and photo of Ballybere Man's head. *Her* man. Someone called Finn Durante wrote this. He's been keeping up with the online streaming, pretty much repeating what she, or Liam, or Mike have said. And he's gone into some details about the museum needing to expand their exhibition space. Huh! He knows more than she does. Clearly Mike has been outlining his vision. She feels a pang of jealousy and determines to speak with Liam. She needs to be in on this.

In the prep room, with Liam working opposite, she continues the messy work of releasing Ballybere Man from his miry casing. She traces where a femur connects with the pelvis and downward. His knees are slightly bent, one resting on the other still partly covered in claggy peat.

'It's such a pity we haven't got the feet,' she says to those watching. 'We excavated all around the body but couldn't find anything. I know some of you have been asking. It's possible they will turn up, but we shouldn't be too hopeful.' *If only she'd been allowed to dig in that pile of peat!*

By the end of the cleaning session, Ballybere Man's anterior is damp and gleaming. Carrie steps back to admire him.

This man had not drunkenly stumbled into a murky bog one dark night. He had been carefully arranged: laid on his back, head slightly angled to his right, arms to his side. An overwhelming sense of pride and tenderness fills her. Within weeks and months tests will reveal more and with each piece of evidence, a picture will form of the man and the world he inhabited. *Patience!*

As she helps swathe him in plastic wrap, work for the day done, she reflects on how he had lain peacefully in his watery grave, then over time, marshy lake plants and sphagnum mosses had died, leaving him to settle deeper and deeper under waterlogged soils. Acidy peat preserved him till Joe Cassidy's digger discovered him, allowing *her* to dig him out.

A smile of contentment spreads. She wouldn't swap jobs with anyone and will fiercely guard her position as Ballybere Man's guardian. Her man. Her find.

5

The Journalist

FINN DURANTE IS AT THE NEWSPAPER KIOSK HE passes every morning on the way to work. A skanky red-top he picks up is leading with a ludicrous story: a close-up of the bog body's face, headlined MURKY MURDER MYSTERY. Now he will be under pressure to follow up. The other day he had waved away the news desk editor, saying, 'Sure, I'm on the case,' before skimming through enough of the museum's live streaming to write something half-intelligent. Now his editor will think he hasn't been diligent, and that there is more of a story here.

Why didn't the tabloids pay attention to those who were dying now? Sure, they did, in their own way, if it suited their purpose: a murder with plenty of blood and gore and high drama was fine, but not the everyday sort of death that smacks of poverty.

The previous week he had written a solid story about homeless deaths. *Those* lives mattered. Seven men and women, all rough sleepers, had died unloved and uncared for on Dublin's streets. Now *that* was tragic. Impossible to ignore the scale of destitution. In his article he had ripped into the authorities, highlighting the loss of public funding, etcetera… Now he is working on a longer piece. He had a graph charting the decline in spending on mental health year on year, had interviewed the head of a homeless charity, and was chasing up the ever-elusive head of department from the council. Once he has nailed that interview, it will make a great piece for the Saturday edition.

While waiting for the traffic lights to change, a Dashboard Confessional favourite blasting through earbuds, he reads the tabloid story. Lazy. So frigging lazy. Any journo worth their salt would never write anything so bad. 'Was this a victim of the Troubles who had disappeared forty years back?' Idiots! This body is much older. Then there is speculation as to whether some long-forgotten peasant had done him in and covered his tracks by dumping him in a bog.

Finn bins the paper, stuffs his hands in his pockets and strides on.

The glass-fronted *Irish Times* building never fails to give him a thrill. Moving from his hometown of Cork's newspaper was a big deal. He had managed this soon after the *Times* had bought the ailing publication. The writing was on the wall for so many regional newspapers with circulation dropping year on year. *Take me on staff*, he had longed to yell to the bosses in Dublin, working his butt off to prove his worth. And they had taken him on. And he was – *is* – grateful.

'Finn!'

Damn! He's not managed to sneak in unnoticed, and wouldn't you know it, the news editor, a guy who's been in that job for years, is waving that effing tabloid front page.

'Morning, Finn. How about heading over to the museum when you've time—'

'Morning. I'll phone them.'

'How about going in person? See if you can get sight of the remains. Take some photos and get someone who knows what they're doing to give you an update – preferably not someone from reception.'

'You know that's all bollocks, right?'

'Course it is. Even so. People like mysteries. Let's get a fix on this.'

'Sure. When I've done—'

'Today. File something before I head home.'

After a quick update story on last night's council planning committee rejection of a controversial development, Finn logs into the museum's livestream to see where they'd got to. He can't see much from the long shot, just the backs of people bending over the body, all of them kitted out in aprons, masks, and gloves as if they are in an operating theatre. He catches a glimpse of the crinkly thing on the table, then the mobile camera guy obscures his view. *Out of the way, ya langer!* All right! Whoever is editing the streaming has cut to a close-up. He squints, realising he can't make head nor tail of what he is seeing. He watches a while longer and figures they are working on the back of the body.

He looks up the museum's staff list, reminding himself of the director's name: Mike Curtis. May as well go for the main man.

'Mr Curtis has a full schedule today,' he is told when he requests an interview. 'We're directing all media enquiries to our marketing team.' But when he is through to that department, he is told, 'My colleague who knows about this project is not at her desk right now. Can she get back to you?'

'Yes... No... It's okay, I'll drop by.'

'I wouldn't waste your time coming over. You'll not be allowed in the lab.'

Even so, he decides he should head over to Collins Barracks as this is where it's all happening. Later. He'll go later. No rush. It's half past two when he grabs a bite from the deli across the road, sticks his earbuds in, selects a My Chemical Romance track and sets off.

At four o'clock he's still at the museum. Bloody waste of good time! The woman from marketing had known sod all about the project so has now gone to fetch someone from the Learning Department.

'Mr Durante?' Finn watches a woman bustle forth buttoning her cardigan. He learns she's been one of those fielding questions from teachers and kids during the live streaming, but it soon becomes evident her knowledge is second-hand:

'I believe that…' 'I'm led to understand…' 'I'm not sure when the isotope analysis will be done.' 'Good question! I'll find out and get back to you.'

'May I talk with Liam Harte?' Finn has checked the name of the Keeper of Antiquities.

'Unlikely.' Cardigan woman shakes her head. 'He'll be back in his own office – at the Archaeological Museum.'

'What about a photo or two?' No harm in asking. 'Can you let me in?'

'Not a chance!' A delighted laugh. 'Marketing can provide you with video and images. They've quite a collection for the media.'

'Is there anyone who *can* talk with me?' He sounds a little desperate.

'You poor thing! Let's see if I can find someone who knows what they're talking about! You need some quality time.' She laughs, turns away, then calls back. 'Photos?'

'Please. The best you've got.'

She waves his business card he'd given her. 'I'll email something to you shortly. That much I can do. Give me a shout if I can do anything else for you.'

Nearly five o'clock and he is still waiting for the promised quality time. He will hang around and maybe catch Mike Curtis, if he's lucky.

But it is Doctor O'Neill he finds himself talking to.

It is her lace-up red ankle boots he spots first as she strides towards him. Cool. She offers a wholesome grin as well as her outstretched hand. 'Carrie O'Neill. How can I help you?'

'Finn Durante, *Irish Times*.'

He looks directly into her eyes. She is his height, made taller by those chunky heels, and looks about his age. He's seen her kitted out in lab gear, and now here she is bundled up in a thick jacket, tucking strands of hair inside a hat. And that accent…

'Australian?'

'No way!' She hoots. 'New Zealand through and through.'

Finn knew already. He'd checked her profile on the museum's website. He is winding her up by way of an opener, knowing something of the rivalry between those two nations.

He appraises her. Yeah, farm-grown, that's how she looks, while he is still a skinny city emo boy at heart, though has tidied his look somewhat since his school and student days. He'd always looked the part, never having to dye his hair to achieve the raven-black look. This he has from his Italian father, while his pale skin is from his Irish mother. He used to peer out at the world from under a long fringe, but these days his floppy hair barely brushes eyes no longer outlined with kohl. That was not the look for the *Irish Times*, for all that their journos were not stuffy types. Today he is wearing skinny jeans and a contemporary-styled tweed jacket, a look that suits his whippet frame.

'What can you tell me, Carrie? Any interesting new angle that is halfway intelligent would be a start.'

Again, that hooting laugh. She looks exhausted but exhilarated. Indicating a quieter spot, she takes off her hat and unzips her jacket. 'Would you like a coffee?'

'I'm good. It gives me the shakes.'

'I thought journalists lived on caffeine.'

'I'm more of a herbal man.' *All sorts of herbals*, he might add.

They settle in hard chairs.

'We can't be sure, but we believe the guy might have been whipped before he died. We spotted some raised welts.'

Finn sits straighter. 'Some sort of punishment then? Might he have been a criminal?'

A slight shrug. 'Who can say? We're unlikely to get particulars of his life – that will be well beyond our reach, the reach of science – but if we're lucky our analysis will tell us a great deal about his environment. Right now, we're at the observation stage. Noting what we can, so we can compare with other recovered bodies.'

'You'll have seen a few of these, I'm supposing.'

'Quite a few. All of them well worked over by others. This one I think of as my man.' She laughs. 'It was such an honour going out there, digging him up, and now getting a chance to be the first to study him.'

She makes a satisfied 'Mmm' as she crosses her legs and he can't help but notice her short skirt, strong athletic legs in black tights and those red boots. He pauses then decides she looks the sort who can take this from a stranger: 'I can see you knee-deep in shite, shovel in hand…'

Again, that laugh. 'The whole thing has been awesome.'

She tells him about specialists who have visited to take samples: a microbiologist and mycologist from University

College Cork. He duly takes note of this, and how they have protected the front of the body with a fibreglass mould before turning it over. Too much detail for his readers, but he lets her explain.

'Will you keep me posted? Regular updates?' he asks.

'Happy to,' she agrees.

They swap business cards, and she gives permission for him to take a photo of her. He will ask about her family another time; the O'Neills must have hailed from Ireland. His mind begins to spin a story. A Saturday feature, perhaps, about this whole bog body business with the lovely Doctor O'Neill in a full-page spread... Finn catches himself.

Back at the office, having banged out the Ballybere Man story, he stays late working on his homeless/mental health feature. *This* is the story he wants to draw readers into.

But the Saturday feature that the *Times* publishes is another from Finn's hand.

A heading, FACE OF THE FIND, with a photo of Doctor O'Neill looking very much alive, and attractive, as a colleague says admiringly, along with an image of a very dead bog man. And a short article. But really there isn't much that is newsworthy.

6

The Keeper

LIAM HARTE ISN'T SURE WHETHER TO LAUGH OR CRY. With the bottom of his sweater pinched between thumb and finger, he methodically rubs his right glasses lens then the left.

There is Carrie, looking Junoesque, being promoted as THE FACE OF THE FIND. Is she trying to undermine him? Had she encouraged this journalist? Uncharitable thoughts flitter through Liam's mind then he places his glasses back on his nose and he can see straight. She wouldn't do that.

He has a soft spot for his staff member. He had been won over by Carrie's enthusiasm and openness at the interview for a researcher and he had not been disappointed. She had worked hard. One evening soon after she arrived, knowing she didn't have her own family around, he had invited her for a meal to meet his wife and Carrie had been totally unfazed when his twelve-year-old daughter kept moving in for cuddles. Liam had eyed this bonding and had milked it. Carrie became their go-to babysitter, and proved herself up to the challenge and rigours of caring for a child with Down's Syndrome and ADHD, attention-deficit hyperactivity disorder. Carrie became indispensable to them. And at work she was good fun. He had laughed when she phoned in a flap having turned up 'at the wrong bloody Churchtown' and she'd had to do a cross-country dash to where they were meant to be meeting for a site visit. 'You are the *researcher*,' he teased.

When a permanent assistant keeper position became vacant, Carrie applied. It was a plum post that attracted interest from far and wide, including from University College Cork's Rachael. On paper Rachael was the obvious choice. But personalities come into it, and – with the support of Mike – they appointed Carrie. There was no question her expertise complemented his. While his first love is for glorious Celtic artefacts of the medieval and Viking eras, her specialism is bog bodies from an earlier era.

Then there are his blind spots. Carrie had made small errors of judgement – not about work, God forbid, but understanding the broader political sphere in which they operate. At a work function, according to Fiona, their chair, she had not been sufficiently deferential with a member of the Dáil who held the purse strings. Although polite, Carrie was somehow too familiar, and didn't recognise social boundaries. She had said quite bluntly, 'Jack's as good as his master,' when he'd had a quiet word with her. It is some sort of Antipodean thing, he supposes, but while Irish society is relatively informal, there are hierarchies and social norms that *do* need to be observed.

Liam heads to the prep room where he finds Carrie already kitted up, chatting with the others, cameras ready to go.

'Morning, all,' he greets the team. 'And a special hello to our Face of the Find.' He cocks an eye at Carrie, raising the *Irish Times* weekend magazine.

Her hands fly to her face. 'Oh, God. Don't! I thought he was a serious reporter. I thought the *Times* was a cut above the trashy press. And to have done that!'

They tease her, and she takes it in good spirit. Headline aside, the article was thorough.

Liam dons a fresh apron and steps towards the worktable as plastic covering and soaked fabric are peeled away. He gazes at Ballybere Man's reddish-brown posterior.

'See, Liam?' Carrie points. 'This is what I could feel the other day.'

'Ah!' Liam runs a hand along raised welts across the thoracic and lumbar spine. 'This fellow's been thoroughly whipped! Ante-mortem for sure.'

'Exactly. No point once he was dead.'

Something is troubling him. What, he cannot say.

With a wet cloth they re-cover the head down to the wrinkled rump leaving the legs exposed. Just the back of the legs still to clean, then they are done. A great pity the body isn't complete. That would have been spectacular.

While Carrie works on a lower limb, scraping between folds of skin, he and Mike stand in front of the table facing the camera doing a back-and-forth, Mike being Joe Public and he the boffin.

'So, let's go over the dating process,' Mike is saying. 'You know, to establish how long he's been in his boggy grave.'

'We've taken a sample of hair, and there'll be radiocarbon analysis of skin and remaining bone. We can be confident we'll get a pretty accurate timeframe of when this fellow lived.' He won't go into the details of decontamination processes and chemical pre-treatment steps. 'And if we find a wood fragment – maybe a bit of a stake buried deep in a wrist – this can be analysed.'

'About the wrists,' Carrie's voice, behind him. 'They're small holes. I wonder if the fellow was pinned down with nails when he was alive.' She straightens and turns to the camera. 'Think of *Horrible Histories*. I've heard stories of criminals having ears pinned to a church door, they couldn't move, or they'd tear their ear off. Maybe he was a thief and pinned to a door and—'

'Doctor O'Neill!' Liam wills her to stop right there. Year 8 students are watching today. He doesn't want these kids thinking this was a normal way of dealing with undesirables in Irish history, or, God forbid, tempted to try something similar on a younger sibling who is annoying them. And he doesn't want their teachers thinking they aren't respecting this body. Carrie's being incautious. He will speak to her...

'Oh!' He flinches, steps back, jogs the table. All sorts of crazy ideas swirl around his head.

Punishments.

'Doctor Harte?' Mike's hand is on his elbow.

Liam gathers his scattered thoughts and focuses on the audience beyond the camera lens.

'I was talking about radiocarbon dating. You know, it's a delicate science. For a start, it's so important that the samples are decontaminated. So pre-treatment is vital...' He allows his voice to drone on, deciding that now *is* the time to go into details about the elemental analyser, mass spectrometer combination. Then he mentions how CO_2 is trapped and reduced to graphite. This will go way over the heads of some of those listening but never mind.

'Super. Thanks so much, Doctor Harte. Fascinating stuff.' Mike beams. 'And be sure, we'll be keeping everyone informed of what's happening. Isn't that right?'

'Absolutely!' Carrie is by his side. 'We'll be here to explain every step of the way.'

Carrie removes her face mask, catching her hair clasp – deliberately or in error, Liam can't be sure – allowing her hair to fall about her shoulders. Dark eyeshadow sets off her blue eyes. He is taken off guard. Did she always wear make-up to work? He isn't one to notice what people wear or their physical appearance, fat or thin. He never judges, being more interested in the conversations they have to offer. But he is noticing Carrie now.

'Please!' Mike gestures her forward to the camera.

'First a shout-out to Ms Foley's science class at Laurel Hill, Limerick. Hi, girls!' Carrie waves and smiles. 'And I seem to remember we have a bunch of lads watching from St Patrick's in Cork this morning, so a shout-out to you guys too.' Carrie gestures to the body. 'The thing we need to remember is Ballymere Man was a real man who lived and breathed, had his good days, and bad days, and might have looked like Doctor Harte, or Mr Curtis, or perhaps like any of your dads. One of the fun parts of this project will be constructing his face. And science will help us in our journey to find out what he looked like, where he came from, his likely background and why he ended up where he did. Many different fields of science come into this.'

Watching her, Liam sighs. Carrie might well be best described as the Face of the Find. No irony, no jealousy, only a resigned acknowledgement that while he has more experience, she has what it takes in this new media world that is alien to him. And he should stop worrying about what she says. Kids like a bit of vicarious *Horrible History*-type of thrill. He'd never been able to enjoy those teasing moments with his own daughter.

Mike steps forward. 'This is all marvellous, Doctor O'Neill. We can all agree this experiment to open a window into our work at the museum has been a great success. Thank you all for taking part. This is our final day of recording, but we'll be posting updates on our website, and I know our Learning Team are in touch with many schools and colleges and you've got some interesting projects underway. Goodbye for now and thank you for joining us.'

All of them wave, call out, 'Goodbye,' and, 'Keep in touch.' Then, thank the Lord, the camera operator calls out, 'Recording stopped.'

Liam feels his legs shaking. What a pity they didn't have Ballybere Man's feet. Recent archaeology in Cambridgeshire, England, had unearthed a skeleton with a nail still embedded in an ankle bone. Dating from the period the Romans had settled England, the man had been crucified, offering proof this form of execution had been practised in the British Isles. But Roman rule didn't extend to Ireland... Liam ruminates on what this might mean.

It had been thought that crucifixion died out with the Romans, and it is purely myth that early Christians killed heretics in such a way in emulation of how their Christ died. Maybe not. Ballybere Man might add significantly to their understanding of medieval Irish history. *His* period of expertise. This could be something new. Something no one else in the world has. Something unique to Ireland. Perhaps an early Christian ritual. He keeps his thoughts to himself as he sinks into the nearest chair.

'Liam?' Mike is looking at him.

'Sorry, what did you say?'

'I'm asking, when can we expect to learn more? I haven't felt this excited since my first visit to the Natural History Museum when I was a boy visiting London.'

It is Carrie who answers. This is her project after all. 'We're waiting for the analysis of hair and teeth, which will tell us location. And we've sent skin and bone samples to Oxford for carbon dating.'

'Good, good.' Mike rubs his hands.

'And we're looking at the locality,' he tells Mike. 'What

there is to find out about Ballybere and surrounding region. Geographically. Historically. How this site compares with our other find sites. You know, I am wondering—'

'Excellent. Yes… Listen, I've got to dash. But the injuries, Liam?' Mike asks. 'These *are* different, aren't they?'

'Quite different. Here, and in Europe, it's common to find obvious signs of hanging, garrotting, stab wounds or bludgeoned heads.'

'Though our man *did* suffer.' Carrie sounds as if this were a competition: which bog body had the most gruesome death. 'We've evidence of whipping, and puncture wounds in the wrists.'

Liam's heart hammers. Their find had been buried near the coast. Vikings and traders from Europe were frequent visitors to these shores. This body might open a window to an unexplored bit of history. Ballybere Man might not even be local but, say, from northern Europe. How exciting this would be. Maybe some spectacular Viking hoard might be hidden to rival the one from Galloway in Scotland. Or, if Ballybere Man proves to be from the Middle Ages, there is a strong case for assuming there could be a long-lost religious community nearby, and who knows what evidence might turn up?

He had dreaded that he might become a jobsworth in the decade leading to retirement. This find is invigorating him.

7

The Kingship and Sacrifice Theory

CARRIE O'NEILL WALKS THROUGH THE KINGSHIP AND Sacrifice gallery in the Archaeological Museum, imagining Ballybere Man taking his place alongside the remains of Cashel Man and Oldcroghan Man. But there is limited space, and she suspects Mike has bigger things in mind for their magnificently preserved find. She's even heard rumours of a museum rejig.

This gallery contextualises well-known Irish bog bodies and other human remains, suggesting that their deaths were associated with tribal sovereignty rituals. Sacrifices for a local king, perhaps, or to appease a fertility goddess. During her doctoral research, she had spent hour upon hour at this exhibition and been given access to the museum's tissues sample bank and other human remains kept in storage. Now, working here, never a day passes without her spending time engrossed in one exhibit or other.

It had been her old professor, Colm Byrne, along with Liam and a team of international specialists, who had researched and shaped the Kingship and Sacrifice exhibition. What can be deduced from each human find? Orientation of the body, manner of death, items buried with them. Then there is the question of land boundaries. These seem to play a significant role. Around forty bodies in Ireland have been unearthed at known tribal or kingship boundaries. And artefacts found at boundaries – hoards, weapons, wooden sculpted figures – suggest some votive purpose.

These liminal places were Professor Byrne's field of study. He had been the one to postulate that ancient tribal boundaries played a key part in where these ritually killed bodies had been buried. His knowledge was embedded in younger brains, and readily available in his own and others' research papers, but nothing about Ballybere Man conformed to these theories. Carrie had pored over maps of old Munster, looking at what is now County Clare, considering what was known about tribal customs and territories. Nothing matched.

She reminds herself that during those days when she was sifting through the Ballybere bog, no other artefact emerged. Then or since. Further trenches have been put in, and layer by layer a team, under the museum's guidance, have continued looking for clues as to who this man was. Soon construction work would recommence. Joe Cassidy would be happy, but she is not. There might be something they've overlooked.

Talking with Professor Byrne was the sensible thing to do, but part of her shrinks from a personal encounter. When she had begun her doctoral studies, she had been directed to Professor Byrne with a suggestion she might like to complete one of his courses. And she had loved sitting in on his lectures, soaking up his knowledge, but the love affair stopped there. She didn't want to complete his essays, and Prof Byrne was all about essays. She had her own research to undertake and write up, so Prof Byrne's course was meant to be light relief, but it ended up a slog, and her essays for him were barely adequate. Perhaps he wouldn't remember her, though she would never forget him.

Every summer – which weren't exactly sun-blistering affairs – and winter, Professor Byrne wore the same scruffy tweed jacket with worn leather buttons and elbow patches. The twill, a mustardy yellow and sage green, seemed to be from the land itself. She remembers with embarrassment how she and other students had not been keen on sitting too close to him in his tutorials. *Don't they go in for dry cleaning in this country?* went through her mind every time she opened his office door. That jacket didn't just *look* like the colours of an Irish woodland; it gave off a fuggy odour, particularly in winter with the central heating cranked up and windows closed. She had thought him quaint, and stories about her batty professor featured in messages home. Nan particularly enjoyed hearing these.

Having plucked up courage to contact the uni, she is disappointed to find Doctor Byrne has finally retired from the Ancient History and Archaeology department. 'A cancer scare,' she is told when she phones to make an appointment. She bites back, asking if he is still alive. News of his death would have circulated. Liam knows him well, and there has been no funeral that she is aware of.

'Is he okay? Is he well now?' she asks the department office manager.

'I'm not too sure. We were just saying we should ring to check. It's been some weeks.'

'Where can I find him?'

'Oh, that's easy. He moved into one of those care homes. I'm told it's very nice. Wait a sec and I'll get you the details.'

When Carrie mentions to Liam that she plans to phone Professor Byrne's care home to arrange a visit, he says, 'Ah, actually Colm's been in touch. He's been following what we're up to and wants to pop along to see our body.'

Professor Byrne is not exactly popping when he arrives at the Collins Barracks at his appointed time. He is pushed in a wheelchair, a woollen rug covering his legs. He no longer wears *that* jacket, and his straggly beard is gone. And much else has changed. He looks frail, back of hands liver-spotted, cheeks sunken.

'Professor Byrne.' Carrie walks forward to greet him, noticing how wispy his gingery hair has become. 'Liam's in a meeting with Mike. We'll see him shortly.' She raises her voice. 'Do you remember me?'

'I do indeed!' A look of irritation crosses his face. 'There's nothing wrong with my brain, or my hearing. It's the rest of me falling apart.'

Having negotiated a time to be picked up, the carer, a middle-aged woman, leaves and Carrie takes over. She wheels the prof across the car park to the conservation block. They have a scan booked at the hospital tomorrow, then the conservation team will commence the preservation process. It is a good job the prof is here, as soon it will be some months before any of them have access to the body while it is preserved.

In the lab, Carrie introduces Professor Byrne to the staff, who unwrap Ballybere Man for this fresh appraisal. She hears a sharp intake of breath and sees the old professor's eyes shining and alert. 'Well, well,' he keeps repeating. 'Extraordinary. Wheel me closer.'

Her guest sits quietly gazing at the uncovered body, occasionally firing questions at the conservators, and she is reluctant to disturb him. He takes his time viewing the body then turns to her. 'You're a lucky girl. What you have here is unbelievably precious – you know that.' There is a hint of jealousy in his voice.

'Oh, I do. I certainly do.' This project will make her reputation. Many specialists are begging her to be involved, eager to be part of the action, and they *will* be welcomed; but she got her hands on the body first and is embedded in the museum team. She is digging in as surely as Ballybere Man has been dug out.

'We are awaiting analysis of his dentation,' she tells him. 'But I wouldn't be surprised if he was in his mid-twenties to mid-thirties.'

'In his prime.' Prof Byrne nods. 'This is often the case.'

'Yes. And these...' She points to the puncture wounds. 'Both wrists. Have you seen anything like this before?'

The professor leans forward in his chair, peering closely, and Carrie resists the urge to hold on to him in case he topples over. 'Never. Intriguing. It does indeed suggest a punishment has taken place.'

'A crucifixion, I'm beginning to speculate.'

'There may be some yet-to-be-discovered practices in ancient Ireland. But Miss O'Neill, as I have said often enough to you in the past: back up your evidence with *thorough* research, and *then* I'll listen to you.'

Her cheeks flush, and she catches the glances of her co-workers. Embarrassing to find herself told off by this desiccated old man.

'All the same,' Professor Byrne continues, 'the position of the punctures is commensurate with a certain kind of crucifixion.'

'And Professor,' Carrie indicates the small incision on the abdomen, 'there is a peri-mortem wound here, clean edges. A sharp blade – knife or something – that may have killed him, or—'

'Or *one* of the acts of violence that killed him. In keeping with the "overkill" aspects of many we've seen.'

'Maybe, but I've been thinking.' Carrie knows she sounds tentative, the end of her sentence rising in that typical Kiwi way. 'It could be an incision for evisceration.'

'Embalming? Unlikely!' The professor scoffs and Carrie flinches.

A text message appears on her phone. Liam. 'When you've seen enough, Professor, we'll join Liam. He's out of his meeting.'

'I'll never have enough, but I appreciate you arranging this.' He looks hungrily at the body.

She wheels her old professor out and back to the admin offices as others cover Ballybere Man and wheel him away, not wanting their mummified body exposed longer than necessary.

'Colm! How are you? Great to see you. And what do you make of our man?' Liam kneels by the wheelchair, Professor Byrne's veiny hand in both of his. Master and pupil, Carrie thinks.

'Oh, he looks very promising!' The professor's eyes rest on three assorted mugs. 'Is that tea?'

She fishes the teabags out and drops them in the wastepaper basket, the stewed tea brick-red with generous amounts of milk. Liam never remembers she drinks hers black with just the whiff of coloured water. Tea weak; coffee strong.

'Is this okay for you?' She hesitantly holds out a mug to Professor Byrne, hoping it is to his liking and that he has strength to hold it.

'Perfect.'

Liam remembers how he likes *his* tea.

Carrie doesn't interrupt as the two of them chat, though her old prof doesn't want to talk about his illness and dismisses Liam's cautious query with, 'Who has time for that? You'll know how I am when you receive the invitation to my wake.'

'Ah, my friend. Not too soon, I hope.'

Professor Byrne shrugs. 'It's in the lap of the gods.' Colm Byrne had been training for the priesthood before he 'lost God and found gods', as he was wont to say. He had turned away from theology and embraced academia, becoming fascinated by ancient cultures in Ireland. Many years earlier Liam had studied under him.

In this room: three generations of individuals smitten by secrets hidden in the landscape. Carrie can tell how much being here means to her old professor with decent conversation firing up his brain cells.

Professor Byrne rests his mug on a knee. 'You'll remember, Liam, when we were considering Oldcroghan Man's violent death... No similarities?'

'It doesn't fit any model we know. In any respect,' Liam spreads his hands palms upward, 'different types of trauma, and no artefacts to go by.'

'And I've been researching everything I can find about known boundaries,' Carrie adds. 'Unless you have fresh ideas to suggest?' She says this to be polite, considering the old professor to be well beyond this, but you never know what story might linger at the back of his brain, what hunch might occur to him.

'Liam, you need to step up your detective work and see if there's any evidence that this might have been a boundary between politically significant places.'

A social limbo between kingship or tribal zones, Prof Byrne will be thinking.

'Yes, Carrie's on to it,' Liam assures him.

She doesn't like the look the professor shoots at her.

'And, Liam, you've ruled out a sacrifice?' Byrne continues. 'A chosen one?'

'We're considering what elements conform,' Liam says. 'Maybe this was associated with Samhain. But again, it's different from anything we know.' He looks to Carrie, and she nods her agreement.

Halloween, the better-remembered pagan festival, has its origins in Samhain, celebrated before the dark of winter sets in. With harvest gathered, the festival saw out the old year while anticipating the coming year would be fertile. This was a liminal time between the worlds of the living and dead. She and Liam have endlessly debated if this might form part of the picture: a local man chosen for one reason or other to be the sacrifice. Winter was usually the time bodies were placed under water: they preserve better this way. But Ballybere Man's traumas? The way he was laid out? She is impatient for the puzzle to be solved.

As the two men talk about academic references, she gets the idea Liam is feeding the old man's ego, allowing him to feel included.

'Consider it differently.' Professor Byrne closes his eyes. 'Consider if that patch of land is *itself* sacred.'

It is hard to imagine a time when that dreary soon-to-be-shopping centre site was significant. She tries to picture men and women, gathering at that forlorn place, all of them wrapped in woollen cloaks. She tries to visualise a significant ritual taking place, but such a thing is too much of a leap. All the same, this body had been carefully laid. It had not been dumped. Some ritual might have taken place. But what?

Later, as Carrie wheels the professor to be collected, he keeps mumbling, 'Lucky girl,' and she finds herself irritated. She is not a girl. She is a well-qualified archaeologist who knows what she's doing. Sure, sometimes her enthusiasm gets the better of her, but better than becoming bitter and forgotten. Apart from speaking to her when she offered him tea, all Prof Byrne's questions were directed at Liam, ignoring her. She grips the handlebars and pushes him faster, watching his hands shoot out to grip the arms of his chair. Good! She's disappointed in both the professor's behaviour and finding he has nothing to contribute to their story. She won't be troubling him again.

In the café she searches for the professor's carer and spots her sitting, hot drink in one hand, folded magazine in another. She also spots Finn Durante's slight figure, an ankle crossed over the other, nonchalantly leaning against a wall, bent over his phone. What is *he* doing here? Sensing her eyes on him, he glances up and is at her side in a flash, his eyes moving from her to the prof as if she owes him an introduction. Cheek! This could be any old codger who has wondered into the museum.

'Hello, Finn…' She hesitates. 'This is my old professor – as in "old" from my time at uni. Professor Byrne, this is a fellow from the *Irish Times*, Finn, um…' She raises an enquiring brow.

'Finn Durante. Pleased to meet you.'

Of course she remembers Finn's name, but is irritated to see him here, waiting for her, she supposes.

Professor Byrne is passed back to the woman caring for him and Finn claims her.

'I'm meeting someone from your Learning Department,' he says. 'I'm doing a piece on the Magdalene Laundries.'

Oh. Finn hasn't come to see her after all.

'Those poor women. That exhibition we held was fantastic.' She had known a little of those women's terrible suffering but had been deeply moved on learning more. The exhibition had been an artistic response to the single mothers' plight. 'Did you see it?'

'Afraid not, coming late to the party. Until I met you here, it had been ages since I set foot in the place. Apparently you've some documents – that's what I've come for. But while I'm here, any updates? What did the revered prof have to say?'

'He wanted to see the body. We're trying to square kingship and sacrifice theories with our find.'

'Oh!' Finn's voice rises a tone. 'If he can see it, any chance I can?'

'Sorry. And not much more to say yet.'

'But you'll let me know when there is?'

She assures him, yes. Her co-worker from Learning is scouring the café so she waves and points to Finn.

Finn touches her elbow. 'Let's catch up over a drink sometime.'

'Sure. This evening?'

'Can't. Tomorrow any good?'

'Netball.'

'Too bad.' Finn turns to her colleague. 'Finn Durante, *Irish Times*.'

As Carrie heads out to catch a tram back to her office, a sense of disappointment settles on her. Does she crave publicity? Has she fallen for that Face of the Find crap? That headline didn't go down too well at work. No one likes an upstart colleague claiming the limelight. But she *is* in a great position to talk about this find. Knowledgeable, personable, and good on camera. She has no false modesty. Professor Byrne had subtly put her down and she's not having it.

Carrie and her conservation staff colleagues take Ballybere Man for his evening appointment at the hospital. She is impatient to learn what his soft tissue might reveal. The small abdominal incision suggesting evisceration that Prof Byrne had been dismissive about continues to play on her mind. Earlier X-rays on their own portable machine showed the ribcage and spine had been remarkably well-preserved and had maintained their skeletal integrity. This had contributed to the body retaining its overall shape across the years.

They'd all been delighted to see this. Bodies survive well in bogs, but bones do not do well in acidic conditions; their calcium phosphate dissolves, leaving a typically saggy body looking as if the air has been released from a balloon. Yet here was Ballybere Man looking he might get up and walk away... if it wasn't for those missing feet.

She helps unload Ballybere Man from his cooled coffin, unswathe his wrapping and place him on the CT scanning bench. Hospital technicians lean close. 'Not our typical patient,' one says, as they carefully line Ballybere Man up. The computerised tomography will digitally peel away outer layers to reveal what is within. At the press of a button a humming begins, and Carrie watches the bench rise and Ballybere Man's head slide into the tube, then his chest and legs. She moves to stand beside the technician at the computer screen to watch as the cross-sectional beam rotates around the body and 3D images emerge. Soon the procedure is done. While others begin to pack their precious body away, she leans into the computer screen.

'Oh, wow, what are we looking at?' She tries to get a handle on the images emerging.

'He's stuffed with something,' a technician offers.

No question about it. Ballybere Man has been embalmed. *Suck that up, Professor Byrne.* She takes pleasure in this spiteful thought. But embalmed with what? She has studied scanned images of Egyptian mummies held in the British Museum and other places, revealing scrunched-up wadding and packing. This is different. On screen she sees the entire chest cavity and abdominal area is packed with small fibres.

Others gather, and she feels warm breath on her neck as they peer over her shoulder.

'My guess is pine needles,' a conservator whispers reverentially. 'I've heard of this. Extraordinary.'

Pine needles! She tries to absorb what this might mean. All of them are curious where this trail might lead.

The next day she is at the lab early waiting impatiently for Ballybere Man to be wheeled out. She gently parts the leathery abdominal incision near his navel, then inserts long tweezers, probes and wiggles. It is difficult to get any purchase on the tightly bound fibres, but with a small tug a bit comes loose and she drops the precious sample into a plastic zip bag. Some type of pine needles, for sure. They decide to send the sample away to a specialist laboratory. She must bide her time.

'Resin from the Boswellia tree,' the chemist analysing the sample informs her. 'Where did you say this is from?'

She prevaricates, offers her thanks, and ends the call.

Ballybere Man's corpse has been treated with great ceremony, expertly eviscerated through a small incision and embalmed: packed with pine needles drenched in melted resin from the Boswellia tree.

Frankincense.

8

The Director

MIKE CURTIS STANDS AND COLLECTS HIS PAPERS. IT HAS been a difficult management committee meeting. Liam had left early so other heads of department felt free to voice their unease: extra workloads due to their new acquisition; concerns about future staffing levels to cope with expected increased visitor demand here and online; peeves that Irish Antiquities were getting so much media attention when another long-planned exhibition on the textual analysis of medieval epigraphs was being all but ignored. Couldn't he, they asked, draw attention to *other* aspects of the museum's work next time he was interviewed on TV? Yes, yes, of course, he promised, stung by their reproaches. In truth there had been little media interest in the bog body for some weeks. There had been nothing to report.

On entering his office Mike learns Liam has been trying to reach him and would he call back? He takes his time, dealing with more pressing things – prep for the upcoming board meeting – and before he gets around to returning Liam's call, Liam's phoned his mobile.

'Money?' Mike tries to catch what Liam is saying against a lot of background noise.

'No, HONEY.'

'I'm sorry, I don't follow you.'

'Pollen. Trapped in the pores. The lab's identified sphagnum moss spores and bits of weed you'd expect to find on skin after being submerged. But pollen!' Liam is talking fast; excited or perhaps trying to make himself heard over his daughter's racket in the background. 'Pollen. This puts a different perspective on things... Evie, Evie!' Liam is at home, having a hard time of things.

'Liam, I can hear you've got enough on your plate right now. How about you drop by my office tomorrow morning? I can spare—'

'No, no, no. Carrie's on her way over with the lab report, we want to share it with you today. All right, honey, I'm coming.' This to his daughter. 'I'll catch up with you later, Mike. Bye... Bye...'

A sharp rap, and Carrie's head appears around the door, sheets of printed A4 in her hand.

'You're expecting me, right?' In a few strides she is by his desk.

'I am now.' He thinks, not for the first time, that Carrie O'Neill can be a little in-your-face. But this is generation Y, he believes the term: millennials who aren't fussed about established ways of doing things. So different from his public school. He can't conceive of this level of informality with any of the masters, let alone the head on the rare occasions they spoke. (Prizegiving, perhaps? Handing out a certificate?) He'd addressed everyone as Sir. Courteous. Obvious. That said, Carrie's personality played out well with the media in the initial buzz of Ballybere Man's discovery.

His assistant keeper tucks her hair behind her ears and drops into a chair.

'Mike. Sooo interesting!' She gives a loud, unguarded laugh.

'What is this about honey?'

'Well.' Carrie leans forward, eyes wide. 'Seems our man was anointed with *honey*. More than anointed. It's likely he was slathered with the stuff.' She places a lab report on his desk, turning it to face him. 'See.' She points. 'Evidence of pollen, and, get this, bits of a bee wing.' Again, that whoop. 'Honey!'

The world of interdepartmental bickering slides away. 'Tell me.'

'It's a way of stopping corpses deteriorating quickly. The ancient Assyrians went in for it. The practice goes back a long way. There's a recently excavated Bronze Age burial mound in Georgia – bodies, funerary items. And food for the afterlife: berries, still red—'

'Honey can do that?' He has tried honey remedies for minor ailments, cuts or sore throats, intrigued by claims of its healing powers.

'It's honey's *bactericidal* properties that's of interest. Chemistry was never my best subject but the thing to understand is that sugar inhibits bacteria.'

'Preserving berries is one thing. But a corpse?'

'Story is that when Alexander the Great carked it, his body was preserved in a whole cask of the sticky stuff to bring him home in a showable state. So, here's the thing.' Carrie's enthusiasm almost tips her off the chair. 'This opens up enquiries into mortuary practices. So many questions. This may not be a local man. We've the evidence of the pine needles and resin he was packed with' – yes, that had been an enormous surprise to him – 'so it's likely that Ballybere Man may have died elsewhere and has been transported to the find site. But from where, and why, we can only guess. *So exciting.*'

Mike fans his face with the lab report. 'Absolutely.'

'You know, Mike, it's so strange. So many of our bog bodies demonstrate overkill – excessive actions to kill their victim – yet Ballybere Man is the opposite. This is excessive action to *preserve* his body. Embalming, anointing, and finally submerging. Fascinating!'

'Absolutely,' he manages again.

From her bag Carrie extracts another A4 with a neat column of bullet-pointed sentences. 'I thought you might like briefing notes to pass through to comms for a press release.'

'Thank you. Well done. Um… When are we expecting more test results?'

'Two to three weeks.'

He takes his time looking at the briefing she has written. It makes a good story, but… He looks up. 'Carrie, we'll hold on a press release till we learn more. And, if you don't mind, we'll keep this to ourselves.'

'Really?' Carrie looks astonished. 'Why?'

'For the time being.' Mike's thinking is they could make an event of the next announcement. Despite the misgivings of some in his management team, he is keen to build up a head of steam about Ballybere Man. Keen to build up interest in what will be the latest addition to their collection. He's been thinking of donors, major donors whom he might tempt to dip into pockets. Yes, it makes sense to hold back and go with something bigger, when they can build a compelling narrative for this bog body.

He is a man who has learnt to be guarded, and keep secrets. Aged eighteen it had taken enormous courage to come out to his parents, choosing his moment carefully. They had been deeply shocked, but they had gradually accepted there would be no daughter-in-law joining the family, though they made it clear he was not to bring boyfriends home – they drew the line there. They had, however, attended his wedding, a small gathering at a register office, and over time had accepted his choices. Attitudes can change given time.

Three days later, while he grabs a quick lunch, Mike's PA messages him. He is wanted. He finds Liam and Carrie hovering outside his office, Liam's cheeks flushed above his beard, Carrie jiggling foot to foot.

'Shall we?' He ushers them in.

'Our man is talking to us,' Carrie blurts as soon as he has closed the door. 'He's a long, long way from home and he didn't walk.'

'We have the hair analysis in,' Liam says. 'Strontium isotope ratios tell us where he was living leading up to his death. He's from—'

'The Middle East!' Carrie shrieks. 'He's been transported by boat. Why? Why on earth…?'

Mike leans against his desk absorbing this.

'Liam, this hair analysis. Where was it done?'

'UCC.'

'And Cork won't go public?'

'No. This is a job they're doing for us. We make the announcements.'

The Middle East… Preserved in honey and brought to Ireland.

He had been looking forward to learning more about their prospective exhibit. The media had been alerted to expect a fresh announcement at any time. Now he isn't so sure. His gaze moves between Liam and Carrie. He begins cautiously: 'I understand it was our own team that discovered the honey?' Nods confirm this. 'And the resin analysis was done at another lab?' Again nods. 'How many people know everything?'

'Well, our own conservators, naturally, but they know not to say anything,' Carrie says. 'I'm leading on the project. Everything comes to me, and I share with Liam.'

'And the age of our find. What do we know?' Mike asks casually. But his palms are clammy.

'We're confident he was a man in his twenties to late thirties, the analysis of teeth enamel confirms this. Test results are in.'

'But the body *itself*?'

'We're waiting to hear from Oxford,' Carrie says. 'They've an AMS—'

'Accelerator Mass Spectrometry,' Liam clarifies. 'They're radiocarbon dating. They've had our samples for three months, so we need to wait a few more weeks.'

'Carrie, when the results come in, call me immediately. And let's meet – the three of us.' He dips his head and peers over his glasses. 'And just to remind ourselves, this stays with us.'

Two heads nod rigorously.

There are times when Mike wishes science was less advanced and technology less capable. He has more of an aesthetic bent, at home in the world of high-concept art exhibitions. In his mind's eye he has been visualising an immersive, highly visual visitor experience with this new find. But science is driving the story. That radiocarbon facility machine at Oxford has done a magnificent job dating a tiny skin sample and sliver of tibia bone that had been exposed where a foot had been ripped off.

Carrie and Liam are back in his office. The two of them yo-yoing between their own base at the Archaeology Museum and the admin hub at Collins Barracks. At this moment his assistant keeper looks as if she might bounce off the walls.

'Two thousand years old, Mike! Give or take.'

'Ah…' He absorbs the news. The team in Oxford, Carrie says, has pushed this job up the queue, equally curious, so the turnaround time has been quicker than usual.

Liam adds a cautious: 'But the team want to run another test, just to make sure.'

His hopes were that Ballybere Man might date to the Middle Ages. Or another good outcome would be to learn they had a Bronze Age corpse, the older the better. Better that Ballybere Man is, say, four thousand years old, making him two thousand years BC... Oh! Those initials. Before the Common Era, or *Before Christ*.

Despite the July sun streaming through the window, Mike shivers. He looks at the two attentive faces across from him. Surely they are all thinking the same thing.

'Oh, boy.' Carrie is radiating energy. 'Just imagine, what if—?'

'Carrie!' Liam glares at her. 'Don't even think of going there.'

Mike had been looking forward to a crowd-pleasing exhibition. Nothing contentious, but highly innovative. He fiddles with his ring, a sensation that can only be described as fear rising in him. He sucks air through his teeth. Yes, he acknowledges he is fearful of where this might lead. His Keeper of Irish Antiquities looks cautious, but his assistant keeper looks to be up for anything.

'When can we go public?' Carrie asks.

'We'll defer for the moment. I want to reflect.'

'But why? I don't get it.'

He can't say why, but he wants to delay a big announcement. Any announcement.

'We will wait,' he instructs his staff. 'Give us time to gather our thoughts as well as the data.'

Carrie shoots him an exasperated look.

Days later, he is at the Archaeological Museum walking through the galleries – yet again – puzzling where they might house Ballybere Man. As their bog body's personal story grows so does the need for space to present him.

Heading towards the entrance, he frowns; Carrie is talking to a middle-aged man scribbling into a notepad. At the information desk he indicates the pot-bellied chap with receding hair. 'Do we know who he is?'

'From a tabloid,' he is told. Mike watches from a distance, then back in his office he emails Carrie, copying in Liam, stating politely but formally that he will do interviews when the time comes, and she is not to speak to the media. Carrie replies: Sorry, sorry. He ambushed me as I was leaving. I didn't say anything. I promise. Everything's under control.

But is it? If so, then barely. It might be time to bring Fiona in on this. The museum's chair is a busy woman. She's been out of the country with her management consultancy work and has recently returned. Fiona had said she might not have taken on the role if she'd known how much work it entailed, so he involves her on a needs-must basis. That said, Fiona is a staunch ally. When he approaches her about something other than the usual pre-board meeting briefings – quarterly accounts or some such – she is always accommodating. 'Tell me what you need from me,' she'd say, and he'd grab her attention with a polished, concise explanation. An elevator pitch: he the writer, she the producer who would make real his ambitions. Mostly these were requests for a word in a politician's ear. Or funding. Money always came into it, and Fiona is well connected.

Yes, he decides, he must have a serious talk with Fiona.

It is not some whizzy high-tech instrument that offers the next surprise.

Mike is called to the lab where he finds Carrie and an assortment of conservation staff bent over the table, all talking shrilly at once.

'Mike!' Carrie makes a space for him. 'Take a look.' The assistant keeper can't contain her joy.

'We have a foot! Look at this. Way to go!'

He stares at the wizened body part.

9

The Ancestor

CARRIE O'NEILL MARCHES, ARMS SWINGING, TOWARDS the city centre in search of diversion. She is bursting, barely able to contain the volcanic pressure building within. How can Mike do this? How can he be so darned cool-headed? The entire evening stretches ahead; how to fill it? Cinema? Bar?

For Christ's sake! They have Ballybere Man's foot, to observe what *that* shows. They have the carbon dating. They have the location of where he had lived. The world has shifted, yet no one is saying anything. Unbelievable!

That morning Joe Cassidy had phoned. 'Doctor O'Neill?'

'Carrie, please.'

'Ye've got yourself one of the fella's feet—'

'What?'

'It turned up at the peat-processing factory. Ye know they were instructed to look out for it. I'm guessing the other foot'll be lost forever. But you'll be wanting this one, yes?'

'Yes! Tell me. Tell me. I'll drive over—'

'No need. I'll be in Dublin, as it happens. It's not, as you might say, factory-new, but still…'

So she found herself being handed a plastic bag with a supermarket logo. 'I hope it's useful,' Joe said.

Later, in the lab, she, Mike and the technicians stood gazing at the shrivelled, mangled right foot and ankle. It was not, as Joe put it, factory-new but it wasn't beyond saving, and the foot anterior and heel was well preserved. Her fingers found it before her eyes, then with a magnifying glass she inspected it closely.

'Looks like an old trauma. The peat factory hasn't caused this. It's like his wrists.'

They inspected the puncture wound from the top of the foot to the bottom of the heel.

'Well, this has got to be a crucifixion, hasn't it?' one of the conservation technicians said. A statement, not a question.

Yes! But before she could say anything, Mike had shut down the conversation.

'Thank you for sharing this with me.' Mike was downplaying the moment. 'Super to have a bit more of Ballybere Man to put on display. Carrie, when you are finished here would you mind dropping by my office? I'll see if Liam is free to join us.'

While the temperature in the lab had been cool, in Mike's office it shot up.

Her: 'Can we say it? Can we at least *say* it? I know you're both thinking it!'

Mike: 'But it's impossible. I can't conceive—'

Her: 'The evidence. Look at the goddamn *evidence!*'

Liam: 'Carrie!'

Mike: 'It's quite all right. There's a lot to process.'

Her: 'It's going to leak. Shit—'

Liam: 'Carrie, please!'

Her: 'We've got scientists and academics from around the world wanting in on this. My email box is FULL. We need to share. Now. And the media—'

Mike: 'You're not to breathe a word. I know you're chummy with the young chap from the *Times*—'

Her: 'Chummy?'

Mike: 'Not a word. I need to consider.'

Liam: 'Fiona must be told. You've got to involve the board.'

Mike: 'I'm fully aware!'

All of them silent. Mike, frowning, twisting his damned wedding ring, fleeting expressions crossing Liam's face, and she, no longer shrill, in a belligerent sulk, staring at the floor.

Nearing Temple Bar, Carrie toys with her phone, considering texting Finn with a casual *meet for a drink?* She and Finn have met three times outside work hours. Professional grooming came into it: him buttering her up to get the goods on Ballybere Man before anyone else. She had teased him, and to be fair, he admitted it. 'You'll not hold that against me? Just doing my job.' Once that was out of the way they found they had plenty in common: indie bands they followed, food they liked, Scandinavian noir they binge-watched on rainy Sundays. No to sci-fi or fantasy books and fan conventions of any type; yes to the right kind of music festivals. But while her idea of a walk is a rigorous countryside hike, weather be damned, in sturdy walking boots, his is a city walk in his usual lace-up canvas shoes which will likely get soaked. She doesn't fancy Finn, but she can imagine him becoming a good mate. She pockets her phone, resisting the temptation to contact him. One drink and everything bottled up will splurge forth.

Friends from University College Dublin? But they are following Ballybere Man's journey. There have been lots of chats over the past weeks and months, all of them curious, all of them envious. But if she were to contact any of them, they would be sure to ask questions and she would buckle. Again, no.

Netball friends? But they will wonder why tonight, why now? Their friendship group isn't given to spontaneous meet-ups. If they go to a bar, it is usually after a game or to celebrate a birthday or engagement. Something arranged well in advance. And she rules out friends from work. A drink or two, and whoosh, the floodgates will open.

The burden of knowledge sits heavily.

How fantastic it would be to offload to Rachel. Carrie has been avoiding her friend in recent weeks. She has seen Rachel's name emblazoned across her phone screen and left it ringing, ignoring Rachel's voicemail requests to phone back. She made one disingenuous return call at a time she expected Rachel would be busy, and thankfully the voicemail kicked in. 'It's me,' she'd said. 'Sorry, I've been a bit busy. Let's talk soon. Um, love to Dan and the kids. And, yeah… yeah… talk soon.'

But she *can't* talk. Not to anyone. Standing on the cobbled street, customers spilling out onto the pavement in this warm summer evening, she imagines herself drink in hand chatting to a stranger about her day: 'Hey, guess what? I've just been looking at Jesus's foot…' No. No. She presses her lips together. The volcano must be plugged a little longer. No pub, and she doesn't fancy any of the films that are showing.

She's due to FaceTime her family later this evening. Nan is expected for lunch at her parents so best to call about midday their time, which will be eleven at night in Dublin. A plan for how to fill these hours forms. She will go home, change into shorts and running shoes, and pound the streets. A run may do something about those two kilos that have stealthily taken up home in her hips and thighs. And it will clear her mind. The thought of preparing food doesn't appeal, so she'll order a take-away and there is wine at home. The run will, hopefully, balance out the calories.

She heads to a bus stop.

'Nan! Look at YOU!'

'You like it? Glenda's done a neat job.'

'Neat's the word. How are you?'

Nan's friendly face fills the screen, her normally permed grey hair styled into a serviceable bob. A bit of home, a bit of Nan. Carrie tucks her feet under her and settles onto the sagging sofa, glass of wine in hand. Her third?

When Mum and Dad couldn't take time away from the farm, it was Nan with whom she had shared adventurous holidays, imagining themselves furry-footed hobbits in *Lord of the Rings* locations; sharing a white-knuckle ride sweeping along a southern river, her yelling her head off and Nan praying for delivery. It was Nan she could confide in after some bust-up with her parents, a fall-out with a girlfriend, or later, when a boyfriend broke her heart. She didn't have brothers or sisters, but she had her nan.

Nan is talking. She is considering giving up her own house and moving to a rest home. There has been a fall, she lets on. 'Your mum and dad swore not to say. I didn't want you worried.' But Carrie is alarmed and needs assurance. Can she cook for herself? Dress herself? Enjoy gardening? Yes, is the answer to everything. Then Nan probes. 'Are you *courtin'* yet?' saying the old-fashioned word coyly, doing the Oirish bit.

'I do have a man in my life right now and he is consuming me day and night. Ask Mum and Dad.'

'Oh, yes, I know a little about that. I imagine it's exciting if you like that sort of thing. But I was meaning a younger Irishman, someone you might fancy kissing and cuddling and what have you.'

Carrie hoots, and her arm shoots out, sloshing red wine over a cushion. What Nan said was funny but not *that* funny. She decides that after this family time, a kitchen disco seems a good plan. With music blasting she can dance wildly. *That will let off steam.*

'My man's older than you might think and isn't even Irish!' *Dangerous water. Stay away!*

'Oh, really? I didn't know that. Blame your dad, he's meant to keep me up with things.'

'No, no. Dad doesn't know anything. Nothing's public yet.' *Stop right there.* 'Tell me about this care home.'

As Nan talks, Carrie looks up the residential home on her phone internet. She likes what she sees: nice units, good grounds. Nan refuses to move out to the farm. Too far away, she complains. She likes her small-town community.

'So, Carrie, love. Not Irish then, this man of yours?'

'Mmm… Middle East… Hey, they've a swimming pool! Take your togs, Nan!'

'Old, you say? How old?' Nan's voice is sharp. 'Didn't I read you found holes in his wrists…?'

Oh, shit! If Nan, tucked away in small-town Otago, can jump to THAT conclusion, what might the rest of the world make of it?

'Woah. Hold back, Nan. I didn't say anything.'

'I should say not! You were brought up to be a good girl.'

Nan attended Carrie's first communion; will she be thinking the conversation was verging on the sacrilegious? Is she subconsciously wanting to spill to Nan? Wrong person. Nan is a simple-living woman she loves to bits, but having any kind of intellectual conversation about the possible origin of this body is not for her. Nan's sense of adventure is physical, not intellectual.

The mood has shifted, and before long Nan gestures behind her and Carrie sees her mother placing plates on the table. Nan makes excuses about not letting food go cold and Mum and Dad call out they'll speak soon, then Nan ends the call. Carrie stares at her screensaver. She'd *almost* said too much. It scares her, and has scared Nan.

A kitchen disco no longer appeals. She recycles the empty bottle – *that went down quickly* – and mashes the Thai take-away container. As she brushes her teeth her brain whirls. Mike needs to take the lead. He's the director. Moreover, she is afraid if he doesn't get on with it, she will speak out of turn. She ejects a gob of foamy spit into the basin and stares at her reflection in the mirror. What must she do to make her boss act and put her out of her pent-up misery?

10

The Chair

Fiona McCormac gawps.

'For the love of God, Mike, please tell me you're joking?'

'I wish...'

On getting to know him, she has found under his posh persona there lurks a man not above smutty schoolboy jokes, and when she's relaxing, particularly with a whiskey, as now, she can cackle and swear like a trooper. Who would think upright Mrs McCormac had such a tongue?

Tonight he turned up at her door. He waited till they were seated, and she had poured a whiskey, before dropping his bombshell.

'Mike...' She struggles to unravel her thoughts. 'I want to give it back. This is a most unwelcome gift. Can I return it?'

'I'm afraid not. None of us can. He's been unwrapped; he's in the world.' There's a slight quiver in her hand as she brings the glass to her lips. What to do? Truly, what to do with this knowledge he has dumped on her?

'But it's absurd. You must know that?'

'Insane to even consider it, yes, but do we have a choice?'
Mike's eyes hold hers. He looks calm, but then he has had
longer to absorb all this.

'Each test you've had done, Mike. Is there any chance they
might be wrong? Misleading?'

'There's no doubt where this man lived, at least for the
period before he died. Pinning geographical locations is
extraordinarily accurate.' Mike's voice is emphatic. 'I'm told
carbon dating may be more variable with such old samples,
but we have to accept the dating as reliable.'

'What about those wounds? Who can prove how they
were caused?' She is clutching at straws, but on firmer ground.

'True enough. The hows and whys will be a matter of
conjecture and we'll look at all possibilities. But people *will*
speculate.'

'Oh yes!'

Fiona is thinking what her poor parish priest might have to
say. Mass was a childhood routine she has continued through
her adult life, and at fifty-two is unlikely to vary. It is a habit, but
she is a true believer, and a staunch supporter of their church
community, one of the dwindling band of volunteers. It is she
who organises pilgrimages to Lourdes: travel, accommodation,
dietary requirements, special support. 'Speak to Mrs
McCormac,' someone would say, and she would efficiently
make necessary arrangements. Fiona imagines sitting in a pew
this coming Sunday, raising her gaze to the stations of the cross
high on the walls. Might she feel the need to unburden herself
at confession? Good Lord! Her priest will think she's lost her
marbles. She places her glass down with an emphatic clunk.

'No, no, no. This is foolhardy. I can't condone any of it.'

'There is no *it*, Fiona. I can't foresee a time when the
museum would ever be so imprudent as to state such a thing.
But we need to share this.'

Mike holds up two closely typed pages. He glances at the documents laid out on the table which she had been looking over in preparation for tomorrow's board meeting. 'We can skate quickly over the quarterly finances and management committee reports. Liam and Carrie will both attend, by the way.' He hands her the report. 'In the circumstances, I suggest we bring this to the top of the agenda.'

The words on the page are stark, clinical, demanding attention.

'I see... yes, I see.' Her hand is at her brow, trying to soothe and smooth it. 'We can hardly dump it into Any Other Business, much as I would like to.' She considers how best to introduce this to the museum's board of directors. And more to the point, 'The crucial thing for us all will be how to control the narrative. We must stay on top of this. We must remain calm and keep it contained.'

'Absolutely. No argument about that. Here's to an intriguing board meeting tomorrow. And here's to our disclosures being met with equanimity.'

'Amen!' She clinks her glass against Mike's.

Fiona observes enquiring faces, all curious about this new paper being placed face down on the polished wooden surface, accompanied by her strict, 'Don't look at it yet. I'll introduce it first.' She could be invigilating a school examination.

Seated around the large table are captains of industry, marketing and brand managers, lawyers, financial wizards, archivists and senior management staff. Carrie is seated next to Liam, both suited up. Liam, she knows well enough. A keeper – of antiquities, naturally – and a good soul. Fiona likes him and expects to keep in touch with him after her time as chair ends. Liam will still be working, God willing, and likely to be with them till he retires. Carrie she barely knows. She had introduced herself at last year's Christmas get-together, a hand thrust out and a confident, 'Hi, we haven't met before, I'm Carrie, working with Liam. Just want to say hello and how much I'm loving it here.' There's an energy about her. Fiona had witnessed this when she had tuned into the live streaming to watch Ballybere Man being cleaned up and examined and Carrie enthusiastically talking to the world beyond the camera. Carrie is the bog body expert, not Liam. For good reason the press have christened her the Face of the Find. Watching her now, Fiona hopes that catch-phrase hasn't gone to her head and the vivacious young woman can be reined in. There will be a lot to face.

Having called the meeting to order she goes through the basics: apologies, minutes of the last meeting, then informs them other items might fall off the agenda. She can see hands fiddling with the edges of the paper, but still she holds off, reminding them of their collective responsibility, the principal functions of the board. Only then does she invite them to read.

Papers shuffle, then there is silence. She notes who the quicker readers are as breaths draw in sharply, eyes dart, murmurs of surprise and no doubt alarm escape lips. She catches a mumbled, 'Oh my God!' and, 'Fucking hell!' and, 'Is this for real, Fiona?'

All eyes are on her now. Relief floods through her, knowing she doesn't have to do the explaining. Where to begin?

'I know as much as you, so I'm passing over to Mike. And Liam and Carrie are here to answer our questions. After we've absorbed everything, we need to agree how the museum intends to handle this. And I don't need to stress that what takes place in this room stays in this room. Understood?'

Nods. Promises.

Mike speaks, then Liam makes some remarks and passes the baton to Carrie, who assures everyone they can trust the science behind the data. The assistant keeper sounds as if she has been practising for this moment, voice steady, words carefully chosen.

'Our goal,' Carrie says, 'is to find out as much as we can about Ballybere Man, using our resources and working with colleagues here in Ireland and around the world. We're so privileged to be given this extraordinary opportunity. This is a journey, and I want to encourage everyone to be open to where it takes us. To be open to where *science* takes us. To be open to *discovery*.'

Glancing around the room Fiona is not sure everyone is as up for this voyage as Carrie appears to be.

'Look,' Carrie continues, 'I know you'll be wondering what I think, and the truth is, I don't know!' She laughs openly, but to Fiona the laughter of others sounds distinctly nervous. 'I want to learn everything I can about the man who has come into our care.' Carrie spreads her upturned hands. 'I'm here to answer questions, and I'll tell you everything we know so far.'

As Fiona listens to the to-and-fro, she gives Carrie credit: she is a good communicator. Without getting too technical she explains how the hair analysis can be pinpointed to Palestine; how she is confident the carbon dating is 'pretty accurate'; how Alexander the Great, who had himself conquered that region, is said to have had his body preserved in honey. 'Given that there's a famous precedent from not long before the time we are dealing with, we can't rule it out.' Everyone is sworn to secrecy; all of them are emotionally drained. Before Fiona ends the meeting they have decided on a plan. They cannot hold back any longer; the media have been sniffing around, curious why there had been no updates for ages.

A press conference is convened for tomorrow morning. She, Mike, Liam and Carrie – 'Team Museum', as Mike calls them – will provide an update on Ballybere Man. They will be cautious. They will focus on the science of this discovery. They will be wary of attempts to trap them into saying what they *should* not, what they *must* not claim. Ever!

Things do not work out as Fiona planned. She is woken far too early by the shrill ring of her phone.

'Fiona! What the hell is going on?' A friend has stopped at a supermarket on her way back from a hospital night shift and the morning papers are in. The trashy red-top has the story splashed across the front page. A close-up of Ballybere Man's face – red matted hair spread out, face serene – the banner screaming IS THIS THE FACE OF CHRIST?

'Jesus wept!' At Fiona's screech, her husband jolts upright gasping, 'What? What?'

'That Carrie!' The Face of the Find must have spoken out of turn. If so, the assistant keeper will be disciplined, might not be a 'keeper'. Swinging her legs out of bed she prepares to face this challenge to her authority. She, Fiona McCormac, is captain of this ship, and if need be the vessel can sail on with or without Carrie O'Neill aboard.

PART TWO

The Truth Seekers

11

The Weight of Blame

CARRIE O'NEILL GROPES FOR HER PHONE AND through bleary eyes glimpses the caller's name. *Finn! Give me a break.* It's just past six. She dismisses his call and closes her eyes. It rings again, and she reminds herself to select a less jangling tone. Nothing Finn wants can be urgent. She swipes left, tries to settle but her mind starts whirling. Best get to work early and prepare the briefing she is charged with drafting for Mike and Fiona. When she steps out of the shower the phone rings again. This time it's not Finn.

'Liam. What's going on?'

'...and saying we might have Jesus! Christ, Carrie!' Liam is uncharacteristically shouty.

Within seconds she has grasped the situation. 'Oh, shit! Shit!' She hurriedly dries herself.

'Carrie! How could you, after everything we said? I've had Mike on the phone, who'd had Fiona on the phone. Mike tells me you've had contact with a reporter from that tabloid.'

'That fat guy, you mean? I spoke to him once, briefly.' One leg, two legs in her undies, reaching for her bra.

'Apart from the banner across the whole page, read the ruddy article—'

'Soon as I can—'

'Don't pay for that garbage, we've a copy here. Says the body came from Israel—'

'Hah! I'd never use that name—' Reaching arms through her sweater. 'I always say Palestine or Middle East. Not that I *did* say anything.'

'Who then?' Liam presses. 'Who's been talking? And don't you dare talk to that one from the *Irish Times*.'

'No. No. Course not.' Carrie hastily dismisses another of Finn's incoming calls. Now she understands. Fully dressed, she grabs her keys, slams the door and hurries to her car, Liam's panicky voice still in her ear.

'You on your way? We're at Collins Barracks.'

'Yep, I'll drive. Quicker… Ah!'

Wallet! Bag! She's panting, running back, key in hand. 'Sorry, Liam, I didn't catch that. What did you say?' Oh God, Rachel's trying to reach her now. Sorry friend, bad time. She swipes away the incoming call.

Early morning sun illuminates the scene. The media has descended. Big time. Carrie eyes the logos splashed across parked vans and cars: TV, public and commercial; radio, national and community. All of them ready to do their job and broadcast news of the day. Crews, wearing earphones, holding booms with outdoor mics, or mics in hand, huddle around serious-looking camera kits atop sturdy tripods. The press is here too, broadsheets, tabloids and probably some of the local freebies. She spots Finn, dressed all in black, chatting to a bunch of other journalists. They are gathered around the fat bloke from the spilling-the-beans tabloid.

She parks far away. She will not be carrion for this lot.

Mike's office door is open, voices within: Fiona's, Mike's, Liam's.

'Ah, Carrie, good, good!' Liam looks like a rabbit caught in headlights.

Fiona, her lipstick a fiery I-mean-business red, speaks sharply: 'Close the door behind you.' She indicates an empty chair in the circle.

Despite being bounced into this, Mike looks calm, but she notices a hand reaching to smooth his tie. His PA is seated at his desk, not her own, laptop open.

'Let me be clear.' Carrie is reluctant to sit. 'It wasn't me. I'm not the one who leaked this.' That anyone could think so! She's a professional. Okay, right now she must look a little dishevelled, but she hadn't time to run a comb through her damp hair.

'Apologies, Carrie,' Mike says. 'We've received a tearful mea culpa from one of the newer members of the board, I shan't disclose who. An error of judgement. That person, highly devout, left the meeting in a state of shock, and, well...' He spreads his hands.

'We are where we are. Let's get our statement prepared.' Fiona turns to the PA. 'Can you read back what we have so far, please. And Carrie, correct errors and add anything significant. Before we go public, the minister has requested I share our statement with her. We're not the only ones to have an early start.'

The National Museum, though an independently governed body, is under the Oireachtas's department with culture in its brief. Carrie imagines they fear ridicule, condemnation. Or both.

After listening to what Mike's PA reads aloud there is little Carrie can add. It is bland. Factual. Consciously undramatic. The statement reiterates when and where the body had been retrieved, its condition, traumas observed, samples analysed with results. And a categorical, 'We are not speculating on the provenance of Ballybere Man beyond the known facts.'

'I refuse to let the words of Jesus or Christ pass my lips.' Fiona is adamant. 'The less said the better.'

A short while later, the statement has been polished and shared with the minister, then Fiona looks at Mike. 'Ready?' Team Museum is to be Fiona and Mike this morning.

'Let's do it. Into the lions' den.' Mike ushers Fiona before him.

'Rather them than me,' Liam mutters as he follows them. 'Or me.'

Outside Carrie eyes the media scrum looking as if they'll make mincemeat of dapper Mike Curtis and the very proper Fiona McCormac.

Earlier Fiona had insisted: 'I know it'll look like we are defending a fortress, and we are being defensive. Even so, we will *own* this story.'

Yes, Collin's Barracks has that look about it. Solid. Military. Impregnable.

Fiona and Mike set themselves up under an arched colonnade, with everyone from the media gathered out in the open. Carrie circles around the back of the media pack. From this distance the two of them appear vulnerable, overshadowed by the huge arched columns. Mike is tall, but Fiona's head barely rises above his shoulders. As always, the chair is immaculate, her hairstyle one of those layered short bobs. Carrie has not yet figured if her hair is naturally brown, or if grey is meticulously coloured and streaked. She has never spotted grey roots showing, and imagines Fiona would be the kind of woman to have regular appointments with a hairdresser.

'Good morning!' Fiona begins. 'We've never seen so much interest in our work. Delighted you're all here.' Arch tone, eyebrows arched to match. Carrie hopes the chair manages to handle this lot. 'We're delighted—'

'Mrs McCormac,' a journalist from RTÉ news interrupts. This well-known TV face has been selected to be opening batsperson. 'We've all read what has been published. What's the museum's response? Do you believe the body you have might plausibly be Jesus?'

A quiver at the corner of Fiona's mouth. A touch of nerves? 'We are thrilled to be in possession of such a magnificently preserved body. Our team is working with colleagues around the world.' She ignores the question, slips purple-framed reading glasses on, and reads: 'As chair of the board of directors of the National Museum of Ireland, it is my pleasure, and *duty*, to share with you all we know, *so far*, about our latest bog body acquisition who we have named Ballybere Man...' The museum's official statement is straightforward, the questions from the media less so, but Mike and Fiona stick to the agreed line: 'We will not stray into uncharted waters.' And they don't. They bat away questions, neither of them mentioning the J word or C word. They refuse to be drawn. Carrie skulks at the back, very happy not to be in the firing line. She shares a look with Liam, who is standing next to her knowing he feels the same.

'Mrs McCormac,' the RTÉ journalist presses, 'there *is* speculation. When may we have access to the body? Have our own cameras in?'

'I'm sorry, no. There are issues of contamination, I understand. Until the body is fully preserved, we can't allow that.'

'But we have excellent footage to share.' Mike is trying to sound helpful. 'We can release as many images and video clips as you wish—'

'Finn Durante, *Irish Times*. If we had access and could see the body for ourselves, it could help demystify things. Dampen things down.'

'We'll let you know when,' Mike says. 'And of course, we're releasing all the data. You can read the reports we have on the tests. We are being completely transparent. Nothing is being withheld.'

Carrie's phone buzzes. Finn texting: Nothing?

She moves into his line of vision and catches his eye. He cocks his head, and she mouths, 'Later.'

'Will you be speaking with the archbishop, Mr Curtis? Our readers will be interested in knowing.' Another voice from the midst. Surely a reporter from the Catholic weekly.

Mike raises his hands, looking as if he is surrendering in some shoot-out. 'Please. We are here to share our work with you. What we *know*. Share the *facts*.'

'But surely you can't contemplate this might be the body of Christ?'

Again, a deflection, Mike not allowing any significant C words – 'church', let alone 'Catholic church', and decidedly *not* 'Christ' – to pass his lips. Instead, he reminds everyone present, 'We are in the early days of our investigation and will not be drawn on speculation of the provenance of our find.'

Questions continue, and both Mike and Fiona do their best to avoid straying into dangerous territory.

But Carrie cannot avoid Finn. He inches towards her just as Mike is wrapping up the briefing, perhaps suspecting she is about to flee into the depths of the building.

'Why didn't you pick up this morning?' he hisses.

'Glad I didn't.'

'Some friend! You sit on something like this and don't tell me?' Finn's face is flushed.

'I couldn't. This is too sensitive. And don't ask me anything. I can't talk about it. Everything has to go through Mike's office.'

'You're the expert. The one with all the facts in her head.'

'It's the way it's got to be. I'm not banned from seeing you – no one can do that – but I've sworn not to talk shop.'

His voice drops lower. 'We might have Jesus effing Chr—'

'Stop! I won't go there. And don't you either.'

'Ah, come on, Carrie. Be grown-up about this. You can shut the stable door, but the horse has bolted. Well and truly.' He jerks his head towards the journalist who had broken the story. 'His headline has been shared hundreds of thousands of times. And you should see what's already out there: all sorts of crap so-called news websites, left-field – or right-field – religious groups. Kind of funny, but the tabloid's website crashed this morning, there was so much traffic.'

'Really?' There is that much interest?

'Here.' He thrusts his notepad into her hand and on his phone search engine types: *bog body jesus.*

Headline after headline appears. What's more, the story has been picked up globally. There is the Sky News banner, The Sun, NBC, Fox, others she doesn't recognise, each more sensational than the last.

'Oh, shit!' Carrie slumps. Mike and Fiona have misjudged this totally. There is no way the narrative can be controlled.

'Is this what the museum wants? *You* want? Mainstream media, and let's be honest, nutjob organisations, picking up and running with it?' Impatiently he scrolls to a Christian news outlet's header: HAS THE TIME ARRIVED? 'They're on the ball. You could've stopped this – or at least been ahead of it. I'm disappointed in you.' Finn's tone is hectoring. 'If you'd worked with me, you could've got an honest, fairly written, intelligent narrative out there and I would have had what old-fashioned journos like to call a scoop. Win, win. Wouldn't that have been better?' His elbow digs into her.

She feels her face flushing but remains silent. He continues, 'Look, promise you'll keep in touch on this? You can at least agree to that, right? We can both make sure stories – *my* stories – are factual, accurate, etcetera… Yes?'

He is right, but… 'Finn, sorry. Right now, I can't speak to the media. Sorry… Sorry.'

'Urgh!' He flicks his notepad shut and turns away.

Quickly she reaches out to grab him. 'But we can meet for a drink later, or there's a movie I'd like—'

'Why? What's the point?' He shoots her a look. 'I thought you trusted me. I don't know where I stand with you.' He pauses. 'Let me ask you, *on* the record. Is the museum being straight up about transparency and willingness to share all the reports?'

'Yes. Definitely.' She nods rapidly, pleased to confirm this.

Finn holds her eye and seems satisfied. 'And strictly *off* the record, where do you stand on this? Is it, or isn't it? Don't say a word, just nod or shake your head.'

But she has not formed an opinion, does not know what to make of the evidence they have. 'I don't know. Truly.'

Again, an 'Urgh'. Finn thinks she is holding back on him. He stalks off.

She has lost his friendship when it has barely started.

And Rachel. What of Rachel? Later, back at her office at the museum, Carrie scrolls through her text messages. The angry one: Carrie. What the f is going on! The concerned one: Hey, please call. We're worried. Where are you? The jokey one: Jeez (am I allowed to use that word?). A message from the other side, please rise and SPEAK!

She takes a deep steadying breath and calls her friend. 'Rach, it's me.'

'Carrie! At long last. God, girl, what in Christ's name is going on... Shit. Wrong words.' Rachel is gabbling. 'I've been worried sick, wondering what the hell – oh shit – is going on. Talk to me. Talk to me and don't dare hang up—'

'If you'll shut up I will!'

'Sorry. Sure, sure.'

'And I'm sorry, Rachel. But if I'd talked to you – and I wanted to – I would've blabbed. Couldn't risk it. You understand?'

'Okay. But talk now. Tell me.'

After Rachel has sucked her dry of the exact test results, with interjections to ask about some precise detail she suddenly thinks about, her friend's tone becomes aggrieved.

'You know, Carrie, whatever happens next, science-wise, right now this is a *story*. I've had Cillian onto me – I introduced you to him, my nephew who reports for the Limerick paper, remember?'

'Oh yes, him.' Carrie cringes, knowing that a good friend would have considered this, would have known that it would be a massive story for a local reporter to have broken: this gathering mystery that had originated on his patch. 'Rach, please understand I couldn't. My bosses didn't trust me, and to be honest, I barely trusted myself. They wanted to get more evidence, draw strands together and present things in a managed way. But it turned to custard.'

'Okay, I hear you.' Rachel's tone is appeasing but Carrie can hear the hurt. 'Don't forget your friends, Carrie. I'm here for you.'

'Thanks, Rach, I know.' And Carrie needs to be here for Rachel, and that means thinking of her extended family obligations. She will come up with a non-contentious angle and feed something to Cillian. That is the least she can do.

She replies to an alarmed message from her parents, assuring them: Not a biggie, just the media playing this up. Speak soon.

When requests for interviews pile into Carrie's email box she forwards them to a designated member of the Comms team. Outlets – from New Zealand in particular – wish to speak with her. It's both weird and wonderful to find Ballybere Man – and she herself – receiving worldwide attention. Why not enjoy the moment?

Some days later she settles with a glass of red wine in hand behind her computer screen and magicks her parents up.

Mum is cautious. 'We don't like the sound of this, Caroline. Are you sure you know what you're doing?'

'No one does. All we can do is keep on with the research – tests and analysis, history and so on.'

'All the same,' Dad says, 'poor Nan's deeply shocked. As far as she's concerned, Jesus is in Heaven, and he should be left in peace. Nan's scared they'll turn her away from the residential home she fancies. Contaminated.'

'You're joking!'

Dad laughs. 'But you know, an old friend wouldn't sit with her at church—'

'Dad!'

'Nan doesn't want to talk with you while you're mixed up in this nonsense.'

'Really? Oh, Dad. Come on!'

'Look. You don't know where this might lead. Think about what you're doing.'

'Yes, Caroline, we're a little anxious here, and you're so far away.' On screen, Mum, normally unsentimental, looks like she wants to reach out and hug her. Nice.

'Love you,' she offers, receiving a gruff, 'And you look after yourself, ay,' from Dad and a, 'Yep,' and dip of the head from Mum.

Carrie refreshes her drink and stares at the screensaver photo: she's a kid, Nan seated behind her, zooming down a log flume, arms flung wide. It hadn't dawned on her that Nan would be upset. It feels as if she is learning to juggle, trying to keep balls in the air, only time after time she misses one and it thuds to her feet. She resolves to get better at it. This is only the beginning. Many specialists – all those 'ists' working within theoretic framework 'isms' – are just getting started: so many post-Enlightenment scientists and historians. And she is one of those seekers in search of provable truths. She will not be stopping any time soon.

12

The Civic Angles

FIONA MCCORMAC WAITS IN THE ROTUNDA AT THE Archaeological Museum, browsing the souvenirs for sale. She loves this building: in particular, this grand entrance with its columns and intricate mosaic floor. She fingers the single strand of pearls around her throat as she waits for Mike to arrive. They have a meeting with the minister, not far away, just along from the museum, but she does not want to be late. Her hand rises from throat to earlobe, where she explores a pearl eardrop. Has she overdone the conservative, I-run-a-respectable-institution look? She smooths the skirt of her pink and grey tweed suit from Harvey Nic's which she has matched with warm pink lipstick.

'Apologies, Fiona.' Mike rushes in pocketing a comb. 'All rather hectic. My phone hasn't stopped. The media. My Lord. Always someone higher up the pecking order: head of news, chief editor, director of something or other. The BBC, someone from Reuters fishing for a fresh angle to feed the global networks.'

'What are you telling them?'

'Comms are repeating our statement, more or less word

for word, but most of them want to speak with me directly. Want a quote, but I won't be drawn.'

The main TV news outlet had given brief coverage, with almost a smile on the newsreader's face: a lighter story amid world crises. But the tone of Finn Durante's opinion piece in the *Times* had been sharper.

> Is there a hint of avoidance in what they said, and didn't say? Are they fearful for consequences? We can respond to the evidence, no longer bound by old superstitions that have dogged us for too long. We are a forward-looking nation. If the National Museum of Ireland is to hold this body for us – the nation, the world – they should get off the fence and declare what they believe they have.

Mike, ever courteous, ushers her out: 'Shall we? Let's see if there are ruffled feathers to smooth at the ministry.'

Fiona admires the woman who has recently been promoted to the mouthful of a title: Minister for Tourism, Arts, Gaeltacht, Sport and Media. She is Gaelic-speaking and keen to promote Ireland as a tourist destination. Fiona is always impressed by her easy-going nature, despite the enormous range of her committee's work.

With coffees to hand, she and Mike sit as if they were about to discuss the implications of latest government policies on grant distribution, with the minister regretful about standstill funding and she and Mike arguing their case. Not today.

'You've been having an interesting time of it, I hear.' The minister, casual and relaxed as always.

'You could say so, Minister,' Fiona responds. 'You'll have seen the headlines and reports.'

'Impossible to avoid.'

'And we're doing our utmost to tamp down the flames.'

Earlier, waiting for Mike, Fiona had scrolled through the latest stories. The ones emanating from the Irish media were tame compared with others, particularly from America. She had been alarmed by some crackpots talking of the Second Coming, while others insisted this was the sign of the devil and a blasphemy to even suggest 'this thing can possibly be our Saviour returned to earth'.

The minister looks sympathetic. 'Are you managing?'

'Thank you, yes,' Mike answers. 'Our assistant keeper, Doctor O'Neill, is our authority. All queries of significance pass through her then back to me.'

'Ah, the Face of the Find.' The minister laughs.

Fiona had scoffed at that moniker but is reassured to know they have someone on staff who has the facts at her fingertips, able to rebuff the stupidest, most ignorant of queries. Carrie's common sense can be relied on.

'So tell me how it's been?' the minister asks. 'And for the record I don't have a religious bone in my body. I'm simply curious. And as you know, your man was dug up on my patch. I have a vested interest.' She laughs again.

Fiona reminds herself that the minister represents a County Clare constituency that includes Ballybere. Naturally she will be taking a keen interest. They fill the minister in on actions they are taking and assure her they will not comment to the media one way or the other about the possibility of this being Jesus. 'It's too absurd to consider,' Fiona stresses.

'If you'd told me when I was a little girl growing up in a tiny town outside Limerick that I'd become a government minister I would have been dumbfounded. If I've learnt anything, it is that life can surprise us.'

Fiona sips her coffee. The minister is not reacting as she

had anticipated. She had supposed the other woman might be horrified by the speculation swirling around one of the nation's revered institutions, or that pressure might have been exerted from above to extinguish the lurid tales. Every so often Ireland could still surprise the world with a gathering of people experiencing a vision of the Virgin Mary or moving statues. Ireland is a modern nation; these things don't fit well. Yet here is the minister ready to be surprised. Maybe her own choice of pearls and besuited 'establishment' outfit has been the wrong one.

'While we respond to the media,' Mike says, 'our work on the body continues. Preservation, further tests and so on. And I'm developing my own plans ready to present to the board. May I share my thoughts?'

'Please do.'

'This is a wonderful opportunity for us.' Mike's voice oozes enthusiasm. 'Whatever the final analysis of Ballybere Man leads us to conclude, we have a fantastically preserved body—'

'Can't wait to lay eyes on him.'

'—that will draw visitors from far and wide.'

'Oh yes.' The minister looks amused. 'We can be certain of that.'

'I want to rearrange the museum to allow an entire gallery for this find. It warrants it.'

'I'm sure it does.'

'Ideally at the Archaeological Museum, close to our current bog body collection, though space is more limited there. The Collins Barracks site offers more flexibility, though it may mean putting some of our collection – part of our rural life exhibits, for example – in storage.'

Really? Fiona is cautious. She and Mike have not discussed this!

A frown creases the minister's eyes and Fiona resists an urge to intervene. Mike is not finely attuned to the nature of

Irish politics, and this celebration of rural life is something that will resonate with the minister's constituency.

'I'm thinking tourism here, Minister.' Mike eyeballs the politician. 'We can expect a substantial increase in footfall when we're able to exhibit Ballybere Man in all his glory. I'm imagining the videos we can install, the contextual information. It will be spectacular.'

'Ah, yes. Tourism.' The minister shifts in her chair. 'That's what I want to talk with you about.'

Fiona smiles invitingly. The minister is taking everything in her stride. Good woman!

'I've been talking with colleagues in other departments: Local Government and Heritage, Rural and Community Development. It's not only me taking a keen interest in how this story unfolds.'

Fiona mumbles, 'I'm sure.'

The minister continues, 'The thing is, there are others who are staking their claim.'

'Minister?' Now Fiona is alert, sitting straight, ankles crossed, and Mike, she notes, is twisting his ring.

The minister speaks clearly: 'Ballybere town wants Ballybere Man back home.'

'Excuse me, Minister?' Her voice sounds far too shrill.

'The leader of Clare County Council presented his case to me, and it is compelling.'

Fiona is floored. She and Mike prepared for this meeting considering all the angles the minister might raise, and they have suitable responses. But not for *this*. Mike's jaw has slackened, and Fiona doesn't dare risk picking up her coffee. She folds her hands on her lap and smiles, inviting the minister to continue.

'My department covers a wide area of government concerns, and occasionally we find there are conflicts of interest to be balanced. Your Ballybere Man, whoever he is, is proving my point. You, on one hand, assume your exceptional find must be housed at the museum—'

'Well, of course!' Mike, indignant.

'Minister, to consider otherwise is preposterous.' Her, defending her territory against interlopers.

'Don't worry too much but please hear me out.' The minister settles back, looking less friendly and not as casual. 'Our policies are to promote and support national and cultural heritage, but also to promote regional development.'

Fiona finds her hands are trembling. She does not like where this may be leading. Ballybere is, after all, in the minister's constituency.

'Supporting initiatives in rural areas is vital,' the minister says. 'We can't just be seen to be supporting our major institutions, so—'

'But we are a *national* institution.' Mike's tone rises a pitch. 'We are geared towards preserving and presenting carefully curated exhibitions of this magnitude. What does Ballybere town hope to do with the body? Convert a village hall? If they have such a thing!'

'Minister,' Fiona jumps in quickly, 'please tell us more?' Mike's cosmopolitan soul has burst forth and this is not a good moment.

'Not a village hall, Mr Curtis. They have ambitions. They changed their mind about a shopping centre on the cleared bog site. They're turning their thoughts to a specialist museum.'

'A museum?' Fiona and Mike repeat the word.

'There's a precedent for this. Silkeborg, Denmark, barely warranted a place on the map, but now look at it, with their own bog body to share with the world in a purpose-built facility. Clare County Council understand the scale of it, can see that wherever it leads, it will put *them* on the map.'

'Are you serious, Minister?' Mike voices what Fiona fears to ask.

'Why not? We must all seriously consider it. I'm asking you to do the same.'

With half an ear Fiona listens to the minister as she talks about the shifting concept of Irish arts and heritage, and how these days we are all linked to a global digital world to share information, stories and whatnot.

'Yes!' Mike interrupts. 'That's it exactly. That is our role as the national institution. Digital technology can make our proposed Ballybere Man exhibition reach the entire world! You know, RTÉ were with us yesterday. We are sharing our story.'

Fiona nods supportively. After their initial cautious news conference they have opened the doors. A current affairs TV crew has interviewed Mike, Liam and Carrie, while the programme researcher worked her way through hours of film of the body being cleaned and examined in the prep room.

'Minister, we are enormously excited about our plans,' Mike continues, leaning further forward in his chair, 'and hope we have your backing for how best to exhibit Ballybere Man.'

'But Mr Curtis,' the minister is very formal now, 'Dublin need not be the epicentre. We need to support the regions. We can imagine, can we not, a scenario of allowing Ballybere Man to drive regeneration in the west of Ireland? Shannon airport stands ready. Don't you agree?'

Fiona does *not* agree, and fears Mike might say something derogatory. The look of his face suggests he might spit out: 'How dare that pitiful backwater think they can take *our* body away!' She isn't sure he has even visited the western rural reaches; his trips are usually to world capitals or cultural centres of excellence. But he recovers more quickly than she does, licks his lips and speaks with admirable calm.

'Minister, thank you for sharing this. It gives us something to ponder, and perhaps something to work with. We are very much in favour of partnerships. After all, Liam and Carrie are busy reaching out globally to the scientific and academic world, and I understand where the town is coming from. I am grateful for the heads-up on the government needing to support rural regions.'

Fiona rallies. 'Yes, thank you, Minister, for sharing this line of thought.' The minister might not have a religious bone in her body, but she has Proud Celt running through her like a stick of rock candy. The minister will promote what she believes is right for the country as a whole and, Fiona thinks, what is best for her constituency. And – feeling waspish now – for her ministerial job.

It is starkly laid out. The museum has competition for the body and soul of Ballybere Man.

13

The Ways of Seeing

THE ARCHBISHOP IS WAITING TO RECEIVE THEM IN A beautiful room in a grand residence, and the man is equally grand in his long black, red-trimmed cassock, white clerical collar and scarlet skull cap. Sudden panic. How to greet an archbishop? Carrie hangs back waiting for Mike to step forward. She need not worry. Years of experience have taught the man of faith how to put others at ease.

'Thank you for coming.' He introduces himself to Mike before turning to her, smile and eyes friendly, handshake warm. And there is tea. And biscuits. They settle in comfy chairs: she, Mike, the archbishop, and an aide whose actual title is lost to her the moment he introduces himself.

'You know, I was watching the news the other night, and I'm intrigued,' the archbishop says, 'and you will not be surprised to learn that my phone has been red hot. So many priests seeking guidance on what to tell their parishioners.'

It had been the Dublin archbishop who reached out requesting a meeting, and Mike contacted Carrie sounding frazzled. 'I imagine this is a polite "nice to meet you and how are things going at the museum" over a cup of tea. Heaven only knows – one is tempted to say – where the conversation may lead.' He gave a nervous giggle. 'You had best come with me as you're the only one who can sensibly answer questions of a scientific nature.'

She resisted at first. She is working her socks off, developing compelling partnership proposals with colleagues around the world, making the case for Ballybere Man staying right where he is. She needs headspace for this, and visiting the archbishop is a distraction. She frowns, focusing on what he is saying.

'Don't worry. The Holy Inquisition is not about to ramp up again.'

The archbishop smiles, so she smiles, and Mike mutters a jocular, 'I hope not, Your Grace.'

The churchman continues, 'We have too many *real* and much more pressing issues to attend to.'

Too right! The sexual abuse scandals opened a Pandora's Box. The church reeled, and has not yet recovered its equilibrium. The Catholic Church still has authority in Ireland, but it is waning as secularisation continues apace. She's seen that for herself the rare times she has popped into a church and, at Nan's insistence, lit a candle for her grandfather. Another time, out of curiosity, she attended a service and found there was hardly anyone her own age in the sparse congregation.

'So yes, intrigued is the right word.' The archbishop smiles invitingly. 'Tell me about your Ballybere Man?'

The archbishop listens without interrupting, nods then looks directly at her.

'The hair test, Doctor O'Neill. How accurate is this?'

'Extremely, Your Grace. And to make sure, we sent further samples to a different lab. Same result.'

He ponders this. 'And the body dating?'

'Yes, we are confident about that.'

'And the markings?' The archbishop touches a wrist, his eyes still on her.

'We can't say what caused them, Your Grace, all we can say is that they, and the one on the foot, are not consistent with post-mortem injuries we've seen before, and might lead to a conclusion this man was…' she takes a breath, keeps her eyes on his, '…crucified while still living.'

Her heart hammers against her ribs, imagining what Nan might make of this conversation with a highly appointed priest. She'd have a heart attack!

'Most interesting.' He sips his tea as if she's told him what was in the sandwich she'd eaten for lunch. He is not ruffled and gives no indication of what is going through his mind. 'Mr Curtis,' he continues. 'You can imagine the unquiet this raises in parishes around the world. In all churches.'

Carrie bites her lip. Yes! Someone at Nan's church hadn't let her sit next to them!

The archbishop continues, 'Our own publication' – the Roman Catholic one, she reasons – 'is asking for my contribution to an article for this week's edition. One of the reporters attended your press event.'

'I recall,' Mike says.

'And ripples are extending. Our representative at the Holy See – our nuncio – was in touch saying he was aware of our small drama. It is my duty to report back.'

'We're happy to assist in any way we can,' Mike offers.

The archbishop hesitates before asking: 'Doctor O'Neill, I am curious how far science can go answering the questions you are asking of this body?'

'A great deal, we anticipate. We're only just scratching the surface of this investigation. This will keep us going for years. In time we hope to answer the question about who this man was by building a compelling narrative.'

'Ah, a narrative.' Now the archbishop smiles. 'Well, he can't be Christ. I am sure of that. And I imagine you, or the museum, will never claim such a thing.'

'Of course not, Your Grace.' Mike's quick response.

She longs to catch Mike's eye with a *why not?* look, but decides to maintain eye contact with the archbishop, determined to stand her ground. The church leader might believe a divine Jesus ascended to Heaven to sit by God, but she is a scientist. A no-nonsense farm girl who has assisted her parents remove animal carcasses for disposal. Life ends, as surely as it had begun through maternal and paternal coupling. And Ballybere Man *had* had a mother, his belly button attests to the fact he had been nurtured inside a womb. The question of his paternity is beyond reach. She hopes the archbishop won't start down the road of miraculous conception. She is not about to be intimidated by this man's authority, God-given or not.

'Your Grace, it's impossible to say what conclusions we might come to. We're on a journey of discovery and we don't know where it will lead us. I would love to believe the world can be open to what we conclude. I believe in the power of science.'

The archbishop gives a loud, heartfelt laugh. 'And I believe in the power of God. I could hardly say otherwise.'

They chat on, and their meeting ends, amicably but with a chasm between them.

Finn texts, I'm still not talking to you, even so, check this out. She follows the link: an open audience discussion organised by Trinity College. BALLYBERE MAN: THE BODY OF JESUS? A spontaneous reaction to events. Two speakers: Pastor Reilly of Grace of God Evangelical church, both unfamiliar names; and Professor Colm Byrne, who is very familiar indeed. Carrie whoops.

Are you going? she texts back.

Course, is Finn's immediate response.

A meal before? On me, she tries.

Finn doesn't take the bait for several minutes. Then, Guess we'll have to talk then. I pick the restaurant. Relief floods through her. She doesn't mean to push Finn away; it just seems to happen.

A Mexican eatery, quick and tasty. They sit, mending their friendship, clutching taquitos and tacos oozing guacamole and refried beans. Finn understands. This is delicate. The museum, and she, as project leader, must step carefully.

'Wow!' Carrie shares a look with Finn, both surprised to find themselves jostling for seats at the back of the heaving lecture hall.

'Hot gig,' Finn agrees.

She looks at the audience. Young people – students? – middle-aged and grey-haired people – academics by the looks of many. And goodness knows who else. Some will be curious churchgoers. To one side, RTÉ has set up. She recognises the crew who interviewed her recently; no doubt some of this evening's exchanges will be included in that extended news package. Or perhaps it's a documentary the TV channel is preparing. She hadn't asked at the time.

There is a tangible charge in the air. Then shushes.

A young, earnest-looking woman, the moderator, takes her seat centre stage. 'From the Student Union exec,' Finn whispers, 'one of these debating society nerds, I bet you. She'll lower the temperature, keep us from rioting.' Carrie suppresses a giggle. A man Carrie judges to be in his fifties walks on stage and sits to the moderator's left. Pastor Reilly doesn't look the rabid sort. He wears a dark suit, and strong stage lights give a sheen to his balding head.

Then, stage left, someone manoeuvres Professor Byrne to his place at the right of the moderator. He looks frailer; in the months since Carrie has seen him he has deteriorated.

Welcomes and introductions then the moderator is straight in: 'The National Museum of Ireland houses a freshly found bog body displaying unusual characteristics. Laboratory analysis informs us this man is about two thousand years old, hailing from the Middle East in a country we now call Israel. Could this possibly be the body of Jesus Christ?'

Bluntly stated. *Very* bluntly stated.

A murmur from one section of the auditorium. Heads twist to friends, or lean close, hands raised to mouths. The moderator waits for the audience to settle, her face impartial, as if she is here to oversee a discussion on whether student loans should be abolished. But this evening's *should* relates to Ballybere Man. Carrie imagines the debating topic: 'We should remain open to Ballybere Man being the body of Jesus.' Something like that. Except this isn't a formal debate. More a chance to air opposing views and influence future debate.

'Pastor Reilly will argue why this bog body cannot possibly be Jesus. Professor Byrne will argue why we should consider that possibility. Gentlemen…' The moderator turns to each of her guests. 'You each have twenty minutes for your arguments, five minutes to respond, then we'll open the floor to questions. Pastor Reilly.'

So, a debate to all intents and purposes. Carrie avoided school and uni debating societies like the plague, and knew no one who belonged to them. This evening she is all ears. Finn takes out a notepad and pen as Pastor Reilly stands, adjusts the height of his microphone, and clears his throat. He doesn't have notes.

'You know, when I received this invitation to speak, I thought long and hard before accepting. But my conscience insisted that I must. In twenty minutes, I am not attempting to cover the entire history of Christology or theological beliefs of different churches. That would be impossible. But I can tell you my deeply researched and deeply held response.' He clears his throat again and speaks confidently.

'This bog body cannot be Christ as his body has *actually* risen from the dead. The resurrection of Christ is *the* fundamental tenet of Christianity. It's cornerstone. Few scholars dispute these facts...' He marks them off one by one on his fingers: 'That Jesus lived. Was killed. Was buried. Disappeared. His tomb – a *sealed* tomb – found empty. Where had he gone? What happened next?

'Here is what I want to stress. *Eyewitness* accounts, *independent* accounts, soon after his death, show he appeared to his disciples, in a manner that led them to believe he was the risen Jesus. Not some sort of vision or weird dream, but an *actual* man. These were what the academics among you' – he shoots a look at Professor Byrne – 'might call *post-mortem* appearances. There is no suggestion he didn't really die on the cross. The Romans knew very well how to kill people.'

A titter from the audience. Sounds of air sucking through teeth. Otherwise silence.

Pastor Reilly continues, 'There is no such thing as a resurrection without an actual body. Consider this. You're one of the disciples who've followed Jesus, who has promised he will be a leader, a messiah, but now he has been humiliated and executed. These men followed Jewish belief, remember – there was no such thing as Christianity back then – and their belief, their worldview, did not predispose them to think of such a thing as rising from the dead. But they *did* come to this conclusion, they were convinced this extraordinary thing had happened. We have no reason to doubt this.'

'Nowhere is it suggested Jesus's body was removed and embalmed in *honey*! Nowhere is there evidence he was transported, physically, anywhere, let alone to the west coast of Ireland and reburied in a shallow lake. Absurd! Why would they do that? And how would the disciples have managed to get into a guarded tomb in the first place? Why would they risk their own lives? So where did Jesus go?'

Pastor Reilly spreads his hands looking around the audience.

'Historical *facts* show Jesus was exalted at the resurrection once his earthly ministry was completed. This is evidence of his ascension. It is said in John 13 *I will come again and receive you myself, and where I am, there you may be also.*' Then Pastor Reilly quotes from Revelations, looking out at the audience. *'There will be no mistake when Christ returns. He will be recognisable to us, personally and literally—'*

'Glory be to that!' a woman's voice rings out from the front seats.

'No one should imagine the divine being of Christ would choose to reveal himself in a bog.'

A titter from some in the audience and Finn nudges Carrie, whispering, 'Don't see why not.' On stage Prof Byrne furiously scribbles on a pad resting on his lap.

Pastor Reilly continues stressing how the resurrection was understood by Jesus's earliest followers. He references the gospels: the evidence, defensible facts.

'Time and again the gospels record how Jesus appeared to his followers after his crucifixion. This wasn't a ghost, or an hallucination. He showed them his scars. We have the testimony of Mary Magdalene, of people on the road to Emmaus, of Peter, of Mary. There's the testimony of the apostles, and Thomas – old doubting Thomas, that sceptic, who's dubious, wants *evidence*. The gospel of John goes into this in detail. Jesus invites him to touch the wounds in his hands – *hands*, not *wrists*, mark you. And – this is important – *The Wound On His Side*. "Reach out your hand," Jesus tells Thomas, "and put it into my side."' Pastor Reilly places a hand under his ribs, repeating, 'Into my side.' He looks around the audience. 'And let's note this fact – though I haven't cast eyes on this bog body myself – there is no spear wound in his side, yet there is evidence Jesus was pierced with a spear.'

'That's right!' A male voice from the audience. Echoes of agreement.

Pastor Reilly's voice rises. 'To suggest this mummified body raised from an ancient peat bog might be the body of Jesus is not to be borne. And as for considering this might be the Second Coming of Christ? Well… well…' Pastor Reilly's face is puce, his bald head almost glowing. 'This is heretical. It would make this the Antichrist.' He is emphatic, jabbing a finger. 'This bog body cannot possibly be Christ. I say again. He has *actually* risen and the sooner this is clarified to the world, the better. Thank you… Thank you.'

Thunderous claps, cheers and whistles erupt as he returns to his chair.

Huh! They like what they hear? Carrie is surprised but doesn't have time to dwell on this.

'Professor Byrne,' the moderator invites her next guest, 'you have the floor.'

Professor Byrne, sunk into his wheelchair, gestures, and his carer, the same woman who accompanied him to the museum, steps out from the wings. Maybe she is a relative. Carrie hadn't asked at the time, and he hadn't introduced her. Now the woman plumps up a cushion behind the prof and he sits up a little straighter. His microphone stand is lowered then he dismisses her with a flick of his hand. If the carer is a daughter, she has her own cross to bear.

Prof Byrne begins. 'How does society, and its institutions, respond to facts and ideas that challenge its basic assumptions? That is a huge question. I want to encourage all of us to keep an open mind and consider why *shouldn't* this body we are calling Ballybere Man be Jesus? It's certainly some man's body from about the right time, from exactly the right place, exhibiting marks consistent with crucifixion.'

Despite his microphone, Professor Byrne's voice sounds thin and reedy.

'The scriptures, those included in the Bible today, are a selection of many documents and gospels created over the centuries. But let's work with the Bible, limit ourselves to that book and consider the *evidence*.'

Professor Byrne's hard stare turns on Pastor Reilly. Carrie is transported back to his tutorials. 'Support your case more adequately, Miss O'Neill, I am not convinced. Where is your evidence?' And with that her latest essay would be flung into her lap. Goosebumps again, this time of gratitude she's not the one in the prof's sights.

'I agree there is historical evidence that a Jewish messianic leader called Jesus lived in Palestine,' Prof Byrne continues. 'There is ample evidence for that. I agree that he irked the Roman rulers, who feared he was planning a new kind of rule. At that time there was a lot of resistance to the cultural and religious assimilation being imposed on Jews. I agree that those Romans were good at getting rid of their prisoners and would have done a thorough job of killing Jesus. What happened next? Sources – and we are sticking to what is in the Bible – conflict. But let's agree he was buried – not in a pit, which was a common end for criminals – but entombed in a cave. Such rock-cut tombs were typical for wealthy Jews, and

Joseph of Arimathea, one of Jesus's followers who was given permission to take Jesus's body, was wealthy. Then what? So far Pastor Reilly and I are on the same page.' He nods at his opponent. 'Is it inconceivable that Jesus's body might not have been spirited away? I don't mean miraculously spirited away, but actually *stolen*. This hypothesis has been around for a long time. Maybe his mother and other women? His disciples? Surely we have to agree it's *possible?*'

'Shame on you! Shame!'

Carrie cranes her neck to see a man in the audience on his feet, shaking a fist. He is shushed, urged to sit, and Prof Byrne continues.

'So, stealing the body of Jesus. Yes, it is plausible and not beyond our imagination to consider possible. We haven't the leisure this evening to look at the inconsistencies in the gospels or consider the time lag between when Jesus lived and when they were written. Pastor Reilly's so-called evidence for the resurrection cannot be proved historically. We have no means of scientifically proving a physical body can miraculously be taken to Heaven. His arguments presuppose a *belief*, a theological belief in God, and that is not something that can be tested by historical or scientific evidence. Where are we if we don't believe in God? How do we begin to find common ground unless we can agree on scientific and historical truths?'

Finn, who has been scribbling, flicking over filled pages in his small reporter's pad, pauses and nudges her. 'Do you? Believe, I mean.'

'As a child. Not now,' she whispers. It had been gradual, like her girl's body growing to become a woman's. You don't notice something happening, until one day you look back and find you have journeyed. That's how it felt.

The prof is in full flow, his voice stronger.

'I ask again. If we don't believe in a god, or *the* God, a

divine being, if we don't have that worldview, that theological framework, then we can surely conceive this mummified body retrieved from an Irish bog close to the west coast might, plausibly, be Jesus.'

Thumping of feet and hisses. A sector of the audience who have obviously come as a group does not like this. Their modest protest is met with a stern look from the moderator and Professor Byrne continues.

'Or Ballybere Man may be from a slightly later period – carbon dating isn't that accurate – so it's plausible this is an early Christian who refused to honour the Roman gods. That would be enough to get you killed. Maybe this man is someone else of importance lost to history.' Professor Byrne raises his voice. 'Consider this…' He takes a breath only to be overcome by a fit of coughing and his carer rushes from the wings unscrewing a bottle of water. He sips then hands it back. 'Consider this. There is evidence of extensive trade links between Ireland and the rest of the known world. Trade was at the heart of the Roman empire. It is possible to imagine that, for whatever reason, a body might be preserved – in honey in this case – and might be transported to a remote site in Ireland and hidden, again for whatever reason. This place we call Ireland was outside the Roman Empire. Safe from scrutiny. And maybe that site wasn't so remote back then. Maybe that bog was known to a group or groups of people.'

Yes! Carrie breathes deeply. Everything the prof is saying is what she has been considering – though not as lucidly as he is articulating – but she has not been allowed to speak. But he can. He has a platform to put forward his theories. While Finn's notepad fills up, she listens carefully.

'For all the research we have done on sacred sites in Ireland,' the prof says, 'there is a lot we don't understand about the past. And this is what is fascinating. I suggest we open our minds – not form an opinion one way or the other – but allow ourselves to consider that Ballybere Man just might be the historical man, Jesus.'

He is done. Professor Byrne sinks back into his wheelchair looking exhausted.

Carrie barely listens to Pastor Reilly's response, which is short and predictable, as is the professor's.

Question time.

Hands shoot up. Assistants rush down the isles with mics. An older man speaks: 'Professor Byrne. What you say is not respectful. Are you trying to poke fun? For those of us who are Christians, you know the time of Christ's death is the most sacred moment.'

'Understood. I hold all religious belief in high regard,' Professor Byrne responds. 'Such thoughts, as I suggest, need not conflict with Christian belief.'

'I just don't see how you can say such a thing!' The man shakes his head, puzzled, seems about to ask a follow-up question before changing his mind, ceding the mic. More questions. Most for her old prof accusing him of going against the scriptures, of undermining the church. All the while Pastor Reilly sits, arms folded across his belly looking smug. There are more people of religious persuasion in the audience than she realised, their hostility barely veiled. She leans across to Finn: 'They don't get his arguments.'

'Your problem is you've been in your academic and secular bubble too long. The same could be said for me. How many people read the *Irish Times*? What Byrne says unsettles people. It asks them to consider reframing their worldview. Even if they're not believers.'

'I would love people to understand about the work I'm leading on. You know, have people see this is, well, *normal*.'

'Normal!' Finn stifles a laugh. 'There is nothing normal about what you're doing. But, you know, Carrie, this might be a good time for a feature: the Face *behind* the Find.'

She cringes. 'No!'

'Seriously. Pics of you on the farm. A wholesome Kiwi kid. Couldn't be more down to earth than that.'

She considers. 'It couldn't be just about me. It would have to be about the body and how we are proposing to investigate. I'd want people to know we are being respectful of the past and respectful of the body. And I want to excite people, get them onside.'

'Of course, of course. All of that.'

'And I'd have to clear it with Liam. And Mike.'

'Understood. But before you change your mind. Deal?' He tilts his head.

'Depending on the official seal of approval.' She extends her hand and they shake.

Looking around at the unsettled audience, she truly realises how disturbing this Ballybere Man conjecture is. Nan hasn't been responding to her emails, but it is not just her who is freaked out. The enormity of being project leader for Ballybere Man is beginning to sink in.

14

The Ripples

Nathaniel Porter is driving his battered Ford pick-up, a Marlboro between stained fingers, elbow resting on the window, radio dialled high. Garth Brooks's voice pierces his heart. Oh, man, too much, too much. Nearing crossroads, he slows and takes a left off the highway. The asphalt soon gives way to gravel as the road narrows. He is nearing the end of a near two-fifty-mile trip out of Kentucky State to drop off his kids. Given that he had made the same trip two days earlier to pick them up, that adds up to an *investment*. And if you put in, you want a return. He'd turned up at Shelly's door rehearsing his, 'Hey, sweetheart, how about we get back together?' line, but on seeing the shape of a man slide out of view beyond her shoulder the words stuck in his throat. He didn't get past the threshold and the speed the two boys scootered past with a backward 'Bye, Daddy' suggested a family reunion wasn't on the cards.

It had been a tough weekend, with his trailer home tucked away in the woods barely containing him and his boys – his occasional family – for all that it had a second bunk room. The boys couldn't seem to pass the time without arguing. Middle of summer, hot as, yet those kids barely set foot outside. It didn't help that the internet came and went. Mainly went. The boys showed him a story doing the rounds, about a body.

'Is this really Jesus, Daddy?' one of the kids asked, holding out a phone.

'I guess it's a joke. Some kinda hoax,' he answered. He was worried they were looking at something unwholesome on a weird platform and Shelly would have his arse. But no, these stories and pictures were on Christian news outlets she would approve of. He and the kids soon lost interest in the story, but it filled a few minutes.

Back home now, with Shelly's new guy playing on his mind, Nate cracks a tab and places the frosted tin against his forehead. He's given in to temptation by stopping at an out-of-town liquor store. *Sorry, God, for lettin' you down.* Guzzling the beer, he opens his phone and flicks through messages. Check this out, urges Ray, one of his buddies. He settles on the cracked leather two-seater couch and clicks the link: highlights of a TV programme about this ancient body dug up from the earth. Man, oh, man. What on earth was going *on* over there?

There is some sort of event in a theatre. On stage, the man on the right, quotes from Revelations: '"Behold, He is coming with the clouds and every eye will see Him."' Yes, sir, Nate agrees, that is so. That is how the Lord will return. Then the guy is saying, 'There will be no mistake when Christ returns. He will be recognisable to us, personally and literally. No one should imagine the divine being of Christ would choose to reveal himself in a bog.'

No way, 'course not! Then the old guy in the wheelchair says, 'If we don't believe in a god, or the God, a divine being, if we don't have that worldview, that theological framework, then why can't we conceive this mummified body that has been retrieved from an Irish bog close to the west coast might, plausibly, be Jesus?'

Nate pauses the programme, not quite understanding the words but feeling shaken, feeling a little sick. He unscrews a bottle of rye.

He knows himself to be a godly man, as were his father and granddaddy: Pastor Porter, founder of Church of Jesus Christ the Saviour. His brother, the sharper tool in the shed, is now pastor, their sisters all good wives and mothers. His own struggles to keep on the right side, the Light side, are well known. Everyone around here knows each other's business whether you want it or not. He has not made a success of his marriage, but hopes bridges can be built… Does he, though? He has kicked the booze – today aside – and regularly prays for forgiveness for that time he weighed in on Shelly and her wrist got broke. She might not be ready to forgive him, but the Lord has.

Nate closes his eyes, recalling that moment of bliss when his worries had washed away with the cool river water of his second baptism when he had repledged his service to God. He can hear the voices of his community clapping and calling, 'Amen.'

One of his aunts hosts the morning slot on the community evangelical station everyone listens to over breakfast or driving kids to their junior, or senior, faith schools. Tuesdays and Thursdays are Bible-reading evenings and Sundays he listens to his brother's powerful preaching. And with his twice-a-week radio slots, *Pastor Porter Preaches*, he never runs the well dry.

This body in Ireland… Nate resumes watching.

A TV presenter is on screen again, with lots of golden curly reddish hair and a cute accent he can just about keep up with. As she talks the view changes. The outside of a big stone building – a museum, he learns – is where the body is. They cut to a close-up of this old leathery thing laying on a table, with people in plastic aprons gathered around. Then there's a pretty lady being interviewed in an office. The subtitle says *Dr Caroline O'Neill*. Nate frowns, concentrating on what she is saying in her different accent, hands flying up, a broad grin: 'Oh, yes, it was so exciting to be the one to dig him out, and an honour to be the project leader. This is a find of a lifetime. Look, I'm a scientist. I am totally open to where this might lead, and with the evidence we have so far there could be quite a story.' A laugh again.

Open to where this might lead? This doctor lady wasn't putting a stop to crazy talk? How could this be allowed?

As Nate is figuring this out, they've cut back to the body when it was being cleaned up some months ago and he realises the doctor lady is one of those wearing aprons and masks. They're in a fancy old building now. A man, the director, so it says, is standing in front of a big red display board headed up *Kingship & Sacrifice*, with words in a foreign language underneath. The man is being asked by someone he can't see: 'But surely you can't contemplate this new body you have acquired might be the body of Christ?'

No! Nate urges him to reply. *We sure are NOT!* Instead, there's some umming and aahing and throat-clearing before Mr Curtis (he sees the name on screen) says, 'It's early days, and we can't speculate what, or who, we have. I'd like to remind you—'

Anger surges up and Nate's thumb presses stop. Why didn't the man say this shrivelled-looking thing could *never, ever* be Jesus? He punches the old cushion next to him. They're giving space to allow Satan in. The Second Coming will be soon. But not like this. Never like this! And, until that time comes the good Lord sits in Heaven next to the Father. Nate particularly loves Thessalonians 4:16. He says it aloud now, reassuring himself.

'For the Lord himself will descend from Heaven with a cry of command, with the voice of an archangel, and with the sound of the trumpet of God. And the dead in Christ will rise first. Then we who are alive, who are left, will be caught up together with them in the clouds to meet the Lord in the air, and so we will always be with the Lord.'

Yes, sir. This is a strong verse. There is nothing soft about the Jesus he loves.

He's also fond of a quote from Matthew – he can't recall chapter and verse – about watching out for false prophets. 'They come to you in sheep's clothing, but inwardly they are ferocious wolves.'

He closes his eyes and prays: 'Lord, let them see the error of their ways. Shine your light, dear Lord. Lead them from darkness.'

That Sunday, Pastor Porter – younger brother Jake – is in good form, striding back and forth helping them understand what had got under everyone's skin.

'We've been hearing things. Seeing things. Reading things these past weeks… y'all know what I'm on about – this old, old body dug up in Ireland. Till now, I've not chosen to use my time here with y'all talking about what's happenin' far away. But it's time… It's time.' Jake pauses. 'Now, we know that Our Lord came down to earth in human form to teach and preach and through his sacrifice saved us. And we know after he was crucified, as we're told, time and again, that he *rose*.' Jake lifts high the Bible in his hand. 'God raised him to Heaven until such time he deems it right to return.'

'Amen.' Nate joins others, voices echoing between the wooden walls of their church.

'And because we know this, we know for a certainty we will be gathered when the trumpets call. We know Jesus will return to save us. Huh?'

'Yes!'

'Amen!' Nate and everyone assure him.

Pastor Porter brings his hands to his chest. 'We hold God in our hearts. We are serious about serving God. Right? Y'all with me on this?'

Yes, they are! They call to him, to each other, to themselves.

'What we hear about, my friends, is the devil's work happening way across the world from us. Now, we know the Revelation will come. Matthew 24:12, "Therefore be alert for you do not know which day your Lord is coming." Matthew goes on to say this will be at an hour we may not think he will. Meaning we are bound to be surprised at the manner of his returning. But not like this, my friends. Not for a moment should we allow this thought. We know Our Lord would never reveal himself in such a way. Found in a bog! Mires like this are portals to hell. This is the work of the devil. You hear me?'

'We hear you.'

'Now, some of your families came from the Emerald Isle. Many of our ancestors did, seeking to escape poverty for a better life in our blessed country. My own family hails from County Armagh, so I'm led to believe.' He opens his Bible to the inside page with names of previous generations of Porters and women they've married, and his finger traces: 'And see here: Daniel Porter M – means married – Colleen O'Neill 1882. Written right here. I guess this Colleen O'Neill, must've been one of the many coming to this promised land. These are my people. Your people. Our flesh and blood. Do you want these misled folks in the old country to burn in hell? Huh? Do ya?'

'No!' Nate does not want that. He recalls the name of that doctor from the TV programme. She might be a far-off relative of his distant grandma. Think on that! That must make her related to him by a drop or two of blood. He imagines that long ago Colleen O'Neill dressed a long full skirt, a shawl, and one of those bonnets. The face he conjures looks a little like Caroline O'Neill. She looked pretty. He doesn't want *her* spending eternity in a fiery furnace.

'We need to bring folks back to God and save them from punishment that is sure to come. Everyone must understand this disgusting carcass, this old saggy bog body dug from the *dirt*, is not our Saviour. Oh, no! This is the Antichrist, the work of Satan and must be destroyed.'

Jake looks real unhappy.

'You know, folks, last night, while I was contemplating the theme of this morning's sermon, my mind was empty, no inspiration. And God came to me. Filled my thoughts on this very matter...'

'Praise the Lord!' someone shouts.

'It hit me hard. I fell to my knees and prayed for guidance. It rattled me.'

Jake does look truly ill as he mops his brow, then his eyes rake the sixty or so worshippers in front of him. For moments his brother's eyes are on him and Nate feels the connection between them.

'Let us reach out to our brothers and sisters. Help them. Urge them to put this demon back in the earth where it belongs. Doesn't it say, Mark 9:29, "And he said unto them, This kind cannot be driven out by anything but prayer." ...*By... anything... but... prayer*.'

Jake – Pastor Porter – joins his hands and lowers his head. 'Pray with me.'

As Nate bows his head listening to his brother's words, he is immediately calmer. Jake is a clear thinker. Nate was never jealous when their daddy wanted Jake to take over the ministry, even though Nate was the first-born son.

Prayer over, Nate stands flexing one powerful arm then the other. On his left upper arm, below the sleeve of his white T-shirt, a tattoo of a Crusader cross with the initials KMC. It was a proud day when he had sworn himself to the Kentucky Men for Christ.

After the service Nate hangs around by the parked vehicles, in no hurry to leave. It's not only him feeling weird about this thing.

'Think prayer makes a difference?' someone asks, not sounding too confident.

'Y'know, it's got me real interested in finding out more,' Ray says.

Nate nods. 'Yep.'

'Let's keep in touch,' Ray says. 'Y'know, share stuff we find out. I'll check out these guys. Might even get in touch with them. Yep, I might just do that.'

For all that Ray is a runt of a man, he's the one to bind them. Nate has known him forever. If he were to be forced to say who his best bud was, it would have to be Ray. Ray had been the one to find a trailer home he could afford and loan him some cash to buy it outright. 'Least I can do,' Ray had said. 'We KMCs stick together, huh?' Nate feels comfortable in his skin around Ray and the rest of his buddies. His sisters and other women in the church sided with Shelly, got all preachy, which made him angry. Across from him and his buds, he watches his sisters and their husbands chatting before herding their kids towards their vehicles. Who will be hosting the shared family meal today, he wonders? He'd stopped accepting their invitations and they'd stopped asking.

'See y'all.' Nate waves to Ray and the other men, climbs into his pick-up and guns the engine. Not a rattle. Smooth as. He's a mechanic, after all. He drives away, figuring that he might look further into this bog body thing and not leave everything to Ray. Besides, it'll give him something to do of an evening after finishing work at the auto repairs. If the internet holds.

Nate heads out of town. Prayer's good, as the gospel of Mark states, but there is plenty else to take inspiration from. *Finally, be strong in the Lord and in his mighty power. Put on the full armour of God, so that you can take your stand against the devil's schemes.* Ephesians.

Back home Nate takes out his gun case and removes his beloved Spike Crusader semi-automatic. He'd had it out yesterday at the KMC's weekly meet-up.

When he had first moved to the trailer he had been lonesome, but soon adjusted. He enjoys hunting small game, hares and such, and sometimes just walks among the trees: hickories, hornbeams, maples, ash, and the rest. And he appreciates the bluebells and other wildflowers.

Out in the woods, some way from his trailer, he fixes a target to a tree. Shooting off some rounds will give him time to think. He loads the magazine, presses his cheek against the steel, left hand supporting the hand guard, trigger finger resting where it needs to be. He lines up the target and squeezes. A rapid burst of fire judders his body. As the sound dies away, echoing through the woods, he sees a bunch of crows circling and cawing above.

'Sorry, guys, didn't mean to startle ya.'

He lowers his weapon, tracing a finger over the engraved words either side and above the trigger:

WAR

GOD WILLS IT   *PEACE*

He's a Bible Warrior and at any time God might call him to do his work.

15

The Harassers

CARRIE O'NEILL NOTICES A CHINK OF LIGHT SHOWING under Liam's door. It is nearly 8pm and he should go home. She's met Liam's wife several times, and from dropped hints, Carrie gets the feeling she would appreciate her husband's presence more often. She isn't too sure about the extent of his daughter's disabilities. Down's for sure, but there's more to it. She means to ask Liam but somehow it is never the right time. What might she say? 'By the way, Liam, what *exactly* is the matter with Evie?' She doesn't want to sound crass, nosy, or use terms that are not acceptable. Whatever, Liam should go home; he's been putting in twelve-hour days for weeks now. She raps on his door.

Liam looks up from his open laptop, pushes his glasses on top of his head, and rubs his eyes. 'Carrie! Why are you still here?'

'I could say the same. I'm sure your wife and daughter would like to see you.' She notices the half-drunk tea at his elbow is scum-topped and looks undrinkable. This is a perfect time to reference the mug, promoting a Down's Syndrome charity, and asking: 'And, by the way, what exactly are Evie's disabilities? I've been meaning to ask.' But in the moment's hesitation it takes to *think* the words it can no longer be spontaneous. Everyone thinks she is a confident, straight-talking Kiwi, but there are things she feels shy about. She pulls up a chair. The real thing on her mind, and no doubt his, is Ballybere Man. And there is something else she wants to mention.

Liam gestures to his laptop. 'Just want to get this off.' He doesn't elaborate what *it* is or who he is getting it off to, but it could be any one of a dozen people or organisations hounding them. 'It's heating up out there. Everyone wants answers. Clarity.'

'What do *you* think, Liam? You haven't said.'

'I wish I knew. Honest to God – no pun intended – this is outside anything the priests had us regurgitate in all my school days. Those creeds were articles of faith. Questioning them wasn't on the agenda, never mind questioning whether the Son of God had actually risen.' Liam's eyes widen. 'Who would have thought?'

'We didn't see this coming.' Carrie's own church education had been cut short after her first communion. The ceremony had been Nan's wish, and she had complied, but she loathed the white dress and felt uncomfortable with the whole experience. For a time she'd attended Christmas and Easter Masses but had long ago backed away from these, only willingly stepping into churches for occasional weddings, christenings and funerals. Grandad's had been the last.

'For sure, this has got us all thinking, but unscrambling the God thing is beyond me.' Liam replaces his glasses. 'And let's face it, getting our heads around Christ the man and Christ as God has been keeping philosophers and theologians busy for two millennia.'

'But people believed he lived. Or at least, few people doubt it.'

'Beyond that there isn't much anyone agrees on.' He smiles. 'But one thing I remember from my catechism is that Christ rose up on high. I've seen enough images of Jesus sitting on the right hand of God with the dove hovering between them to know that much.'

She's seen tons of such illustrations or paintings in churches, often tacky or garish, with Jesus looking uncommonly white-skinned. The body they are analysing is now stained a chestnut colour, but in life his skin would have been some tone of olive brown. That much she is sure of.

But she hasn't come to discuss the body.

'Liam, yesterday I had a strange email to my work address. I ignored it, but today I had another from the same person. Have you received anything out of the ordinary?'

'Usual suspects.' He shrugs. 'And, oh, I want to tell you I've had a long email trail with Frida. She's keen to come and view.'

Carrie has also been talking with colleagues at the Silkeborg Museum where Tollund Man is exhibited. Everyone there was over the moon about this latest Irish find.

Liam begins to scroll through an email. 'She was saying—'

'Wait. I mean, umm, not exactly freaky, but not normal either. It might be nothing, but I thought I should tell you.'

'What is it?'

She has Liam's full attention. 'The one yesterday started off very formally with "Dear Doctor Caroline O'Neill..."'

'So far so good. Not unusual from our friends in Germany, you know that!'

They laugh. She had been caught out by how formal – even emails – could be from colleagues there and had been gently reprimanded by Liam when some of her early responses had been considered overly casual.

'Here, read it yourself.' Carrie opens her phone to her work email account and passes it to Liam.

'Have we got the rite person...' Liam looks up. '*R.I.T.E.?*'

'Exactly. Read on,' she urges.

'...with that body thing? We want to no if youv got it get rid of it. Apart from not knowing how to spell, it doesn't say who "we" are. Carrie, you said there was another?'

'From the same address – and by the way, I've reported it to our IT team, and they'll block it.' She finds the message for him.

Liam reads: 'Dear Doctor... etcetera... Shuld of said you get back. Tell us when youv put the body back in the earth.' He looks at her with concern. 'This is not nice. Unsettling, I'd say.'

Carrie is relieved Liam takes her view. 'Yeah, a little freaky. What should I do if more come?'

'Log them. Keep them in a separate file. Others on staff might find themselves facing the same. I'll let Mike know and I'll share with senior management.' Liam looks pensive. 'You know, we – that is, the museum – might find we've taken on more than we bargained for. Passions can run high. We have to step gingerly.'

'Finn – you remember, the guy from the *Irish Times* – was saying something similar. He wants to do a feature. About me...' She feels herself colouring, expecting Liam to stamp on the idea, but he tilts his head waiting for her to continue. 'The Face Behind the Find kind of angle. Showing I've come from a normal background, that what we're doing is normal—'

'Except it's not!' Liam chuckles.

'That was his point.' Carrie rushes on, not wanting Liam to think she's an egomaniac. 'I said I'd only be interested if it was about our teamwork. And I said I'd ask you, get permission. What do you think?'

'It's a great idea. I'm mindful of Mike and Fiona's wish to

"control the narrative", as they like to say. I'll get back to you, so you can do it with Team Museum's blessing.' He laughingly makes the sign of a cross. 'I am sure Mike will agree. They're alarmed at the worldwide attention this is receiving.

'Thanks, Liam. And go home!'

She and Finn have fun working up the feature. It requires a few pub interviews with pints in front of them, him scribbling on a notepad; it's too noisy for the phone to record. Today is a glorious summer day and they're sitting at a pavement table browsing stock images on the internet.

'That's Geraldine, where Nan lives,' she points out. 'The closest town to where I grew up. I'd be surprised if there are two thousand souls.'

'Will you look at those mountains? You really get that view or is it photoshopped? A distorted lens to make you think they're really close.'

'Oh, they're real!' On seeing the Southern Alps cloaked in winter white her heart gives an actual tug. 'And the sky's piercing blue, compared...' She gestures to the moist sky above her, clouds scudding. 'Clear night views. The Milky Way is spectacular.'

Finn looks intrigued.

'You should go there,' she tells him. 'Pick up work at shearing time. That will build some muscle.' She squeezes his skinny arm.

'Maybe I need a tour guide. What do you say?' He cocks his head.

She can imagine showing Finn around. Could be fun. 'Maybe. One day.'

Carrie shows him photos from the last time she was home. 'There's some neat ones with me and Blue. This is my favourite.' She is squatting in a paddock, grinning broadly, an arm across

Blue's back, his tongue lolling. In the background, a line of high macrocarpas form a windbreak against those piercing southerlies. Another tug of her heart. Home.

When Finn's article is published, in print and online, she copies the link to her parents, who tell her they are chuffed to bits, and emails Nan. 'Talk to me!' she begs. So, when Nan next visits her parents, there she is. FaceTime!

'Nan, good to see you! I'm so sorry that someone was mean to you.'

'Don't worry about it. She's a strange one.'

'All the same. Nan, I don't want you worrying.'

'You're quite the celebrity heh? I saw you on the news. *Our* TV news!'

Nan is grinning and Carrie thinks she must be a little proud.

'Nan, do you find anything about Ballybere Man interesting?'

'Well…' Nan's lips press together. 'As far as I'm concerned, I'd rather you found something else to do.'

'Aren't you curious to follow this? To find out more?'

'NO!'

That's emphatic. 'Why not, Nan?'

'Some things are best left alone. Don't expect me to be following what you're up to.'

Carrie will not be telling Nan about those two weird emails. Or the next one. Or the fourth. Each from a different email address but each beginning Dear Doctor Caroline – or Carolyn, suggesting this was a different writer – O'Neill. The last quoted something that must be from the Bible: *You cannot drink the cup of the Lord and the cup of demons.* It had unsettled her. No, Nan will not be told about any of this. She moves to neutral territory.

'Tell me, how are you? Any further developments with your residential home plans?'

Nan has been to visit and likes it but is still thinking, not sure she's ready to give up her independence.

She's about to end the call when her dad appears.

'Carrie, love, just to say Blue's been a bit crook.'

'What's the matter?' Their collie isn't that old and is always in the peak of good health.

'Vomiting and had the runs. Think he must've found a dead animal... He's okay now. Out and about somewhere.'

'Thank goodness for that!'

'Anyway, I'll leave you with your nan. Speak soon.'

She ends her call on good terms with Nan, both extending arms to the screen in air hugs, and pursed lips smacking.

Rachel calls. 'Are you keeping up with what's going on over this way, in Ballybere?'

'I've heard they've plans for a museum or something similar.'

'Yeah, but not that. It's the tents springing up. Cillian's been over to report for the *Limerick Leader.*'

'Tents?'

'It started with one, and before you know it a dozen of these wee pup tents appeared, making quite a camp of it out bog side. The devout crowd have landed, Carrie. They're convinced some miracle has taken place.'

'Jesus!'

'You might say so. To start with the council tried to clear them off the land, but they weren't having any of it. Cillian showed me a photo – they've constructed a frigging cross out there!'

'You're kidding!'

'I tell you, Carrie, this is going into strange places. You need to take care now.'

Yes, she knows that but doesn't want to alarm her friend with these bothersome emails. Rachel continues: 'Hey, by the way, I loved the feature *The Times* ran. I almost know a celebrity!'

'Rach! The idea was to try and keep things grounded. Make me, and what we're doing, seem *ordinary*.'

'Sorry, pet, it's not working. Not judging by our Ballybere campers, waiting for some sort of sign. It would be funny if it weren't so serious. I'd say, keep a low profile. You take care now.'

'Sure. Love to—'

'Dan and the kids. Will do. And how about a visit before long? Dan only makes his veggie lasagne when you're here. It's been a while.'

Carrie promises 'soon' and makes kissing sounds towards the phone.

That evening, Carrie checks her messages: a cancellation of netball practice, a friend sharing a photo of a night out, another forwarding that pic of her and Blue with a message. She grins. Wait… This isn't from anyone she knows. A random stranger has seen that article, discovered her private social media account, and sent a message: NICE DOG! NEW ZEALAND, HEH?

Is this friendly or threatening? Blue! Her precious collie. Had he been deliberately poisoned? No one would hurt a farm dog in the depths of the South Island… Surely… But she is not sure of anything.

She deletes it.

Dodgy emails continue to arrive at work. They are easy to spot. Most genuine emails end dot org or dot ac. If a sender's name is unknown, their email address suspect, she bins it. They are on to her. DONT IGNORE US, one subject line threatens. Another: OPEN THIS WHORE!

She does not report them, as she's been instructed to but deletes them immediately without opening.

Best to hold some things close to her chest. Lots of things.

16

The Fallout

CARRIE O'NEILL THROWS HERSELF INTO WORK, putting the final touches into a section of a funding proposal. A major foundation with bags of money has indicated they are 'very interested in being involved'. *Yes, please.* The thrust of this application is a multi-disciplinary approach to Ballybere Man: paleopathology; historical research; ethical considerations of appropriate, contextual display. She is working on the methodological approaches and expected learning outcomes. On and on.

Soon the Oxford team confirm the results of further radiocarbon dating tests. There is no doubt about the age of Ballybere Man.

Then, the best moment for ages. Digital modellers have been working with 3D scans Carrie and her team have supplied and, with specialist photo-editing software, have recreated a digital version of Ballybere Man's face. The lead modeller is telling her something.

'Sorry, repeat what you just said?' She wants to be certain.

'I said we can, with a considerable degree of certainty, place him from the Middle East.'

'Yes!' She's on her feet, bouncing up and down.

'Several morphometric traits of the skull indicate this. It's very good, yeah? And you'll like what you see.'

A short video of this digital facial reconstruction will form part of the exhibition, and the museum is getting a bust made. Forensic artists – magicians – will create a resin replica skull, adding muscles and flesh in layers of modelling clay. And Mike's talking about having a bronze cast made. 'Part of the experience,' he explained. 'We can encourage visitors, especially visually impaired people, to *feel* the face.' Before long, she will be confronting her man in more ways than one.

She urges the 3D modeller, 'Send images! Want to see him!' She is shouting, like a kid in a sweet shop yelling, 'I want... I want...'

It will take a while to convert their program, so they mollify her and send her a screenshot. As Ballybere Man's face fills her screen she jerks back. It is a psychological shock, and she stares and stares. There is no doubt of this man's ethnicity.

'Wow,' she manages to say to the recreators, still on the line with her. 'Oh, wow. Incredible.' Then she remembers to say, 'Thanks, guys. This is magic.'

'You're welcome. We're absolutely loving working on this.'

When Carrie shows Liam, he too is fascinated by the screenshot. This digital reconstruction project will be kept under wraps till the big reveal. 'Understood,' she says, 'but shall I prepare something for the media? Confirmation Ballybere Man is definitely from the Middle East?'

He surprises her by saying, 'I know we've agreed to share all our research – transparency and so on – but Mike and Fiona feel there might be such a thing as over-sharing. Perhaps this is a case in point. After all, this isn't major news. Let's just quietly get on with our work, mmm?'

She's disappointed but doesn't feel this is worth fighting for. 'Okay,' she says.

Liam doesn't say, but it is rumoured that Mike is regretting giving the go-ahead for Finn's article. Perhaps this is also categorised as over-sharing. Well, she isn't sharing any more about herself. In fact, she's not sharing much at all.

She deletes a fresh bunch of emails she doesn't like the look of.

The Ballybere find site camp is expanding. A cluster of twenty or so tents including some family-size ones appear and will not be deterred. Carrie follows Cillian's reporting for the Limerick paper and Finn messages to say he's been out there doing a feature. She isn't that interested. More weirdos. Let them enjoy the summer weather while it lasts. Others tell her they've seen something on TV, and Liam mentions that the BBC have covered it, and, 'You'll never guess.' He looks amused. 'There's a Christian TV channel all the way from America out there.' Carrie brushes it aside. She puts her head down, keeps to herself, and works. Her only social commitment is weekly netball practice. Here she can let off steam.

Growing up in rural New Zealand all her friends took part in team games, and netball was her thing, with goal defence her favoured position. On that sector of the court, she would fiercely keep her eye on the opposing team's goal attack. More than just her eye. She would leap and spread her arms, a 'back off, bitch' look plastered on her face, fair hair scraped into a ponytail, cheeks flushed in the winter chill. Her five-foot-eight solid build was a boost to the school team, and later to the University of Otago team, where she had taken her first degree in archaeology. 'Tough tarts,' they'd called each other fondly. She'd flown back for two weddings, putting up with the teasing. 'We'll come over for yours, just give us a yell.' That wouldn't be happening any time soon. The girls in her Dublin netball club are good mates, but there's no one here she's really close to.

When Finn suggests joining him at a favourite nightclub where a local Emo band are playing, she turns him down. Maybe it would be fun, but she is saying no to most things right now.

God! She stares at her left hand. When had she started biting the skin around her nails? She buys bright blue nail varnish in the hope this might give a visual 'finger alert' before they reach her teeth, but it isn't working; the skin around her nails is becoming more ragged and red. Running is taking a back seat, and what occasional exercise she gets is not countering the bottle of wine with dinner. When had this become a regular thing? Jeans that fit one day are too tight the next and she is becoming too rough on the netball court.

'Ow, that hurt!' An opponent thumps to the floor. She apologises, helping the woman to her feet.

She is not great company, and better away from everyone.

Each time Carrie opens her private email, she is gripped with anxiety in case some stranger has got hold of it. Without causing alarm she finds ways of reminding friends and family to 'please not share my personal accounts with anyone'. Dad teases: 'My celeb daughter's hiding.' And she goes along with the gibes, determined to keep a low profile, determined not to be distracted.

But she can't ignore the miracle that occurs at the find site: one of the campers, a mute, finds his voice. Cillian scoops this. Apparently, some guy who has been traumatised in the armed forces and hasn't spoken for five years attributes his recharged vocal cords to divine intervention. 'I feel the healing power of this place. Christ reached out to me, unlocking something. He was right here. I know it.'

'For heaven's sake!' Carrie shakes her head in irritation. Then the Catholic weekly publication is on it, reporting campers praying and fasting, speculating Ballybere might become a holy site, a place of pilgrimage to rival Croagh Patrick, even Knock. The article ends by urging the Catholic Church to take an interest.

The whole thing is snowballing. A TV reporter speaking with a slightly arch tone interviews the returned serviceman, who tells of the doctors and shrinks who've previously tried to help him before tearfully insisting, 'I was touched by something that night. I can't explain it... The Lord didn't talk to me, I didn't see a vision, but I know it was *Him*.' Carrie is an atheist, without belief in a divine being. She would describe her younger self, still under Nan's influence, as a theist – believing in a creator God but also in natural laws which shape the universe. Over the years she stopped thinking about God, looking to science to explain the world around her. So, though she's happy for the guy who's found his voice, such talk makes her queasy. It concerns her that the find site is becoming a focus for desperate people.

The quicker she can lead a team of scientists and academics to prove who Ballybere Man might have been, the better. And they have a dead man – Jesus or not – being cared for right here in the museum. After initial examinations Ballybere Man has been conserved – anointed – in a twenty-first-century way: submerged in a solution of polyethylene glycol preserving fluid for a month before being freeze-dried for several more weeks.

Carrie's schedule is full. Two visits arranged for next week: colleagues from Drents Museum in Holland and Moesgaard Museum in Denmark, and more visits to schedule for the coming weeks. All of them with research proposals, and money to back them. Bring it on!

Liam appears at her desk. 'Mike's here and would like to see us both.'

'Now?' It isn't a good time. It is never a good time.

'Right now, I'm afraid.'

Mike is waiting in Liam's office. And so is Fiona. What could Team Museum be wanting from them now? A soon as she sees both sets of eyes on her, she senses an ambush.

'Please.' Mike indicates empty chairs. Carrie's mind races. What is this? She glances at Liam, noting his eyes flicker away. Whatever it is he knows too.

'Carrie, the tech department's been doing a check on our systems,' Mike begins. 'Regular monitoring and maintenance.'

'Okay...' She wonders where this is leading.

'That includes scrutiny of emails. They noticed unopened binned emails in your account—'

'Oh. I can explain. It's because—' Heat rises from her neck to her cheeks.

'No, listen!' Fiona's sharp voice.

'You must have suspected what was in them otherwise you wouldn't have deleted them,' Mike says. 'We've read them. They're nasty. You agreed you would report anything like this that came through.'

She bobs her head.

'There are people out there who don't like what we are doing, and you seem to be in the firing line. And it's my duty to protect my staff—'

'*Our* duty!' Fiona stresses.

'I don't need protecting!'

'Carrie!' Liam's hand is on her arm.

Mike continues, 'There's talk of our find being associated with the Antichrist, talk of heresy. We know the emails are coming from the States. One signed off as Kentucky Men for Christ.'

Carrie's eyes widen. 'Kentucky?'

'And look…' Mike swivels Liam's laptop to face her. She views a news item with a short video clip, ten seconds or so, on a repeating loop: men, all white, some wearing combat outfits, all with face coverings – and all of them armed with semi-automatics. Carrie turns from the screen to Mike, but it is Fiona who speaks.

'A far-right Christian collective of all sorts of extremist groups. It acts as a magnet. Those men from Kentucky are affiliated.'

'But, Fiona, surely this is a political movement, nutters set to overthrow secular governments, seeing conspiracies every which way. What threat are they to us?'

'Nothing, we hope. But we know how easy it is for something to spark. On the one hand, those messages show we have unwanted attention from far-right evangelicals who want us to destroy the Antichrist, and on the other hand, we've got believers setting up shop over in Ballybere. Believe me,' Fiona huffs, 'I don't want to find myself organising tour groups out there, or finding a statue of the Virgin Mary or Christ erected… You're smiling, but I'm serious.' Fiona pauses. 'I had the minister on the phone earlier. Religious leaders have been having a quiet word. All wanting an end to this speculation. All concerned about maintaining the integrity of belief systems.' Carrie feels Fiona's eyes drilling into her. 'And you are the face they are attaching grievances to.'

Carrie tries to absorb this.

Liam clears his throat. 'I've decided – we've all decided – you need to step back.'

'What? What do you mean?' She looks from face to face. They are ganging up on her.

'For a short time,' Mike assures her. 'You've leave owing—'

'Too busy to take any! Anyway, I'm saving my leave for a trip home. Liam, we agreed this.'

'Yes, um, but...' Liam takes a breath. 'I'm taking over your upcoming meetings—'

Her head snaps from her departmental boss to her director. 'I've a full schedule!'

Mike is emphatic. 'You're taking time out. That's official. We can honour your held-over holiday leave. We all agree. Not because you didn't report the emails – though that hasn't helped your case. We need to lower your profile. *Our* profile.'

'And lower the temperature,' Fiona adds. 'When I took over as chair, I never imagined I'd find myself in this position. Carrie.' She takes a breath. 'You've come from a highly secular country, and for all that Ireland is a modern nation, our church history, our *Catholic* church history, is very much with us. We have to tread very carefully. We want to keep Ballybere Man here—'

'Oh, yes!'

'But we are under a great deal of scrutiny.'

'Two weeks, Carrie.' Liam smiles at her. 'Take a break, the weather is great. I'll deal with what I can, and, well – other things I'll delay until you're back.'

'But—'

'Two weeks.' Mike is emphatic. 'We'll take stock after that.'

Liam's eyes are compassionate. 'Looking at you, I honestly think you do need time out. Truly I do.'

'Wrap things up today,' Mike instructs. 'Rearrange things as you see fit.'

Carrie is gutted. All because some religious fundamentalists across the Atlantic believe she is doing the devil's work! And now a bunch of religious leaders here are putting pressure on the government. Her face feels fiery. Knowing she is in danger of bursting into tears, she jumps up and hurries out. For now she is no longer part of Team Museum.

17

The Pathologist

Rachel Muloney hears Carrie's wail down the phone: 'Rach! I'm not allowed back into work!'

'What do you mean?'

'Sort of gardening leave, but not exactly.' It sounds as if Carrie has been crying.

'Oh, pet. Why? What's happened?' Rachel moves out of the living room away from Dan's hearing, concerned where the conversation might lead. She sits at the kitchen table, always the best place, and listens.

'Okay... Okay... I hear you. You know, this isn't the end of the world for you or your project. Be glad Mike and the others have your back. I understand their concern. They'll be wanting things to chill for a while. A week, you said?'

'Two!'

'Ballybere Man waited two thousand years to be discovered. You can be sure he can wait a wee bit longer for his mum to come back to tend to him.' She tries to coax a laugh, but across the country in Dublin, Carrie will not be consoled, fretting about appointments and looming deadlines.

'Carrie. Stop now. Come over to us. What are you going to do otherwise? Sit at home? Mope?' *And drink?* Carrie sounds a little slurred. 'Please, you've been promising a visit for ages, and there's so much I want to know about our man. I'm invested.'

True enough. Rachel longs for a proper in-depth, face-to-face discussion with Carrie. Their relationship is both professional and personal. 'So when should we expect you? Tomorrow?'

'The girls won't mind?'

'No prob.' Claire, seventeen, will be fine having her twelve-year-old sister room-sharing for a few days. Rachel is blessed with easy-going, level-headed kids. Fourteen-year-old Sam too. 'Tomorrow, then. Safe journey.'

Rachel's mind turns to her own work and family commitments. School summer holidays have ended, she has taken all leave due to her, but will see if she can arrange to take Monday off to give herself a long weekend. Dan can drive Sam to football. And didn't Jessie have something on? Her mind whirls.

'Getting it!' Rachel rushes to the door.

There's Carrie, standing on the step, travel bag at her feet, looking woebegone.

'Poor lamb.' She hugs her guest. 'So glad you're here.'

'Oh, Rach!'

Rachel steps back and Carrie dumps her bag in the narrow hallway where jackets, scarves, and woollen hats overflow coat hooks. A moment later her family rushes forward in a messy, noisy, huddle, with Dan's 'Carrie, good to see you'; Jessie's 'Hi, Carrie, give me your bag'; Claire's 'Come on through to the kitchen, the kettle's on.' Even Sam's 'How was the trip? Traffic okay?' And Buster, squeezing between legs, tail thumping.

'Oh, wow!' Carrie staggers back in mock surprise before returning hugs and kisses.

Rachel observes her friend as she bends to remove her shoes. They have spoken, but it is many months since they were excavating in their wellies and waterproofs. This project is taking a toll on her friend, that's obvious. As Carrie moves a dog lead, making room to hang her jacket, Rachel notes chipped blue nail polish and ragged nail edges. Straw-blonde hair, normally glossy, has lost its lustre, and eyes are surrounded by bruised-looking skin... And, it surprises her to note, Carrie has put on weight.

Later, Rachel watches as Carrie begins to uncoil. It is wonderful to witness the simple healing power of good food and drink, and sympathetic company. Having her here is the right thing.

Next day Rachel opts for a favourite walk, a fraction of the Wild Atlantic Way coastal path, with Buster, a bundle of golden fur, leaping to catch or chase the green tennis ball she or Carrie throws. Walk. Talk. Toss.

'Rach. I wasn't put off by those nutters who were messaging. I just don't get how any sane person can think something like that. You know, believe that there can be anything, well, *unsavoury* about this find, and that anyone should be fearful or feel threatened by knowledge. This is the twenty-first century. Can't we all be rational human beings?'

'Fat chance.' Rachel accepts the saliva-covered ball from Buster's mouth, draws back her arm and chucks it. 'Those religious extremists in the States are something, aren't they? And what do you make of the campers over here?'

'Oh, them. Honestly!' Carrie rolls her eyes. 'One lot thinks this is some sort of heresy to even suggest it might be Jesus, while others seem to be hoping it really is, or are waiting for all sorts of miraculous stuff to happen.' Carrie pauses to tug the ball from Buster's jaws. 'Really, why can't people be *sensible?*'

'Proven truth. Probable truth. Truth by consensus. That's what you're hoping for?'

Carrie looks surprised. 'Of course! And you as well.'

'Umm. Sure, but...' Rachel stuffs her hands in her pockets. Maybe this is a good time to talk – for her to offload, rather than absorb Carrie's woes. There are things she doesn't talk about with her family. Things in her work that are too gruesome, too upsetting. Such as the time she'd been required to analyse a five-year-old girl drowned off the coast, her corpse recovered a week later, skin waxy and soapy, nibbled by fish and sea lice. No mother talks about this with her children. And Dan had pulled a face when she had shared some of what her work entailed. She has not talked about her experiences of last year. Not even to Dan. Carrie then.

'You know I was with the International Red Cross team. Assisting the Working Group on Missing Persons?'

'Yes. Kosovo. I remember you being out there. Justice needs to be done.'

'Sure, it's about seeking justice, but really it's about closure. Thousands went missing and thousands have been found buried in mass graves, but there are still more to be located. The whole purpose was to try and identify *individuals*. I thought of all those mothers waiting to give a proper burial to sons and husbands. I looked at news footage of mothers gazing at photos, holding on to cherished belongings. I wanted to help those women. God forbid if something like that happened to Sam or Dan...'

Rachel thinks how her own kids push back at her 'love you' every time she sees them off to school, ends a phone call and says goodnight. Even so she sneaks in her 'love you's once a week or so and settles for daily bedtime rituals of 'night night, love' with Dan. And he says the same. With kisses, cuddles, and the rest.

'Rach?'

She has stopped walking, thinking of a particular day in Kosovo. The diggers had been at work, and she and her forensic colleagues were all kitted up in hazmat suits waiting to get started. Twenty or so years after that vicious civil war, mass graves are still being discovered. She picks up her story.

'We weren't sure how many were there – eighteen men and boys, as it turned out – as all we could see was a mucky mush of filthy jackets and jeans with skeletal corpses. It was a grubby trainer that caught my eye, and—'

'Why are you telling me this?'

'Because I want you to understand something.'

She pauses, sees Carrie nod, then continues. 'We exhumed those bodies, stripped them of those clothes – nylon wind breakers, jeans, trainers. After the corpses were taken away to be examined the clothes were hosed clean and they began to come to life as the men and boys who wore them could not. Reds, blues, checked shirts, colourful hats – though previously white cotton T-shirts had seen better days. The shirts with logos printed on them were great in helping to identify who had been wearing them when bullets tore through. But that trainer was important. I watched it become a whitish colour with a purple stripe. Size 10. I recall that. I watched it being catalogued. And you know, that shoe helped identify the seventeen-year-old with a bullet hole in the back of his skull. Yeah, *I* recorded that. That was my professional contribution to allowing one more family to grieve and find some sort of closure.'

She feels close to tears. 'This is why I sign up for international work with other forensic pathologists. It's gruelling dealing with decomposing bodies—'

'Rach!'

She laughs harshly. 'That's why I don't bring my work home. But when I hug Dan or my kids, I revel in the warmth of their very alive bodies.' She looks directly at Carrie. 'As I said, this was about allowing space for grief and closure. I find it rewarding to achieve positive identification of real people who were victims. For mothers to receive bits of body to bury. It's not the *science* they care about, Carrie, that is only a means to an end. It's something far deeper – a spiritual longing to connect with someone who was loved.'

Carrie touches her arm. 'You okay?'

'Here's what I'm trying to say. You may never know who Ballybere Man was. It's too long ago. And maybe it's not right to even try to figure this out. Who will it help to know if this is, or is not, Jesus? Either way, you'll end up upsetting a lot of people.'

Buster is objecting to being ignored, so she half-heartedly tosses another ball.

'You don't agree with the work we're doing?' Carrie sounds confused.

'Of course I agree. It's fascinating. But I'm saying you might *never* have definite proof of who it is. And this man has no family waiting to claim him. Leastways, no family that's alive, unless you count the church. It's all too contentious.'

'We can agree about that!' Carrie scuffs her walking boot on the track. 'But I *am* hoping for what you said: that we discover the truth of who he is. What we can prove. What is probable. What we can agree.'

'And if we can't? Agree, that is? How will you feel?'

Carrie laughs. 'I'm persistent. I am confident that many good minds putting their intellect to work through a host of disciplines *will* arrive at consensus.'

'In that case, my friend, let's hope truth will out.' Rachel glances at the gathering clouds. 'Let's head back. And Carrie, don't mention what we talked about.'

'Of course. And, Rach, thank you for sharing with me. I appreciate it.'

They link arms.

'Oh, Cillian's coming this evening. He wants to show you something. No idea what. Perhaps an excuse to invite himself over. His way to get a foot in the door and winkle out something fresh from you for a story he's doing.'

'But I can't talk shop.'

'Sure. Don't worry. I've warned him.'

Cillian is already installed on the sofa alongside Dan when they get home, her three kids perched on arm rests or lolling on the floor joshing and teasing. When Buster bounds in her family knows she's back.

'Auntie Rachel… Carrie.' Cillian uncurls and greets Rachel with kisses, then offers Carrie a firm handshake.

'You've got something for me?' Carrie asks.

'Ah, yes… tell you over supper.'

Dan glances at the clock. 'Speaking of which, I'd best get the oven on.'

Saturday meals are Dan's department. Judging by the deep oven tray smothered with creamy sauce resting on the sideboard it's lasagne.

Main course dishes have been removed, and Jessie, wearing thick oven gloves, carries over an oven dish, its sides dripping with sticky juices. 'Great stuff, love.' Rachel rewards her daughter with a smile. No one will complain about apple crumble. She refills her wine glass, happy to see Carrie relaxing and laughing.

'Cillian. You've something for Carrie?'

'Ah.' He pushes back his chair, retrieves a folded sheet of paper from his bag, then spreads it on the table, revealing a few handwritten paragraphs. 'I thought Carrie might be interested. You all might.'

'So, what's this about?' Dan asks.

'Remember Annie Donovan?'

'The folk singer? Surely, she's not still at it?' Rachel is surprised. 'She must be a hundred.'

'Not singing now, no. She used to go around collecting old songs, began that in her twenties, from the old codgers, some still living in turf houses, no electric.'

'And?' Rachel prompts.

'Well, a friend of a friend knows her grandson. When Ballybere Man hit the headlines, he said his grandmother wasn't surprised. He told my friend, who told me. That's how stories get passed on, yeah? Thought I'd go and see her, while she's still with us. She's an ancient old biddy but good fun.'

Carrie is reaching to take the paper, but Cillian places his hand on it.

'I recorded it but wrote it down too. I'll read it out loud, shall I?'

Everyone is encouraging him.

He begins.

18

The Tale

On the west coast of Ireland, not far from the village of Ballybere, is an ancient bog. In times past it was a marshy fen where spirits might be seen drifting through shreds of fog covering the area like a blanket. People seldom go there now but, according to legend, this was once different. It's said that many centuries ago, before history was written down, it was a place where people used to gather at certain times. Why they would have come to this place has been lost, but there are tales that speak of seafarers from a faraway land who once visited. Over the years, stories have accumulated as they do, with mention of secret meetings and ancient rituals. You know how it is. Stories of apparitions, people possessed by unexplained forces, and so on. But these are all old stories, and today there's little in the place to indicate anything special or extraordinary ever happened there. Though you know, my ma used to cross herself on those occasions she passed that spot. It was just the thing people did, she said, and had been for as long as anyone could remember.

That's all I know.

19

The Pathologist

CARRIE O'NEILL LISTENS, ENTRANCED.

'May I see?' She wants to read for herself. *People gathering, seafarers from far away…* 'Wow.' An involuntary shiver passes through her.

Sam teases his cousin: 'Cillian, you're making this up.' And Dan looks sceptical. 'Has Annie still got all her marbles?' But Cillian isn't having any of it.

'Sharp as a tack. That woman is full of stories, local tales, that haven't made their way into any anthology of myths. You know, stories that aren't developed into long sagas of heroes or gods, just snippets like this one.'

The paper passes around.

'I love this.' Rachel is smiling. '*Spirits can be seen drifting through shreds of fog…* You know you would've had will o' the wisps in those places. People didn't understand how bog gasses cause them. Imagine…' Rachel reaches to hold her younger daughter's hand, lowering her voice. 'You're a lone traveller. It's night. Ahead you see all these darting, flickering lights. Fairies? Ghosts? Are these friendly or malevolent spirits?'

Carrie watches Jessie make a face and grimace.

Dan picks up the narrative. 'And you'll remember the story we read to you when you were little: Jack and the Devil. That had a jack o' lantern—'

'Dad, cut it out!' Jessie laughs. 'That used to terrify me.'

Sam leaps up and lowers the light, and the family segue into scary stories. Carrie loves this about the Muloneys, so different from her own childhood singledom. 'Female problems,' Mum said, when Carrie had wondered why she didn't have brothers or sisters. She had never asked further, and Mum had never explained. She refills her glass.

As Sam starts with some story, upping the ghoulish stakes, she thinks of Annie's tale. Why mightn't Ballybere bog have been a magical place back then? A revered place? Some sort of sacred place? If it had been, the only way of passing on things was by word of mouth. Stories change in the telling, they always do, but main events, important characters, vital *facts* remain a constant. Two thousand years ago there had been a compelling reason for an embalmed man to be transported to a faraway land. She imagines his bearers finding the perfect place to lower him into chilly water, though however Ballybere Man had been anchored to the weedy pool bed was unknown. Maybe linen, which had rotted…

'Carrie!' She jerks at Cillian's voice. 'And? What do you think? Annie's tale?'

'I love the bit suggesting it was a sacred place where people gathered.'

'And,' Dan speaks up, 'it's well documented how common it was for people to travel by boats along the shores, from well before Roman times actually.' He interlaces his hands behind his head. 'As soon as the Romans arrived in Britain, they began eyeing us. Didn't conquer us—'

'Nah, we would've seen them off in any case.' Sam pumps a fist.

'You bet,' Dan says. 'But they did set foot on our soil. Always handy when someone drops a coin or two only to have them discovered centuries later leaving clues to who's passed through.'

'So I can tell Mrs Walsh that Jesus was dropped off on our shores to be found centuries later.' Sam sniggers and Claire reaches over and knuckles his head.

'His RE teacher,' Rachel explains. 'Seriously, Carrie, I said earlier you might never know who you've got. He's a man from a long time back and from far away, but reading too much into his traumas may be a mistake.'

'Might further analysis show you've got the date or the location wrong?' Cillian asks.

'No. No. The opposite. The Oxford team ran more tests: body and peat samples. They've confirmed the dating, absolutely.'

'Nailed it then?' Cillian is cautious.

'Yeah, anyway, the digital software reconstruction has…' Her voice trails off, and she knows she is blushing. This is the bit Liam and others didn't want to share.

Cillian is refilling her glass. 'What's this about, then?'

Rachel is on to him. 'Hey. No underhand tactics in my house, thanks very much.'

'Ah, go on, go on.' Cillian does a *Father Ted* riff, dares to wink, and Carrie finds she is laughing. Oh, stuff it! But Finn? What kind of friend is she to withhold fresh information from him only to blurt it out now allowing the weekly *Limerick Leader* to scoop the prestigious *Irish Times*? She is not handling friendship with Finn at all well.

She takes a deep breath. 'Okay. The shape of a person's skull reveals everything you need to construct a face. Ask

Rachel.' The pathologist nods, and Carrie continues, 'Eye socket structure, the angle and width of the nose, jawline. But with Ballybere Man, we have the soft tissue as well. Win, win. So sure, this man was definitely from the Middle East about two thousand years back.'

Silent faces stare at her.

Cillian speaks: 'So I can report this? Just want to be sure. Don't want to upset my lovely aunt here.' How will Liam and Mike react? Never mind. She is annoyed with office politics. 'Sure,' she says to Cillian. 'Go for it. It's not a biggie.' Anyhow, Liam will love Annie's story, given his fascination with narrative threads that trace cultural influences back to Viking trading routes. And heaven knows, there are plenty of early Christian sites near west coast inlets. It is totally within the stretch of imagination to consider they might discover historical evidence proving Ballybere bog was a long-established sacred place. Why not?

Monday morning. Carrie keeps out of the way. Breakfasts, lunches packed for those that take them, homework books and PE kits to fling into backpacks. The routine floods back. School, including Dan, a maths teacher at the local tech. The car doors slam, engine starts, then Buster settles back onto a scrappy blanket near the range cooker.

'We have a day to ourselves,' Rachel says. 'Do you want to go to Ballybere? Are you curious to see the camp?'

'Yes! I'd been planning to swing by there when I leave but I'd love to go together.'

'Or we can go into Limerick, if you'd rather, and find somewhere nice for lunch.'

'No, no. I want to see the camp.'

'It might have to be the Ballybere chippy then.'

'Or a bog-standard caff.'

Laughter. This feels good. Normal.

The find site is much changed from when Carrie had last been here, kneeling in a squidgy trench in chill late winter, Joe Cassidy's excavator standing idle at the side.

They are experiencing an extended summer, and with the September sun at its zenith the camp has a festive air. This is nothing like environmental protest camps she has seen on TV news: a mix of improvised tarpaulin shelters and a tepee or two in the countryside, a sea of multicoloured self-supporting tents on paved city centres. This bog-side cluster of tents has a different feel, more like a music festival, the campers here to celebrate.

'Look at those yokes.' Rachel draws her attention to two green portable toilets, with wooden planking in front. 'The council is going all out on the posh facilities.'

Carrie points to a group sitting on folding camp chairs, one playing a guitar. 'They seem a happy-clappy bunch.'

She and Rachel meander past an open tent, where a middle-aged couple lie fully clothed in a loose embrace, and beyond to where a group sit around a barbecue with glowing embers, mugs in hand. 'Hi, guys,' she calls, receiving a friendly wave. None of the campers ask why they are here. They pause by the cross. It looked okay on the TV news, filmed at night decked with glowing lights. Now, the cobbled-together piece of carpentry standing six foot high is in a sorry state, propped up by rocks, a string of unlit fairy lights dangling limply.

A man approaches: thirties, bearded, wearing old jogging pants, a grubby sweater, feet in wellies. 'Coming to join us, or checking us out?'

'Checking you out.' Rachel laughs. 'How're you doing?'

'Good. Really good. The Lord is doing his work. We all feel it.'

Is this man for real? He looks sincere.

'Any more miracles?' Carrie asks, making sure to keep her voice neutral. 'Is the man who found his voice still here?'

'Gone. He found what he came for. A guy bowled up the other day, had some sort of leg deformity, hoped to be cured. He didn't hang around.' The man laughs. 'But there are other ways to heal. This place has a vibe. Know what I mean? A kind of healing vibe.' Carrie's eyes dart away, uncomfortable with this sort of talk. 'I'm not kidding. And we know He's behind it.'

The man is staring at her. 'I thought your face was familiar. Now hearing you speak…' He grins, twists around and yells, 'Hey! Look who's here: the Face of the Find's come to visit with a friend.' He whoops and hugs her, and the whiff of unwashed body fills her nostrils.

She and Rachel are invited to the barbecue. Within moments more camp chairs are unfolded and the circle grows as guitar man's group joins them. And the cuddling couple. Carrie introduces Rachel, saying it is really the pathologist who first laid eyes on Ballybere Man. Soon water bubbles in an old billy-can and Carrie is nursing a chipped enamel mug with a floating teabag. Two large crusty loaves appear, still warm, wrapped in old tea towels. Not from Ballybere. That store didn't run to anything artisan. Have they been baking? A Dutch oven or something? She is salivating. It smells great. Someone is cutting a slab of strong cheddar with a penknife, and she is handed a thick slice of bread and cheese.

They ply her with questions. What did it feel like to uncover the body? And those wounds on the wrists… what did she think? Her answers are cautious, professional. They are eager listeners, bodies attentive, eyes on her.

She finds her empty mug replenished, not with tea but red wine. Bottles have appeared. She and Rachel won't be exploring the delights of the local chippy after all. She stretches her legs, sinking back into the manky green camping chair.

Two hours pass in easy company.

On the drive home Rachel chats about Claire: subjects she's taking and where she wants to go to college. Carrie half listens as she checks her social media messages and her heart contracts. Security has been breached. He, or she, or they, have more to say: We do not consent to your satanic ways.

'Rach!' With shaking hands, she holds her phone up.

Rachel brakes and pulls to the side. 'This is disgusting!'

'Yeah.' She deletes the message.

Rachel reaches across and stills the hand Carrie has unconsciously brought to her mouth. Her poor nails are bitten to the quick, but she can't stop biting them.

'Carrie. There are disturbed people out there and I'm worried about you. You've got to report this. The museum has got to do more to support you.'

'But how? They've sent me away for a break. I can't hide. I need to get back to work. I want to get back.'

'Delete that account. I hate this anonymous crap. Shouldn't be allowed.' Rachel drums the steering wheel. 'Okay. Here's what's going to happen. Every evening I'm phoning you or texting and you are going to answer and tell me everything that's happened in your day—'

'But—'

'Uh, uh.' Rachel wags a finger. 'Every day. Promise?' Her eyes are hard.

Carrie raises three fingers, thumb and little finger tucked in, remembering how aged ten she joined the Brownies. 'Promise.'

Rachel her mentor. Rachel her friend. Rachel her guardian.

20

The Fallout

MIKE CURTIS'S EYES WIDEN IN DISBELIEF. THOSE sneaky bastards have stolen a march on him. While his staff have been at the coalface preserving Ballybere Man, liaising with scientific and curatorial colleagues from around the world, and he has been doing the rounds of the media and keeping the big picture in mind, *they* are scheming out west.

He rereads the minister's email. A delegation from County Clare Council have met with her to share an impressive plan for their proposed museum, which I am sharing with you, at their suggestion. We would value your input as a key partner.

Key partner! Mike opens an attachment, noting the logo and name of a well-known award-winning architect's firm. He scrolls through the concept design report. Aims and objectives to design an environmentally sensitive yet architecturally vibrant museum with the sole function of displaying Ballybere Man. The summary of the project outlines how the council expects to create a visitor attraction on a par with Silkeborg Museum in Denmark where Tollund Man is housed. The architects talk of making visitors feel like explorers to this hard-to-reach part of Ireland, where they can discover a rare jewel...

Mike flicks back to the minister's email; two councillors have visited Silkeborg *and* Moesgaard Museum outside Aarhus, where Grauballe Man is housed. They returned with two economic impact reports showing what a difference the museums make to the wider community – hotels and restaurants etc. They suggest you contact them directly, and they'll be happy to share these reports with you.

I bet! Smug bastards.

These Danish museums are as remote from Copenhagen as Ballybere is from Dublin, though nearby Aarhus is a vibrant city. He visited both museums in preparation for his interview for his current post. He understands how creating a unique site of world interest can work, even in remote locations.

Damn them!

The architects' report includes sleek concept drawings. Exterior images show a low-lying building, blending with the environment, green-credential rough grey bricks looking like blocks of peat. He notes the turf roof and floor-to-ceiling windows of a gallery and the ramp leading to the door – easy access for wheelchairs or pushchairs. Another sketch shows landscaped grounds with happy families picnicking or looking out towards a brilliant blue sea. The floorplans flow well, leading visitors from the foyer to a vast gallery. And, of course, a café, education room, shop...

It isn't just the minister who is impressed. This is the problem with his own museum – certainly the Archaeological Museum where Ballybere Man rightly belongs. Space. Space to expand. Space to vision something new. Collins Barracks offers possibilities but the fit is wrong, though there are facilities for coaches to park, and he envisions many of these. Insidious green fingers of envy squeeze his heart. Every bit of his being assumes Ballybere Man must be theirs: the National Museum's. He has glibly imagined he can see off his country cousins.

Ballybere Man is going to stay right here!

He sends a polite email back to the minister thanking her, saying he will share information internally, stopping short of saying he looks forward to being a partner. As an afterthought he adds, Minister, I am aware you haven't yet seen Ballybere Man. May I invite you to view our find and hear about our plans?

If possession is nine tenths of the law, they have the advantage, and he needs to push it. He thinks of the great and good he can call on: directors of world-renowned cosmopolitan galleries and museums, curators. People who can be relied on for a soundbite and photo op. And Fiona. He needs to ensure Fiona stays on side. He forwards the minister's email to her suggesting they chat about this when she has time.

He puts all things west of Ireland to the back of his mind, then three days later Liam draws his attention to the weekly *Limerick Leader*.

'Quite a splash, don't you agree?' Liam reads the online heading. '*A museum for tomorrow to house a man of yesteryear.*'

'Yes, yes.' He knows he sounds tetchy. The architect's concept drawings of the proposed museum do make a splash.

Why has Liam come to see him anyway? To rub this in his face? The Keeper has plenty to do: his own work plus overseeing Carrie's. Even so, insisting Carrie took time off had been the right thing to do. Those messages were gross, and more continue to arrive. He's instructed they be logged but has no time for them, or for Liam, right now.

'This is where it gets interesting.' Liam scrolls to another article. '*Ballybere Man: new mysteries, new facts.* There's a myth they've dug up about the find site. Insists it was known as a sacred place, and get this—' Liam's eyes gleam. 'People were said to have travelled by sea… I love it! Doesn't surprise me one bit.'

'It says so?' Now Liam has his attention. 'Where has this story sprung from?'

'A local folk song collector. And Mike…' Liam hesitates. 'It seems Carrie has had a hand in Cillian's article – I know he's Rachel's nephew and I also know Carrie's been out there – so she'll have been the one to have told him about the digital facial reconstruction – *confirming without a doubt this man hailed from the Middle East.*'

'It says that?' Mike is exasperated. This is not a major piece of news, and perhaps they should have released it earlier, as Carrie had suggested to Liam. He feels the narrative… everything… slipping from his grasp. 'When's Carrie back?'

'Monday. And if you're thinking of reprimanding her, don't. I need her here. Work is piling up.'

It isn't only Carrie that Mike needs to consider. Liam looks dishevelled and he has been longing to brush a crumb of potato crisp caught in his beard.

'Liam, when Carrie returns, we'll all meet to take stock.'

'Coffee and tea are on the way.' Mike welcomes Fiona, Liam, and Carrie into his office. 'From now on, I want weekly meetings which Fiona has agreed to attend as and when she can, so we can move forward with our Ballybere Man plans. Whatever develops out there' – he flutters his hand, unwilling to name that godforsaken backwater – '*we* are doing the big reveal and I mean to fight to keep him in Dublin.'

'Hear, hear.' Liam taps his chair.

'Time-wise, how are we doing, Carrie?' She looks alert and refreshed from her days away from work. Good, good. He hadn't been sure it was the right thing to do, but now he is certain he has shown the right level of compassionate leadership. These things increasingly matter, and he doesn't want to get a bad reputation. At some stage he will want to move on to a greater institution. Perhaps back in England.

'We had the same tissue samples dated using ultrafiltration,' Carrie tells them. 'It's really accurate, and sure to remove any contaminants. Everything concurs. We can be super, super confident our man dates from exactly when we've said, and from the location we've said. Even without additional contextual analysis – you know, grains, seeds. Given that our man had his stomach and all his innards removed we'll never know what his last meal was.'

'And thank heaven for that!' Fiona sounds relieved. 'I can just imagine, Sunday, after service, fending off a myriad of Last Supper jests.'

'There's been plenty of that, regardless,' Carrie says. 'More and more weird and funny memes.'

'Oh?' Mike has no idea.

Carrie dives for her phone and passes around images: the head of Ballybere Man transposed into Leonardo da Vinci's Christ presiding over the Last Supper; a golden halo photoshopped around Ballybere Man's head with his matted hair spread out; Ballybere Man rising from a peat bog, a speech bubble: 'It's been 2,000 years, I thought I should show myself.'

Mike sucks his teeth, discomfited, and returns Carrie's phone. 'There will be some who don't like these jokes.' An understatement if ever was one.

'I received a letter yesterday.' Liam hesitates. 'A rather nasty one.' From his pocket he extracts an envelope, then draws out a single page. Mike catches sight of an image of a shield with a cross in the centre, and notes the letter is handwritten.

'Where's it from?

'The States,' Liam says. 'A pity the postmark's blurred. I'll read it, shall I?'

We are writing the old way coz our emails get dumped.

The Bible says And the beast was captured, and with it the false prophet who in its presence had done the signs by which he deceived those who had received the mark of the beast and those who worshiped its image. These two were thrown alive into the lake of fire that burns with sulfur.

That body you have needs to be got rid of. No way is this Jesus. He would never of risen from a dirt swamp. When He comes back to rule the world we will be ruling by His side keeping His law.

Get rid of it before we get rid of it for you.

Warriors for Xist

Who on earth...?

Liam catches his eye. 'Before anyone asks, I've looked them up. Warriors for Xist is a hub for a sprawling online community. A network of evangelical, extreme right-wingers. The gun-toting brigade.'

Mike is horrified. 'They're *threatening* us? We have never claimed – would never claim – we have Christ.'

Fiona looks green around the gills. She mutters, 'Unsavoury!' He knows that she, as a staunch Catholic, is uneasy about where Ballybere Man's personal story might lead them, and now, hearing the message, Mike fears Fiona might be pleased if Ballybere Man *were* to be housed in County Clare. The thought has barely registered when Fiona speaks: 'You know, Mike, the sensible thing might be to hand our find over...'

No!

'...to the council as quickly as possible. Wash our hands of this project.'

'Oh no, we can't do that!' Carrie is looking aghast. 'I told you I've changed my personal social media account.' She explains to Fiona: 'I got a creepy message from someone saying they didn't consent to my satanic ways. I don't need to hear that kind of thing, but we must keep hold of our man. We'll never get such an opportunity. I can't bear the thought of him not resting in the museum where we can see him every day. Let's not be put off by these pumped-up extremists!'

'Extremists who have their eye on us,' Mike reminds her.

'If not their sights.' Liam lifts his arms, holding an imaginary rifle.

'Please, Liam!' Fiona says. 'I don't hold with this nonsense. I wonder if we should alert the police?'

'That seems a little melodramatic.' Mike's mind is focused not on rabid fanatics from across the Atlantic, but on the threat from County Clare, and he needs Fiona as a champion, and a buffer, at political level.

'Fiona, I believe an invitation to the minister would be appropriate coming from you. A special viewing.'

'What if she wants a photo op?' Fiona is frowning. 'Likely, I should think. And likely posed in front of Ballybere Man.'

'Ah, yes, that won't do. We get to reveal him fully to the press.' Mike's turn to frown. 'Perhaps a group photo in the lab, the minister with hard-working staff bent over microscopes. Just a hint of what is beyond view on the table... a hint of Ballybere Man's red hair, or some such.'

'Happy to invite her.' His chair snaps her mauve handbag shut – Burberry, if he's not mistaken – and stands. 'Please remember, we must all keep a low profile from now on.' Her gaze is purposely fixed on Carrie. 'We must take our foot off the pedal. Nothing must make us newsworthy. Unless it's the minister visiting, then it's best foot forward.'

'And the best china mugs,' Mike promises.

They all laugh.

Mike breathes easily as he ushers everyone out of his office. No police. Team Museum are back on track.

21

The Harassers

FINN DURANTE ANGLES HIS BODY, SQUEEZING between shoulders to get closer. Being thin has its advantages. He can see it now. Sort of. A pity the pig's head has been covered by a black bin bag, but with the right angle he figures he can get a photo of the snout. If that doesn't work, the cordoned-off sticky blood spilling down the Archaeological Museum's steps provides colour. Actual colour. Red. The farmer who dumped it cuffed himself to railings separating the museum from Leinster House compound and is at this moment being arrested. Finn films one of the Garda grasping long-handled bolt cutters, his arms opening and closing, with each squeeze urging the chain to snap while other guards struggle to keep the resisting farmer from thrashing and squirming.

For the second morning in recent months Finn is outside one the National Museum's sites alongside others from the media. It's not exactly a crush, but there's been enough interest to turn up. This story will fill space in an otherwise quiet late October day.

The farmer is led down the steps yelling: 'Public money to places like this and that new fancy museum in Ballybere. All this attention on some old duffer dug up from God knows when. He's dead! What about us? We're on our knees…'

Disgruntled Farmer Protests. Finn snorts; he's getting more tabloid by the minute. Still, he might suggest it as a caption. For fun.

And what of the other protestors? His gaze takes in the handful of men and women, outnumbered by the media. One protestor he knows and has said hello to: a guy who works for the homeless charity in Dublin. *Food Water Shelter For All* is the message on his banner. Others clutch Bibles or a handwritten message: *Holy Bible Read It And Heed It.* Finn watches as an old guy with matted hair who is well known in the city centre finally finds an audience for his sandwich-board message: *Believe In The Lord Jesus Christ And Thou Shalt Be Saved And Thy House.* On the occasions Finn comes across sandwich-board man patrolling his regular patch of pavement of a Saturday, urging passers-by to repent, Finn gives him a wide berth. But here, outside the slippery bloody steps, piggybacking, *ha-ha*, the farmer's protest, the man has found his opportunity. On the pavement beyond the gated entrance, a reporter from RTÉ talks to camera, and sandwich-board man sneaks in behind, getting his message broadcast. Kudos.

Okay… Finn pulls himself together. This is a pathetic grab-bag of protestors without a coherent message, though he will make space for the homeless appeal. What other connections might he weave into a story? Something about Christian views on poverty and wealth? He will look up some references.

The farmer is clearly pissed off at the others who are trying to share the limelight. This is *his* gig. Finn is intrigued by how Ballybere Man has become a focus for all sorts of grievances, even farming subsidies. Perhaps *this* is the angle of the story he should write.

Carrie is inside the museum. They've texted each other: she curious about what is happening on their steps, keeping in touch with her man on the scene, as she put it. Another message pings: Want to meet for lunch?

Finn considers. Whenever he thinks their relationship – mate-ship – is solid, she does something else to piss him off. The last time had been that nugget about the shape of Ballybere Man's eye sockets, nose and so on. *There* was a story, and she hadn't given him the heads-up, so that weekly out west had scooped the lot of them. He had been so angry, and his editor had foamed at the mouth. 'Durante! She's your contact, isn't she?' The entire newsroom had been scornful at his lack of chops.

Her man on the scene! Carrie's casual words sting. He does not feel her man, on the scene or in any other way. He likes her. Enjoys her company, yet she lets him down. Is he getting things muddled? Is this about personal trust not being accorded, or his journalist's ego being ignored? There is that. He wants – expects – her to put him first when there is news to share. Is that too much to ask? Sure, she'd apologised, telling him: 'I know, I know, but after a glass or two of wine and, well… sorry.'

He considers Carrie's suggestion, but as he rarely takes a lunch break he texts back: After work?

Carrie responds: OK. What time?

He names a time and a popular cocktail bar. If it takes alcohol to get Carrie O'Neill to talk then let's find out what her favourite tipple is.

He arrives early and watches Carrie pause at the entrance scanning the room. It's been some time since they met. She looks different, though he can't say how. He stands and raises a hand. As soon as she spots him, her grin is as broad as usual, and she bounds over: 'Hi. Good to see you.' Kisses on both cheeks. Okay. That's cool.

He indicates the drinks menu. 'What shall we start with?'

'Start with? Whoa…' Carrie slings her jacket over the back of the chair and gives serious attention to the menu: cocktails described and illustrated in a dizzying array of colours, types of glasses, fancy bits and bobs such as cherries or ridiculous little umbrellas. She goes for a fruity margarita, and he opts for a vodka martini.

'So, how's it going?' He raises an eyebrow. An open question.

'It's good to be back at work, that's for sure. So many partnerships we're working on.'

'Great, are you allowed to tell me?' He makes a pout.

'Come on!' Carrie lightly punches his shoulder. 'Course I can, it's just the Jesus thing we need to avoid. I shouldn't have said anything to Cillian. We can't find ourselves falling down a rabbit hole.'

'Okay.' But he is interested in this rabbit hole, and he senses she is too. *Slowly does it.* 'So, that aside, what are you working on?'

'Well, now the conservators have freeze-dried the body, I'm about to start on a project with colleagues at Silkeborg. Comparisons with Tollund Man: find sites, context and so on.'

The drinks arrive. Fishing out a curl of lemon – too fancy for him – he sips the chilled liquid. He is genuinely interested in what Carrie is telling him. 'I can follow this up? Get details?'

'Oh yes! Mike will happily agree to that.' Carrie laughs. 'And you might like to talk with him about his plans to introduce Ballybere Man to the world. The "big unveil".' She makes air quotation marks.

'Oh? That will go ahead, then? What about the proposed museum at Ballybere?'

Carrie is dismissive. 'If that gets built. *If*. It won't be for ages.' She crosses her arms and speaks emphatically. 'We get to keep him for some time yet.'

He can imagine the museum board – and clearly Carrie – wanting ownership. 'Are *we* getting a wee bit possessive about our man now?' His turn to tease her as he knuckles her arm.

'You bet!' Her laughter is honest. 'Oh, and Professor Byrne phoned the other day wanting to speak with Liam, but he was out, so he settled for me.'

'Glad to know he's not carked it.'

'Far from it. Ballybere Man is perking him up. He loved reading about the myth Cillian had dug up.'

'Dug up!' The first cocktail is going down well.

Carrie rolls her eyes. 'Anyway, he said, "My word, I would love to be younger. This puts a fresh perspective on the matter, Doctor O'Neill" – I was pleased he didn't call me a chit of a girl. Then, "Consider this. Myths frequently contain nuggets of fact. What fun to consider we might indeed have Christ in our hands." The prof sounded sad he wouldn't be around to investigate.' Sipping the last of her drink, Carrie is becoming chattier by the second. 'Oh, you might like to know University College Dublin Archaeology department are planning two digs at promising locations near the find site.'

'Interesting. I'll follow up.' He gestures to the menu. 'Another?'

Carrie shakes her head. 'I'm cutting back on booze…'

So much for his scheming.

'…pinch more than an inch.' Through her sweater Carrie pinches her midriff.

'You look fine.'

Finn regrets his ulterior motive for the meet-up. Carrie doesn't deserve this. It's as if he is a pervert looking to date rape her. No way! This isn't him. He needs to separate work from private life.

He picks up the menu. 'Something non-alchy then... and work aside, what's up?'

Carrie talks about what her family is up to and tells him about an upcoming netball match. 'I'd like to see it,' he tells her. 'Spectators allowed?'

'Sure. It's only a local thing, but I enjoy it. It helps me relax and take my mind off things.'

That's it. Carrie looks strained, he realises. 'Take your mind off things? What do you mean?'

Carrie fiddles with the empty glass then looks at him directly. 'Off the record?'

Off the record? He nods. 'Cross my heart, hope to die.' He gestures across his chest, as he'd done as a kid.

She winces. 'The IT guys are screening our emails now – but you can't write about it. Can't tell anyone. Promise?'

'Promise!' He isn't sure what he's promising but sees she is burdened.

'They're horrible, Finn. Just horrible! Religious weirdos.' Carrie tucks her hair behind an ear and leans her elbows on the table. She spews out the hate-filled crap that she, and Liam now, have been receiving.

He tries to keep up. 'A letter, an actual written letter?' She nods rapidly. 'And to your personal media address?'

'Yes. It creeped me out.' Carrie tries to laugh it off. 'Am I over-reacting?'

This alarms him. All this Bible reference stuff, increasing threats, trolling. Now he understands the stress Carrie – *his friend* – is under.

'The police? Are they involved?'

'No. We're logging everything at work. The board know and will decide what to do.'

'Okay. Is that enough?'

She nods. 'I guess so. Emails are hard to track as they keep opening new accounts, but the letter from Warriors for Xist was quite upfront.'

He will research them later.

'And the thing is,' Carrie continues, 'we can never say, one way or another, that it is Jesus – even if we wanted. But I want to remain open-minded. Let science do the work for us.'

'Lead us to the Light.'

'Ha ha!' Carrie pokes out her tongue. 'I don't get why people are so riled up and angry. And you know, that Face of the Find article has had consequences. Some weeks back a weirdo sent a message saying, "Nice dog. New Zealand, heh?" I've been checking with Mum and Dad, asking casually how Blue is. He was really sick for some days and I was worried it might happen again. The idea of poisoned meat being put out for him crossed my mind, then I figured I must be getting paranoid.'

Finding he has contributed to any of this is a punch in the gut.

'Carrie, Mike and your board are taking the right lines, I see that now. Don't go talking about this to others.'

'I'm not!'

Early that day he had joked about how Ballybere Man was becoming the focus of attention for all sorts of random causes. Suddenly Finn is worried. He squeezes her hand. 'Promise me you'll take care, and keep me in the loop.'

'You and Rachel both. I've promised I'll contact her every day.'

'Good. Add me to the daily list. A text if nothing more.'

'Okay, partner,' Carrie laughs, 'and if you don't hear from me by a certain time, you can start to worry.'

Carrie leaves before him, and no sooner is she out of the door than he messages her: Just testing.

Immediately she pings back: ☺

Returning to his phone's internet screen he taps in *Warriors of Xist*. This web of alt-right red-necks is something else. They've tentacles everywhere. He clicks through to one of their YouTube uploads.

22

The Ripples

NATE PORTER IMAGINES HIMSELF ONE OF THOSE GUYS
on screen. He and a bunch of others are at Ray's watching
some truly inspirational videos on YouTube.

Nate's in awe of these tooled-up warriors ready for the call
– any call – to do battle to protect the Christian way and fight
for Christ and country. The leader has the gift of the gab, just
like his brother, Jake.

'The guy's a vet,' Ray says. 'Served in Afghanistan. Knows
what's what – about political shit and what can be done about it.'

'Man, this is a well-put-together film, huh,' someone says.

'Yep, sure is,' Nate agrees. 'Awesome.'

It's kind of like an avatar in his favourite sniper computer
game, but real life. Nate knows he has the body for it, and with
some imagination and special effects it could be him wearing
combat gear, splatting the bad guys and running in that slow-
mo way, the glow of a massive explosion lighting the sky behind
him. Nate has tried the *Samurai Warriors* games, but finds the
dynasties and rules complicated. Too many characters and he

got bored. There was a time he had toyed with the idea of buying an actual Samurai sword and practising, but he got put off when a bunch of local kids did a dumb thing with one. The sword arced through the air ending up embedding itself in a forehead. Sniper warrior games are much easier to participate in.

He gives his full attention to these Warriors of Xist Ray is introducing them to.

'They're the real deal,' Ray assures them. 'And know what?' He grins. 'They've reached out to us.'

'Yeah? No way!' Nate is stunned these top guys have even heard of them.

'Oh yeah!' Ray beams.

Ray's the networker – the one who knows what's happening out there. The one keeping track of undercover forces operating within 'our so-called government'. The one who directs them to the trustworthy media outlets.

Some days later Nate goes onto the Warriors of Xist website and is stoked to see the KMC name and logo added to their affiliate list. 'Mother trucker!' He stares and stares. Pride fills his heart.

It's practice day. Nate pitches up at the regular meet-up, parks next to Ray, and steps down from his pick-up. 'Hey y'all.' He raises a hand to the Kentucky Men who've arrived before him then reaches for his gun case. If those gun control freaks could see how careful he is with his weapons, they would not be after his hide. He lights a Marlboro, leans against his vehicle and sucks in the beauty of this place. The trees are in their fall colours: vivid splashes of orange, red and gold. Awesome. This is God's own country, and he is blessed to be born here.

They sort their guns and amble the short distance to the firing range.

When they've shot off some rounds Ray happens to mention: 'Those WXs are having fun with some serious messaging to those folks in Ireland.' It takes Nate a second or two to figure out who the WXs are and a while longer to realise he's referring to that dug-up body, Ballybere Man. Nate hasn't given that any thought. He catches the drift and laughs hearing the Warrior for Xist guys had written: 'an actual letter – on paper – and bought a stamp! Can you believe it? Shit. Who does that these days?' Ray looks impressed.

Such a cute name, Ballybere, like it's straight out of a story for kids. His brother, Pastor Jake, hasn't mentioned it again at church, but every so often Nate remembers to pray for those misguided folks in Ireland, as his brother had urged. After all, he knows he must have some distant relatives there. Even that doctor lady might be related. Now it seems those WX guys are getting hot under the collar. Nate would have thought there is enough going on with political stuff on the home front: rallies and marches for one thing or another. Some of these guys like to bowl up and create a presence. Nate has no interest in travelling up-country to these events and anyhow doesn't have the bucks in the bank… No bank account either.

At the next KMC meet-up, Ray chews on a stick of gum.

'You know that Ballybere Man thing we've talked about?'

Sure, they all did.

'Thing is,' Ray says, 'we all gotta take this serious. We're keeping ourselves ready for the resurrection – the signs show it will be here soon—'

'Reckon so,' someone agrees.

'—and this darned thing happening over there is confusing people.'

Ray looks around the gathered men. 'It's like this. The WXs want that body got rid of but they are too, what ya might call, high profile to do the job. FBI – everybody – got 'em in their sights. Word is, they're looking for a foot soldier to do the Lord's work. Hear what I'm saying?'

'Whattcha mean, Ray?' someone else asks.

'They're wonderin' if one of us…'

'One of us, what?'

'You know. Go over and take it out, any way they see fit.'

'Shit, Ray!' Nate stares. 'You serious?'

'Damn right. If y'all want to pave the way for the Second Coming, then conditions need to be right. The Bible says nothing about Jesus coming back in this lousy way. We gotta make things pure. Listen…' Ray plants a foot on the step-up of a vehicle. 'These boys, they've got it sorted. We wouldn't have to take out a loan or anything. They'd pay and they have contacts there – in the north of the island. The job they want done is in the south and there's some sort of state border, but they say they can get weapons and bombs through.'

This wasn't making sense to Nate. 'But Ray, I don't get it. It's a body, dead as can be, why are you talking about weapons? A saw would be better.'

'The thing's protected, ain't it? Can't just walk in and say, "Excuse me, sir, would you mind handing over your body?" or, "Ma'am, we're instructed to collect the body from ya." There may be some what you might call resistance.'

'Why can't someone over there do the job?'

Ray smiles. 'Good question. I asked 'em that. Like I said, no one thinks as clearly as we do on this matter and that's a fact. There're folk over there that'll support us, can get hold of stuff. Know what I mean? But they want a Soldier of Christ from here. Guaranteed committed.'

Nate stands straighter, marvelling there are folks out there who admire guys like him.

'Course, I'd put myself forward,' Ray says, 'but I got my business to run, the kids 'n' all…'

Nate shakes his head. Some of the others weren't working, but he also has a job, can't take time off. Anyhow… 'Ray, you'd need a passport, wouldn't ya?'

'Sure. But that can be fixed.'

Nate shares a look amongst his buds. None of them owned such a thing. None of them had travelled outside the States. Shit, none of them had travelled much beyond the southern states. He knew that for a fact.

'I don't know, Ray,' someone says. 'Sure, this is Satan's work, and someone needs to straighten them out and get rid of the thing. But, heck, it's a bit crazy to come looking to *us*.'

Ray lays a hand on the guy's shoulder. 'They think crooked over there. Y'know, like some folks up north.' Ray would be meaning city folk from northern states. Or Canada.

Nate shares a look with one of his buds. Ray is way ahead of them all while he is struggling to keep up.

'Look guys, okay… Okay, damn it, I'm in!' Ray dusts his hands on his thighs. 'I'm willing to draw a straw with all of you, willing to put myself forward. Don't chicken out on me now – don't chicken out on doing the Lord's work.'

Whoa! It's as if the air has been sucked out of him. Nate comes to target practice to enjoy company. It's the only time he really talks with anyone outside church, or work. A farmer might drop by to order a tractor part, or get a panel beaten straight after a collision with a tree or some such. He and his kids might text a few words. That was all. He looks around and finds everyone is looking at their boots.

Clearing his throat, Nate speaks slowly: 'We're Bible Warriors, ain't we?'

Booted feet scuff dust; caps are re-angled on heads; hands fiddle with holsters.

'I guess,' someone eventually says, the words dragged up from deep inside. They can't back down.

'So, how'd ya want to do this?' Ray asks. 'A draw? Matches would do it, blades of grass'll look different. There are six of us—'

'But Tony's not here today,' someone adds quickly. 'Let's do this next time.'

Ray shrugs. 'His loss.'

'I'll mark up this one.' Someone holds up a cartridge.

So that's what they do. Using a hunting knife, a cross is scratched on it and added to unmarked cartridges in Ray's upturned cap.

'First a prayer.' Ray clasps his hands, and they all bow heads, eyes squeezed closed.

'Dear Lord. We Kentucky Men for Christ take as our inspiration from the Good Book – *Blessed be the Lord, my rock, who trains my hands for war, and my fingers for battle.* Lord, guide us in your mission, this day.'

'Amen,' they say.

Ray holds out his bulging cap, metal chinking. 'Mine'll be the last one. That'll be my fate. Let's do this thing! No cheating, heh? Hand straight in and grab one.'

Nate watches first one man, then another, draw out a cartridge, concealing it. He wipes clammy hands on his jeans. When he'd left home, he had been considering where he'd stop off to pick up a bucket of chicken wings on his return trip. Now this.

'Nate?' Ray invites him forward, the remaining cartridges nestled in the sweaty cap. He keeps his eyes on Ray, as Ray jiggles the cap, 'to make sure they're mixed up,' he says, then Nate reaches in and grabs. He doesn't look to see what he has as he waits for two others to draw their lot, but while the cartridge is concealed in his right hand his fingertips probe the smooth metal... *Shit!*

Silently they open palms to reveal their draw.

'I dunno…' Nate looks from one to the other, seeing relief in their eyes. 'I dunno, Ray.'

But before he can say what he doesn't know, Ray has placed a hand firmly on his shoulder. Others do the same. A strong hand is planted on his head. His legs are giving way. He sinks to his knees.

'Oh Lord, hear us…' Ray begins.

With Ray's prayer filling his ears and the weight of his buddies' hands pressing on his body, a violent thing happens. At this moment he understands what it means to be chosen by God. This is nothing like the time he had been baptised and promised himself to God. That had been a warm and tender feeling of surrender. This is hard, as if his heart is being torn from his chest and he wants to yell, 'Stop!' but he has no breath and can only surrender to the weight of it all. He finds he is sobbing but is not ashamed. Suddenly. Bam! God has spoken to him in no uncertain terms.

He is the chosen one. But is he up to this thing?

Nothing in his life has made him stand out. Nothing suggested he is special. He'd dropped out of school – a mutual parting. There had been some fight, and he swore to God it had not been his fault, but he never found the right words to explain. Same with Shelly; he doubted he would find the right words to tempt her back. Other folks had that gift. In his family, all the smart talk had been doled out to Jake, leaving his own mouth parched.

Ray grips his shoulder. 'Body, tools, mindset. Everything has to fit, Nate, and you're our man.'

Lashing rain and wind buffet his trailer. Nate blocks out the sound as he continues with his press-ups. A new song: a well-known female singer covering Cash's song about a trumpet of the Lord sounding, backed by a banjo-picker and string musicians. Sweat drips off his nose as he forces his way beyond fifty, nose close to the rank carpet. Up… Down… She is singing about when the roll will be called. Sixty now and counting… *Done.* He drops back on his haunches and runs a hand across his brow. Takes a moment. Stomach crunches next.

Before long it arrives in the mail. With reverence he withdraws it from the envelope, takes a moment to admire the dark blue cover. 'Well, well, who'd have thought it?' He opens the passport. There's his name, Nathaniel David Porter, and there's his non-smiling don't-mess-with-me stare straight into the lens.

'Shit.' Getting real now. He strokes the passport. Best let Ray know flights can be booked.

Knowing that he is the one chosen to clear the way for the Lord to make His *true* entry back to earth, as the scriptures foretell, takes some getting his head around.

23

The Ways of Seeing

BALLYBERE MAN IS CAUSING A STIR — HERE AND abroad — and it is Finn's job to keep track. One right-wing group in America he is following has posted a real doozy.

Warriors for Xist

The signs are everywhere before us that the time is coming. We know to look for the Antichrist who will appear before the last hour. This son of Satan, the beast that will rise from the earth, the beast that will rise from the sea.

Fact: the world is heating up, hurricanes and wildfires ravage our lands, pandemics surge across nations and nations are at war as never before.

Fact: a west of Ireland bog, close to the sea, where an old body was unearthed, is being revered as a holy place.

Fact: Jesus was raised bodily to Heaven. The bog body, Ballybere Man, who is the same age and from the same place as Christ, is NOT the Lord.

Fact: Ballybere Man is the Antichrist – an evil thing. It must be destroyed to hasten the Coming of Christ that we welcome.

An evil thing? An Antichrist? Finn decides to head out west for a different perspective.

Ballybere's campsite, or Seekers' Camp, as it is now known, is a magnet. Seekers from far and wide are flocking here.

Finn walks past five stinky porta-loos, surrounded by mud, and approaches a row of stalls looking like a Christmas market. He pauses at one selling T-shirts and sweaters bearing an image of the bog body's serene face, framed by a ring of burnished hair, a slogan stating IN CHRIST WE BELIEVE. Judging by the family gathered there, a brisk trade is going on. The little girl is clutching a small pink sweater while the man is sifting through a pile of practical black ones with white logos. Finn's almost tempted to say, 'Sure you want to buy that shit?' Among the merchandise he notices carefully stacked sturdy white mugs with the same image printed on them. Aren't there always mugs for sale amongst the merch?

Flickering light catches his eye, and he moves to the stall selling prayer candles: glass containers with an image of the bog body, lit candles within. Should he buy one of these for Carrie as a memento? He sniggers. Perhaps not. There's a stall doing a brisk trade selling hot food and drinks and – a chuckle escapes – another displaying throw-rugs embellished with THE IMAGE. 'Here,' he imagines himself saying to Carrie as he thrusts one into her arms. 'Snuggle up with your man.' Yeah. He will stop by later and get one for her.

He takes photos, fascinated by the commercialisation of the bog body, then sets off in search of camp leaders, if there are such things. He supposes this makes him a seeker too. He wants to understand different responses to Ballybere Man, but most of all he wants to get his head around how sane people can fall for this: expecting some long-dead man to ease their pain, physical or mental, and heal their suffering. It is not for him to figure this out, but he can ask questions.

It's getting seriously cold and far too late in the season for camping. As he trudges through the churned-up ground he regrets not buying wellies. Didn't Carrie go on about this? His good shoes are getting ruined.

He circulates, introduces himself, chats to people. 'Are you aware,' he asks, 'of online rhetoric stating "for a fact", that Ballybere Man is hampering the second coming? That the bog body is evil?' Heads shake. People say they are saddened by such talk.

'It's hard to define, exactly,' a misty-eyed woman tells him. 'But I feel nourished. I had a hard time after a second miscarriage, and I'm getting perspective on that, and all sorts of other things. God is present here. I feel it. We all do. Are you just here for the day, or can you stay longer?'

A man tells him, 'I'm not stupid enough to believe that the body found here is Christ. But we can sit up and take stock of where we're going in our lives.' He lays a hand on Finn's shoulder. 'We can all do with that every so often. Why don't you stick around?'

Whoever he speaks to makes him feel welcome. Perhaps this is the thing: a sense of community spirit – the human kind of spirit rather than the godly.

It hasn't all been sweetness and light, he discovers. There has been dissent. 'A guy tried to set himself up as camp leader, a spiritual guide, you might say,' someone shrugs. 'We got rid of him.'

'That's right,' a woman agrees. 'No patriarchal hierarchies here, thank you very much!'

No, Finn thinks, looking at her determined face. None of that shite for her.

Back in Dublin Finn writes a story about the camp then puts Ballybere Man aside and addresses himself to another of his articles about inequalities in Irish society. This one is a follow-up to the baby death atrocities in church-run mother and baby homes. It was decades ago but the trauma is still felt.

Tentatively he requests an interview with the Catholic archbishop in Dublin, assuming he will be politely brushed aside. But no, a day later, he learns he has an invitation.

He finds himself at Archbishop's House in Drumcondra, as Carrie had some months earlier, and finds the archbishop to be an amiable man. The Irish government has apologised for the past; now this senior churchman apologises again, for the church's failing to respect and protect the unmarried women in their homes and respect the bodies of the babies. Finn records the interview, takes notes, gently presses his interviewee to make sure he has the quotes he wants then moves on to the second topic on his agenda. He has not given the archbishop the heads-up on this.

'Your Grace, we've been talking about ripples – giving due respect for bodies, and how the past touches the present. You'll have been following the Ballybere Man story?'

'Ah, yes. I am certainly engaged. How could I not be?'

'I've recently visited the camp at the find site. What do you make of it?'

'One might question the need for certain elements…' Maybe the archbishop takes umbrage at the market traders, Finn thinks. 'But if it brings people closer to God, who are we to object? And I understand they wish to build a shrine there, near the new museum, perhaps?'

'I believe so. But, speaking generally, what do you make of the overall story as it's unfolding?'

'The narrative that the bog body might possibly be Christ?'

'Or the Antichrist, as some would have it. But yes. Have you spoken to colleagues? Might you issue a statement?' Finn is fishing. A statement about what exactly? He suspects it suits the church to keep a low profile.

'Opportunities for spiritual renewal are always welcome.' The archbishop speaks carefully. 'Contemplating who he was allows us to question the mystery of existence, and in doing so, become closer to God.' Seeing the archbishop glance at his phone still on record, Finn takes the hint and switches it off.

'Off the record,' he assures the senior churchman.

The archbishop leans back, stretching his legs. 'We have a fascinating theological conundrum. No man, or woman, can possibly know God's plan for them. Whether this recently discovered body is, or is not, considered to be the actual body of Christ, it makes not the slightest difference to my belief. I live with Christ every day and spread God's word every way I can.'

'Are you concerned that mainstream churches are losing congregations to evangelical churches—?'

'How people choose to worship has shifted more quickly than I could have imagined when I was ordained. I am tempted to say that if Ballybere Man were to be esteemed and venerated, then – as I have thought throughout this episode – it might bring people closer to God.'

So, Finn smiles, the church feels able to absorb another relic. He wants to keep the archbishop talking, and is mindful of that scene in *All the President's Men* – a classic as far as he's concerned – when Dustin Hoffman's dogged *Washington Post* reporter drinks coffee after coffee to keep a reluctant host-cum-interviewee talking. Finn indicates the teapot. 'Might I have a top-up?'

As the tea flows so does the talk.

'Whoever he was, this man, he suffered,' the archbishop says. 'His suffering is evidenced by his wounds, yet the love and care he was given is evident from how he was cherished after his death. Might this body be serving a purpose by reminding us all what it means to be Christian?'

Nice angle. Finn likes it.

The archbishop continues: 'I was talking with our nuncio recently, and—'

'Nuncio?'

'Ah. Consider him a two-way channel for church matters here to be funnelled to the Vatican, and revised canon law to be chewed over in terms of implications for the church in Ireland. His Excellency feels we must consider the uniqueness of what we have. No one could, no one should, leap to conclusions about "who" or "how" but we can agree we are seeing this bog body become a magnet for the faithful. This will not diminish. If anything, it will grow. Therefore, the question is, should we embrace it as a gift?'

'A gift? How exactly, Your Grace?'

'Might not this body be displayed in a spiritual context within Ireland? Or is it possible we conceive it being housed *outside* the country?'

Finn dares not move a muscle. *The Vatican wants the body?*

'Your Grace. I'm not recording, or taking notes, but, well… can we go on the record? What you are saying is very interesting.'

The Archbishop sighs. 'I understand.'

Irish Times

In the question of who will ultimately house Ballybere Man, the 2,000-year-old body retrieved from the west coast bog, a new voice has entered the arena. In a statement from the Archbishop of Dublin's Palace, the archbishop is quoted as saying, 'The body we are calling Ballybere Man has gained interest from around the world including from followers of the Christian faith. We might consider a different arrangement for this Everyman to rest. A place that is not a museum but a space that has a spiritual function.' The Archbishop of Dublin wasn't prepared to go further.

On the east coast, in Dublin, The National Museum of Ireland's director, Michael Curtis, defended the museum's right to house the body, saying, 'We have the expertise, facilities and comprehensive international professional networks. Ballybere Man will be ready for a spring unveiling. People will be able to see for themselves how fitting for this wonderful exhibit to take his place in our gallery.'

On the west coast, Ballybere town has advanced plans for their own museum, with finance partly in place, thanks to a major donation. When pressed about how the remaining hole in the €9,000,000 budget would be met, Cllr Mullen said they had submitted to a central government grant scheme and were hopeful of a favourable outcome. If all goes to plan, they expect to open to the public within twelve months once they are on site.

Finn can't help but smile at a tabloid's take:

Far from being no room at the inn, everyone is opening their arms to welcome Ballybere Man. Rumour has it the Pope has weighed in. Could it be we should imagine our man from the west of Ireland being enshrined?

…but he frowns at the *Limerick Leader's* coverage:

The Ballybere museum project is moving forward swiftly. At the last council planning meeting, council leader Cllr Mullen thumped the table, stating, 'For the record, we'll bloody well steal him from that lot over there if we have to!' His tone now is more measured and optimistic; he told the *Leader* 'We are enormously grateful for the generous donation from the Ryan family.' Members of that family live in Limerick, associated with Thomond Aviation, and a relative, Gavin Ryan, represents Ohio in the USA Senate. Details of the exact amount of money Senator Ryan is raising has not been disclosed. Cllr Mullen says, 'We expect...'

Senator Ryan? Who the hell is he? Finn does a rapid internet search. That Limerick reporter, Cillian Muloney, is breaking far too many news stories for his liking. Okay, he himself began his career in a regional weekly, but he has since moved on to bigger things. It would be concerning if he were to fall behind the curve of the multiple strands of this story.

24

The Civic Angles

CARRIE O'NEILL SAYS 'HI' TO SANDWICH-BOARD MAN who never misses a day, or says no to a snack if anyone is kind enough to offer a packet of sandwiches or a coffee. She is returning from her lunch break, then, having paused to take in today's gathering, she decides to engage with one of the regulars. This woman, who would be in her thirties and looks completely normal, carries her horrible placard: an image of a goatlike creature with a DESTROY THE ANTICHRIST message. That any rational person could believe *her* man was evil.

'Hi there. I'm Ca—'

'We know who you are! You're the one guarding that Son of Satan!'

'Excuse me?' Carrie steps back. Gross!

'It's obvious why we're here, isn't it?' Another woman is by her side, boxing Carrie in. 'We want our message to be clear and you're not getting it. None of you. What needs to happen before you take notice?'

Meeting the eyes of these self-righteous women Carrie has never experienced such a gulf. She shivers, feeling the power of the hatred directed at her. They are bonkers, these women. She navigates past them.

Ballybere Man isn't stored at the Archaeological Museum, he's at their conservation department at Collins Barracks, but the protestors have settled on their central city site as it is next to Leinster House's political hub. More visibility. But this is where Ballybere Man *will* be housed, sensitively curated as with their other human remains.

A thought strikes her, and she turns back. 'Have you seen our Kingship and Sacrifice gallery? It's just inside and I'd love to show it to you and talk about what we've got and what we plan. There's nothing to be anxious about.'

Carrie thinks she hears a hissing sound escape from lips. 'We're not going in,' one says.

The other jabs a finger: 'You should think about what you're doing.'

'My offer stands. I'd love to show you around.' She feels their malign presence at her back as she hurries up the steps and wishes the police would do something more permanent about getting rid of them. The protest on the pavement outside the museum is always carefully gauged. Never massive. Never obstructing visitors. Always complying with police requests to disperse. Should the authorities – police or city council – come down on them, or would this only fuel the fire? Mike's attitude, Fiona's too, is, 'Let them have their moment in the limelight. They'll get fed up when winter sets in.'

Can't be too soon.

Next day, there is a Team Museum meeting. Free lunch. Fiona and Mike want a catch-up after a meeting with the minister. At the Italian restaurant, she and Liam make their way to where

Mike and Fiona sit, an opened bottle of wine before them.

Liam rubs his hands together. 'Ah, excellent. Something to celebrate?'

'Afraid not.' Mike looks rueful. 'The minister was not in the best of moods. Some of our embassies—'

'Poland, USA, Brazil, amongst others.' Fiona purses her lips.

'—are being pressured.' Mike explains. 'Insisting the Irish government isn't doing enough to put an end to speculation about Ballybere Man. Destabilises things. Not good for world peace, she would have us believe.'

Unbelievable! Carrie drops into a chair, wishing all this interference would simply stop.

'And?' Liam ventures to ask Mike. 'The proposed museum out west?'

'She confirmed the government's proposing to back Ballybere Museum with a substantial grant.'

'Oh, Mike!' Carrie's hands fly to her face. She is desperate to keep Ballybere Man under her gaze where she can cherish him. She is a guardian and means to fight to keep him.

Liam strokes his beard. 'Is this definite?'

'As good as,' Fiona says. 'The minister told me it needs a final sign-off. Personally, I think the further away Ballybere Man is from her office the better, as far as she sees it… White all right?'

Carrie hasn't yet finished her alcohol-free spell, but she doesn't hesitate to hold out her glass.

They order, then Carrie learns what has taken place. The minister, it seems, believes the county has a compelling case and have shown themselves capable of bringing in partnership money. This will be the senator's family cash. Carrie imagines a plaque fixed to the museum wall. Or, God forbid, naming the museum after the family. Or might the Ryan family claim a right to rename the body!

Steady. Steady.

As a waitress lays meals on the table, she enviously eyes Mike's and Liam's bowls of saucy pasta while she has limited herself to salad. Still a few kilos to go.

'We're in a sound position,' Fiona insists, 'and I'm all for ploughing on regardless. Best-case scenario is that we keep our man and Ballybere town gets its museum, but they refocus on local folklore. I can see it now. It could be lovely… Thank you.' She nods to the waitress placing a bowl of soup before her. 'Failing that I suggest we hide him away, till the county council backs down.'

'Great plan!' Mike laughs.

'Anything else I can get you?' The waitress hovers, and she is assured they have all they need.

Carrie listens eagerly as they get down to business.

Between twirling pasta on his fork, Mike outlines his thinking beyond the big reveal event, looking four years ahead. 'Imagine a bog body tour,' he says. 'I'm talking with Moesgaard, Silkeborg and the British museums. And that's just the start. We hope others will join us. The most famous bog bodies there are in the same travelling exhibition: The Bog Body Phenomenon.'

Liam's eyes light up. 'It could be as big as the Terracotta Army exhibition.'

'Absolutely! It could be stunning. Huge.' Mike spreads his hands and Fiona's head bobs rapidly.

This sort of talk fires Carrie up. She missed seeing the Chinese sculptures – all those thousands of terracotta guards buried with the first Emperor of China – but had watched documentaries. How thrilling to see the scale of what had been hidden for so long and was now being revealed and shared with the world. She glows, imagining the spectacle, and the wealth of information they can share about Ballybere Man and the others.

'The public will love it.' Liam dabs his beard to remove a spot of sauce.

'They will *adore* it,' Mike stresses. 'The more we double down on our international partnerships and long-term plans, the better our case will be.'

'I love the idea, Mike,' Carrie says. 'How can I help?'

'By coming up with robust partnership projects.' Her director is quick off the mark.

'You know we're already working with Silkeborg and the British Museum?'

'Absolutely. Well done.' She is grateful to see Mike beaming at her, acknowledging her work. 'I'm delighted with the funding you've secured. Don't stop! Look at other institutions.'

Carrie wonders how thin she can stretch herself.

'Carrie.' Fiona catches her eye. 'We're going to ramp up our publicity machine. We've been rather cautious until now. Mike has suggested bringing someone in to run a campaign, and demonstrate to the minister—'

'The entire government,' Mike clarifies.

'—that as a national institution we must lead on this, and we expect their backing. You're to be the Face of the Find. Again.' Fiona laughs, seeing Carrie's surprised look. 'I loathed that term when the tabloid used it, but talking with Mike we believe we need a fresh face—'

'A media-friendly face,' Mike adds, 'who knows the details, and will fight to hold on to what we've got. Liam? A little more of Carrie's valuable time?'

'Ah.' Liam pats his lips. He catches her eye, then glances away.

This isn't right, Carrie thinks. Mike should have discussed it with him first.

'Of course,' he says. 'We'll manage, and I agree absolutely, we should not yield to the government's wish and – well –

yield the body.' He raises a glass. 'To the campaign. To the Face of the Find.' His smile looks a little wistful.

'A thought!' Fiona snaps to attention. 'I can do this. I can coordinate the PR. It will allow me to get close—'

'Conflict of interest.' Mike shakes his head.

'Voluntary, naturally. I wouldn't charge and I needn't step back as chair.'

Carrie thinks Mike doesn't look entirely convinced, but what can he say? What can anyone ever say to deter Fiona?

'Most generous.' Mike has recovered and oozes charm. 'To Team Museum. The next phase.'

Glasses chink. It feels good to find herself at the heart of work politics. Carrie sips her wine. Up until Christmas, she will stick to her healthy resolutions: stay sober, lose weight, keep fit.

With crisp hand motions Fiona is exploring what a profile-raising campaign might look like. 'We must thrash out our role in public. Day after day highlight our international profile and national reach. I will not stand by and let our institution be diminished.'

'Absolutely not!' Mike is looking aghast. Carrie likes this fighting talk. *Go Team Museum!*

'First our grant was reduced, then standstill funding forecast, yet they can find a substantial grant for this new museum.' Fiona's eyes have narrowed. 'We'll rally around Ballybere Man. Make him our standard bearer.'

Carrie images them planning a field campaign around this white tablecloth scattered with breadcrumbs, dots of tomato sauce, and an oily smear of salad oil. Fiona the general, playing politics, using Ballybere Man for her own ends, determined to make sure her time as chair is a success, wanting to prove to the government she is a worthy adversary. Mike a colonel, perhaps, with Liam a major and she as what? Captain? That's about right. A mid-ranking second-in-command role, but still out there in the field doing battle. Oh yes, this assistant keeper will keep her eye on the prize, will fight to keep Ballybere Man in her control.

25

The Weight of Blame

CARRIE O'NEILL SPENDS CHRISTMAS OUT WEST WITH Rachel's family and celebrates New Year in with a bunch of people back in Dublin – including Finn, though they barely see each other. Then it's back to work. Another day on the treadmill. How has this come about? Work she normally loves has become frantic, the pressure unbearable, with someone always wanting a piece of her. She finds herself back in front of camera doing a series of interviews with colleagues – lab assistants, conservators, Learning Department staff – and with specialists from abroad, all of which is rapidly uploaded onto their website. Material to feed the beast. She barely has time for her real work.

Are you squeezing me out? Finn protests, on one of their daily text message exchanges. You planning on being a journo?

No! ☹

You'll run yourself into the ground, Rachel cautions.

I'm OK. Thanks! ☺

Liam should step in, set the limits. He is her immediate boss. All this extra PR stuff is not in her job description. And yet. She wants to – *needs* to – make the case to keep hold of her man. And with the ever-efficient Fiona McCormac getting involved, this complicates things, muddies the water. Carrie has complained to Liam about too many chiefs and Liam cleared his throat, nodded, promising to talk with Mike. While Liam is the perfect boss in normal situations, these aren't ordinary times, and she wishes he would display a little more backbone.

One morning as Carrie arrives for work, protestors are already gathering, at least a dozen or so, with that ghastly banner being unfurled. She sees the devil horns emerge and moments later the full Antichrist message is on display. Devil-banner woman is early today. Usually, she appears around lunchtime with a bag of apples to keep her going. Doesn't she have a life beyond making herself unwelcome? Carrie lowers her gaze and is about to head inside then, remembering her Face-of-the-Find, spread-the-good-work-of-the-museum role, she calls cheerily, 'Hi, guys. Going to rain soon, I wouldn't hang around.' She registers glowering stares then hurries away. Shortly she's doing a filmed to-and-fro with her counterpart at the British Museum, live-streamed, with plans to edit and add to the growing amount of content on YouTube.

The interview starts well, talking about Lindow Man and the importance of contextual and sympathetic displays of human remains, then somehow the conversation veers to other mummified bodies held by the British Museum. She chips in, 'And, of course, you've got preserved tattooed Maori heads. A sensitive thing for the Maori tribes concerned, and New Zealand society in general is much more aware these days.'

There's a slight pause, her colleague sounding defensive: 'Absolutely. Guernsey Museum has repatriated theirs. We hold some.'

Carrie winces, but having started on this track she can't abandon it, so mentions the calls for repatriation of these heads to New Zealand. Then somehow it seems the British Museum – any national museum – are the bad guys for not letting go of things others have a better right to retain and respect. Each time she tries to turn the topic she digs herself deeper into cultural appropriation of sacred objects and human remains. She winces, a menstrual cramp making her fully aware of what it means to be a woman, to be human. What it means to have a bad day at work. Finn is right: she is *not* a journalist, and needs to extract herself from this public role. She focuses on the screen, where her colleague in London is waiting, then manages to steer the conversation back to safe territory. Not her greatest moment.

The rest of the day gets worse.

A European partnership grant she is angling after has rejected her stage one application as 'not closely enough aligned with our priorities'. When she prepared it, she wondered if she should focus it differently; now she is certain, and it will be another six months before a fresh funding cycle begins. A missed opportunity.

Liam doesn't rub it in but purses his lips. 'Perhaps if we'd spent more time discussing it.'

She nibbles the rough skin around her thumb, knowing she had rebuffed his offer for input, partly because she was tight against the application deadline, and she knew how ponderous he was about such things. And partly because she didn't feel he could add much. It had been wrong, personally and professionally, not to involve him more.

Thank heavens it's Friday: a lazy night in to recharge batteries. Tomorrow: run, shop, house chores. And in the evening, clubbing with Finn.

It is one of the Temple Bar nightclubs. 'Not my usual scene,' Finn says, 'but I like the DJ. He presents a thoughtful mix. You can really let yourself go.'

And he does. And she does. Against the pulse of thumping music, flashing lights, purple, green, orange, they gyrate and leap as much as the press of bodies allows. Her arms flail above her head, sweat trickles down her neck and her dress sticks to her back. By the end of the set they are exhausted. Exhilarated. A guy sidles up and catches her eye, and she glimpses what nestles in the palm of one hand: pink, green and yellow pills, with indents of hearts, clover, and smiley faces.

'No, thanks.'

'If you're not in, I'm not.' Finn motions the seller away.

At uni in Dunedin, she had occasionally done club drugs – but not for years.

Is she getting too old for all of this? Most of the girls around her look easily a decade younger, and have spent more time and money on beauty-bolstering aids than she has done. She admires their beautifully styled hair framing faces with strongly drawn eyebrows and eyes made larger with black liner and false lashes. They threaten to spill out of low-cut necklines. And those nails! So long, so polished, so artificial. She catches herself, realising she sounds like Nan. Her eyes follow the seller making his way across the room; she watches an exchange and sees a guy pop a sweet little upper into his mouth. Perhaps…?

No. Not tonight.

A new track: throbbing repetitive beat, the laser light display catching the sparkle of earrings and necklaces, T-shirts dazzling in their whiteness. Finn tugs her into the fug of bodies where she abandons herself. Through the tips of her fingers, flung upwards toward the crystal-coloured ceiling, she releases work worries and responsibilities. From her belly, up through her throat, and out of her wide-open mouth she frees herself, yelling and yahooing. She is in the moment. A hedonistic type of mindfulness. Against the insistent bass throb, she eyes Finn, hair flying as he shakes his head, shirt sticking to his skinny chest, narrow trousers riding low on his non-existent hips. Does she fancy celebrating *his* body and *her* own body later? He's never made a move on her. She tries to picture them together...

No. Not tonight. She abandons herself to the music. Free. Liberated.

Finn catches her eye and grins. She's glad he's her mate.

Sunday morning, Carrie wakes, feeling exhausted. She is not sleeping well and doesn't know what to do about it. She's arranged to join a friend from netball for a run but the idea of getting her body moving is too much of a stretch. Instead, she reaches for her phone, intending to make her excuses, then notices a message from her parents: Sorry to tell you but Nan's in hospital. A stroke. We tried phoning. XOX

Nan! She punches the landline icon, not caring what time it is in New Zealand, not caring if she wakes her parents – if they are even at home – maybe they're at the hospital... *Answer the phone!* Oh God, Maybe Nan's...? Dad's mobile then. Again, she punches in a number and waits. Finally, a sleepy voice: 'Hi, dear.'

'Dad! Where are you? How's Nan? Is she... Oh shit, is she—'

'Hold your horses. She's not dead if that's what you're thinking.'

'Oof!' A long wail of relief.

'We're staying over in Geraldine while she's in hospital.'

'Tell me! Tell me!'

'Luckily she was with people. Bridge club. Must've been an exciting game—'

'Dad!'

'Listen. Life's uncertain. If she'd popped her clogs playing cards with her friends, that wouldn't have been so bad, heh?'

Carrie squeezes her eyes shut. Her parents are always matter-of-fact about life and death. 'Goes with running a farm,' Dad always insists. 'Get used to it.'

'But is she okay?' Carrie asks.

'We'll see. Her left side's looking pretty ropey: mouth's dropped, left arm and so on.'

'Can she talk?'

'Kind of slurred. Hard to—'

'Dad.' She has to ask: 'Any brain damage?'

'She'll be in for a while, being assessed. Not sure yet. She had a bit of a fright for sure.'

Carrie is out of bed. 'I should come. I'll book a flight, I'll—'

'No way!' Her mother's voice. 'Caroline. Don't think of it. You've got your life there. Nan will recover, and we'll do what's necessary.'

Carrie sits slumped on the bed. The people she most cares about are far away and she wants to be near them.

'Carrie?' Dad's voice now. 'We're on it and don't want you to fuss. Look, it is what it is.'

'Okay.' The initial shock is wearing off. 'How can I contact her? What can I do?'

'We'll keep you up to date. Tomorrow, when we visit, we'll take a photo.'

'Okay. Yeah, okay. Promise me.'

Late Sunday night, Monday morning for her family, a short video of Nan arrives. Carrie stares at the grey-haired woman lying in a hospital bed: Nan, ashen-faced, the left side of her mouth droopy. Dad sits by the bed raising Nan's right hand to give a feeble wave. *Oh, Nan.*

That night she barely sleeps.

Monday morning, Carrie just about functions at work, though her input into a shared research proposal refuses to coalesce. She presses throbbing temples. A year. An entire year since she had been called out west to dig out Ballybere Man. She had intended buying a cake to share with colleagues to celebrate the anniversary but, earlier, standing outside a bakery, this no longer felt the right moment. Instead, she purchased packed egg sandwiches.

At lunchtime, muffled up in a warm jacket with Nan's scarf slung around her neck, she heads for St Stephen's Green. Slipping past the imposing Wolfe Tone statue and into the park, she notices signs of colour are cautiously returning to the February landscape. She walks around the ponds and sits on an unoccupied bench to eat her lunch. Grey clouds part, allowing a weak sun to reach her. She closes her eyes, tilts her face upwards. Leaning back, she hooks her elbows over the bench seat, stretching out her legs, taking deep breaths, allowing her belly to soften.

A shadow passes over the pink tinge of her closed eyelids. Moments later the planks she is sitting on shift slightly as someone shares the bench. It makes no difference really, but she craves personal space.

'D'ya mind?' A male voice.

Reluctantly she opens her eyes and twists to see who has joined her.

A man sits less than a metre away staring straight ahead. His deeply tanned face is out of place in Ireland, as is the type of peaked cap few wore here. Her eyes travel down his stretched spread legs, noting his square-toed cowboy boots. Under a padded jacket she senses he is hench, one of those guys who lives at the gym.

'Pretty, heh?' The drawl places him in the southern states somewhere. He's not looking at her but studying the flower beds: crocuses, dwarf irises, cyclamen. She makes a move to gather her bag, uncomfortable with this intrusion.

'All part of God's creation.' He shakes his head, marvelling.

'Yeah, I guess.' She stands, not wanting to engage. The American lazily turns his head and she meets his gaze. The muscles around his grey eyes tighten as he stares candidly. She flicks a wave. 'Enjoy your day.'

'You too, ma'am.'

As she hurries back to work, she doesn't give the tourist another thought.

PART THREE

The Upsurge

26

The Chair

FIONA MCCORMAC POPS A SLICE OF BREAD IN THE
toaster, tops up her coffee, and speaks loudly in the direction
of her phone balanced on the sideboard. 'But the CCTV
cameras will have captured the culprits. Surely the Garda can
sort this?'

Mike's voice reaches her. 'Sadly no. Balaclavas obscuring
faces; nondescript dark jackets and jeans. They were enterprising,
though.' He chuckles. 'No ladders or vans. Arrived on foot. We
saw one chap being hoisted on to the shoulders of another then
scramble over the railings. Looked like he had a grappling hook.'

'This sort of behaviour is so unnecessary.' Fiona checks the
time. 'I'll swing by before my meeting.'

'Oh, no need. Really. But I thought you should know.'

'Thanks. All the same, I will drop by.'

'In that case, I'll let Liam know to expect you. In fact, I
may still be here.'

As she emphatically spreads butter over the toast, she
thinks, yet again, she could do without further fuss emanating

from the museum. The chief exec from Thomond Aviation is in Dublin and she's meeting him to discuss a piece of work she has agreed to do: an external consultancy related to planned management change. But first the Archaeological Museum. She bolts her breakfast.

'Oh, for Pete's sake!'

The graffiti is bigger and more offensive than she had imagined, and she wonders how easy it will be to remove the filth. Filth in more ways than one.

She had parked at the back and walked the short distance to stand where visitors approach the museum. *Some welcome!* She stares at the black-railed gate, now open to the public, the stone pillar to the left decorated with an upside-down pentangle star filling the surface. The bottom point is intersected by a slash forming an inverted cross. The letters SA are written to the left of the upside-down T and AN on the right: Satan.

'Charming!' she mumbles, manoeuvring through a braying bunch of protestors. Twenty of them, perhaps?

On the cream stone façade above the columned entrance, large, no, massive red letters have been sprayed: BODY OF THE ANTICHRIST. And one of the columns has another of those stars with the word Satan worked into the design. How had this got so out of control?

'Out of my way!' She brushes past a young woman with a small backpack who looks like she's settling in for the day.

The backpack woman shoves her, shouting, 'Hey!' and Fiona trips, hands outstretched. Ooph! Her right kneecap crunches on the edge of a step the palms of her hands connect to the hard surface, sending shockwaves up her arms, and her neck whips back. Stabbing pain blinds her.

'Oh God. Sorry!' The backpack woman reaches out. 'Didn't mean that. Are you okay?'

As she is hauled to her feet Fiona's outrage simmers. How dare they assault her! How dare they defile this institution! *Her* institution: the holy of holies she is charged with protecting. She brushes her stinging palms. 'Is this your doing?' With a shaking hand she points to the messages that have appeared overnight. She glares from face to face. 'Well?' Her knee is killing her. 'Well?' she demands again. Eyes slide away. Heads shake in denial.

'But we want that body taken away,' someone says.

She wants *them* taken away, and the chaos that seems to be gathering. She negotiates the steps, refusing the arm of a scruffy protestor. The body is not even here yet, she could have told them. It is stored elsewhere and won't be brought over till much nearer the exhibition opening date. Gritting her teeth, she limps on.

'Fiona!' Mike rises as she staggers through to Liam's office and sinks into a chair. Stretching out her sore leg, she notices a hole ripped in her tights. *Damn it!* She touches the bony plate of her knee and winces, then her fingers probe the tender muscles around the kneecap. Being out of action is not to be contemplated.

'Fiona. What happened?'

'A small contretemps with some of those outside.'

'They attacked you!' Liam is on his feet now, eyes wide.

'No, no. But, Mike, this is altogether too much. We cannot bear the brunt of every misguided person's gripe.'

'Totally. The ministry's been in touch and has agreed we need extra protection. The demos are being banned, from today, and there's going to be a police guard—'

'But for how long, Mike? Initially I thought it would have tailed off and everyone would have calmed down. But not a bit of it. And you know, I fear that once we have the body on display here, this mightn't stop.' *There.* She's said it.

Liam looks aghast, a hand placed on his chest: 'Fiona!' Liam's eyes are widening; Mike's have narrowed.

'You're not saying we should wash our hands of Ballybere Man and hand him over to that… that bloody—'

'No, no,' she hurriedly assures the director. 'We must keep him here, but I am genuinely concerned these agitated souls we have on our doorstep might continue with this onslaught.'

She rubs her knee. 'Have we any ice?'

Liam is immediately attentive, and a few minutes later someone appears with ice cubes in a plastic bag with a souvenir museum tea towel wrapped around the chilly parcel. The logistics of her morning are getting complicated. She doubts she can drive. That means she'll need to get a taxi to her meeting. She glances at her watch… she'd better ring and delay it if she can. Liam's admin assistant is hovering. Can she get her anything else? Tea? Coffee?

'A new pair of tights, please, as quick as you can. I'd be very grateful.'

'Put that away,' Mike says as she fumbles for her wallet. Liam's assistant hurries out. 'Fiona…' Mike hesitates. 'When I had the minister on the phone, she mentioned her office had received a rather nasty email. More of the same. More of what we've come to expect.'

'They're still arriving?' Fiona assumed they had nipped these in the bud.

'Oh yes! Email, social media – every which way – by the dozen. And now the minister. Sounded like a veiled death threat, actually.'

'Shocking!' The minister is bound to think the museum board – *her* board – is not in control. She doesn't relish the prospect of being replaced. 'Is she concerned?'

'Not so much for herself, I'd say, but she's more conscious of Ireland's image on the world stage. All of this is not consistent with a modern nation. She didn't quite use those words, but that was the drift.'

'The conference should sort that out,' Liam tells her. 'I'm sure the minister will be more settled after that. It will lower the hysterical pitch and provide an opportunity to place Ballybere Man within a scientific context.'

Fiona nods. 'I hope you are right.'

The Institute of Archaeologists of Ireland (IAI) is to host an international conference. Long planned, but now with an added agenda to include initial findings on Ballybere Man. And Carrie is the one who'll be presenting a paper. Fiona understands the assistant keeper has been liaising with top scientists from around the world, some of whom have visited and laid eyes on their find, giving their opinions, and getting excited about obscure research projects.

'Yes, I do hope you are right.' She moves the ice pack to the other side of her swelling knee. Ballybere Man is proving to be a bigger project than she had anticipated. But she is not one to back away from a challenge.

When Fiona arrives at her meeting, she is almost carried into the building.

'Mrs McCormac. Are you sure you shouldn't see a doctor?' she is asked. 'Or pop up to the hospital?'

'Don't worry, just help me in there.' Supported under her armpits she allows herself to be half-lifted into the meeting room... Oh! ...*Two* men stand. She had been expecting to meet with just the CEO for an informal briefing. Immediately she recognises the second man, who hastens towards her.

'Gavin Ryan.' Senator Ryan is at her side. 'Allow me.' Strong hands grip her elbow, assisting her to a chair. *What on earth is he doing here?* Reading the question in her face he offers, 'When Gus' – he cocks his head to the industry boss – 'said he was meeting with you I begged to crash the party for a minute or two, and then I promise I'll be gone from under your feet.' He flashes a toothy grin.

'Fiona, and allow *me* to introduce Senator Ryan.' Gus looks a little shamefaced, and so he should! Fiona suspects the meeting has been hijacked and what they will discuss has nothing to do with the business of management restructures at Thomond Aviation but everything to do with that wretched museum out west. She puts on her brightest smile, holds his eye, and extends a hand. 'Senator, delighted to meet you.'

'Mrs McCormac, we are truly fascinated by what's going on in that museum of yours. And as I was here, and as Gus was meeting you, he kindly offered—'

'We?'

Again that flashy grin. 'I refer to myself, and others of my acquaintance back home. Knowing I was planning a trip here, we wondered if I'd be able to set eyes on your Ballybere Man.'

'Shortly, Senator Ryan, shortly. We'll be delighted to include you on the invitation list for the unveiling.'

'Ah, but I'll be back home by then. My people phoned the museum to request a viewing but were turned down flat. I was wondering if you might kindly arrange something for me.'

She wishes he would stop flashing those teeth.

'Unfortunately not, Senator. At this moment the body is undergoing some treatment that must not be interrupted.' This sounds unscientific and feeble, but the senator seems satisfied.

'Understood. Though a great pity, I must say.' He leans towards her, his face earnest. 'You have had the honour of viewing this body. Are you able to say—'

'No, Senator. Please don't ask!'

'In that case, Mrs McCormac, I won't press my case. But before I leave you and Gus to get down to business, will you join me in a prayer for guidance?'

What? She stiffens. This is not the way they do things in Ireland. She glances at Gus, who has the decency to look even more shamefaced than he had been earlier, and she detects a slight shrug of his shoulders.

'Senator,' she says. 'I'm not sure what this is about?'

'One way or other, Mrs McCormac, you have a body that the world is interested in. And *I* am interested in seeing housed fittingly—'

'Ah, yes.' She can't quite control the spite in her voice. 'I've heard you've raised a significant amount for that Ballybere museum project.'

'We have: a museum *and* a shrine.' Senator Ryan grins proudly.

We again. Some fraternity or Irish networks in the States? She doesn't ask as she is not inclined to give him time to explain.

'Though you know,' Senator Ryan eyeballs her, 'calling it a "museum" sounds kind of fusty. "Foundation" seems more fitting. Don't you agree?'

Foundation! That makes her think about under-structure. A base to grow from.

'The thing is, Mrs McCormac, none of us can know what God has planned for us. Maybe it is not on his agenda to remain hidden...' The senator's voice trails off and his eyes become misty.

Christ almighty! Senator Ryan is hoping Ballybere Man is truly Jesus and the Americans want a piece of him too! It wouldn't surprise her to hear him say the body properly belonged to the promised land of America. *Politics.* Fiona's mind whirls. The senator already has the Catholic vote in Ohio. His seat is secure. She steals a look at him. Maybe he has his eye on a higher political prize? Perhaps this man wishes to be associated with a 'foundation' dedicated to preserving (possibly) Jesus because he plans on running for president… What a fillip that would be to his prospects! She stills her tumbling thoughts.

This is what it is like to feel skewered. If it weren't for her incapacity, she might be tempted to politely suggest to Gus that they reschedule their meeting. Instead, she watches fascinated as Senator Ryan laces his fingers, bows his head, and asks God for guidance on where this body should be housed.

The cheek of it! She refuses to comply with this nonsense, but Gus avoids her icy stare by closing his eyes and joining Senator Ryan with an 'Amen' of his own.

The writing is truly on the wall: literally sprayed on the museum, and figuratively in the air. The antichrist lot want poor old Ballybere Man to disappear from the face of the earth, and Senator Ryan's lot is no better than those camped out at the bog site hoping and praying this might be a sign from up high. A thought passes through Fiona's head about being caught between the devil and the deep blue sea, and a wry smile tugs the corners of her mouth.

All she has ever wanted is for the National Museum to *appropriately* acquire and display Ballybere Man, and she is not backing down. Before long she fears someone might get hurt in this tussle – and she's not thinking of sprained knees.

27

The Ancestor

Carrie O'Neill heads towards the museum
entrance, head buzzing with all that needs to be done. The
façade is gleaming; the graffiti has been removed with some
sort of paint stripper. And thank goodness that ragbag of
protestors has been forced to disband. The police are finally
on the case, protecting the museum as well as investigating the
sources of those tweets and emails. Into their hundreds now.
Carrie suspects it is only because the trolling was lapping the
ankles of a government minister that the police have acted.
But police investigations notwithstanding, the internet is a
broad church, and no one can stop fake news proliferating.
Outlandish stories, sometimes naming *her*, are brought to her
attention daily by members of staff. Or Rachel. Or Finn. One
ridiculous story hinted at Ballybere Man being the centre of
occult practice. She had joked with Finn: 'So there's me, in the
dead of night when the museum's closed, leading the rituals.'
    'Oh yeah,' Finn egged her on. 'Tell me more.'
    'Holding candles and chanting and—'

'How's your singing?'

'Lousy. And my dancing's more of a galumph.'

'Ah, no, I wouldn't say that.'

'Anyway, there we are shuffling in a circle around our man laid out on a slab.'

'Can I join you one night? Maybe I can bring some enhancing substances. That might work.'

All this was funny, to a point, but didn't she have a hard enough time defending *sciences* against the loonier religious fringes without this? Perhaps she should stand on the museum's steps and shout: 'There's nothing secret. Nothing hidden. Nothing paranormal.' Her whole focus is on rational explanation, and uncovering the mysteries of their find. Honestly! Some people!

She sloughs off her jacket and plonks down at her desk. The IAI conference is a week away and she has a lot to pull together for her presentation. This will be her platform. Her time in the limelight, not for the media but for her peers. It is a big deal, and her paper will be published. Many more will follow, naturally, but these initial findings are a start. She presses fingers to flickering eyelids. These past days a tic has developed. Nerves, in part, with the pressure of work, but she is exhausted. At night sleep eludes her and she is fearful she is becoming over-anxious. Just as these internet nutters fear something secret is going on at the museum, she is afraid she is being stalked. *Paranoid or what?* Carrie tries to shake the thought off.

Some days earlier she walked the short stretch from tram stop to flat. It was late; the street was empty. Hearing footsteps, she looked back to see a male figure some distance behind. He paused, and she found herself slipping her right hand into her pocket and gripping her keys pointy ends out before hurrying on. When she glanced back again, she neither saw nor heard anything. She found herself fumbling with her keys in the lock. Ordinarily she enjoyed living by herself, but at that moment she wished the hall light had been shining and there was a housemate, or boyfriend, ready to welcome her home.

And not only that. A day later she'd arrived home to find a religious pamphlet from one of those fundamentalist churches wedged in the letterbox, urging her to accept God and not be tempted by Satan. She'd never received anything like this. Ever. Why now? She told Rach and Finn about the leaflet but had been too embarrassed to tell anyone about the phantom stalker. Then last night, she was lying awake, at some ungodly hour, and she could've *sworn* there were footsteps outside her window. Back and forth. To settle her mind, she crept out of bed and thumped the curtain-covered window. After a moment she took a steadying breath, drew the fabric aside and peered out. Beyond the small frontage where the bins were lined up, and beyond the low brick wall and iron railing boundary was an empty pavement and quiet red-brick houses opposite. But if there had been someone – and why would there be? – her banging would have alerted them. And it was dark outside, no streetlight, so she couldn't be absolutely sure...

Perhaps she should tell Rach and Finn how she is feeling? She promised she would but didn't want either of them worrying. Carrie sighs, opens her computer, and plans her day.

She skips lunch, no time, then early that afternoon she finds Liam's beaming face bending over her.

'Carrie. The bust has been delivered. Come. Mike's inviting us to unpack this together... If you want to?'

Carrie pauses for a split second. 'Yeah, I do want.' This is worth putting aside her work. She'll stay late this evening.

They head downstairs and through the back entrance to where Liam's battered Ford is parked, and she endures Liam's appalling driving for the short ride over to Collins Barracks. In Mike's office they gather around as he opens the plastic crate on the floor beside his desk and removes the top packing.

'Please, may I?' She lays a stilling hand on Mike's. The men acquiesce.

Carefully she reaches in and draws out the bubble-wrapped parcel. It's heavy, awkward, and for a moment she is afraid it might slip. Resting the life-sized bust on Mike's desk she peels away swathes of plastic wrapper, until… 'Wow.' Her utterance is almost a sigh.

Stepping back, she gazes at this man's face as he might have been. Brown eyes stare out over a strong slender nose. Thick black hair falls to his shoulders and his beard is a little unkempt. Olive-toned cheeks have been dabbed with a damp sponge to simulate textured skin, and fine wrinkle lines are etched around his eyes. He seems to be in the room with them, his humanity palpable. Tears prick her eyes. And Liam and Mike are equally moved; the three of them become a small chorus making appreciative humming sounds.

She can't resist touching a corner of the mouth. *What might you say, if you could speak?* She is not sure which of their reproductions she prefers: this hand-crafted craniofacial model or the 3D digital visualisation using photo-editing software that shows Ballybere Man's old leathery face morph into a modern man's visage.

Carrie stares and stares at the bust and can't get enough of it. This is, she supposes, a form of ancestor worship. We gaze at the past from our perspective of the present. She touches a lock of hair. At a ringtone, her hand jerks away. She considers letting her phone go to voicemail but decides to check. Her father. He never usually calls during work hours.

'Excuse me.' She moves to the window. 'Dad. What is it?'

'I'm so sorry. I didn't want to disturb you...'

'Dad?' She is alert. Ready. Guessing.

'It was a massive heart attack that took her.' His voice wobbles.

'Oh, Dad! Tell me.'

'Apparently she'd just had tea when it happened. When the nurse came to collect the tray, she was dead.'

'I'd wanted to see her! Hug her!' She chokes as tears well up and spill down her cheeks.

'I know, I know. But these things can't be planned for.'

Liam's hand is on her back, Mike thrusts a box of tissues forward and she pulls out a handful. She needs to get outside, so gives a half wave to Liam and races out.

'When's the funeral? I want to be there.'

'That's not necessary.' Mum's voice now. Always the practical one. 'We'll let you know when arrangements are made but you mustn't think of flying back. Far too expensive, and what's the point? I know how much Nan meant to you, but she's dead. Best remember all the fine times you had together.' Her parents never talked about someone 'passing' or being 'gone'. Death was death.

'Mum!' Carrie is walking up and down under the arched colonnade, a wodge of tissues to her eyes, the paper soggier after giving her nose a good blow.

'Look, dear.' Dad again. 'You've got your life, and if Nan could leave a message to you, it would be to live it to the full, ay?'

Hadn't this always been what Nan said? Enjoy your life. Enjoy being young. It had been Nan who encouraged her to come to Ireland and study. 'Spread your wings and fly,' she had said, stretching out her arms and leaping around her garden next to the flowerbed. One of her gardening gloves had slipped off her hand and sailed through the air. 'See.' Nan had laughed. 'It's a sign. You are meant to leave.'

On the phone it is Mum who is speaking. 'Let it sink in. Your dad or I'll keep you up to date.'

'Carrie...' Her dad now. 'The cremation will be a small affair. We can film it for you if you'd like?'

'Yes, I would!'

'And perhaps you'd like to suggest some music?'

'Okay. I'll have a think.' She tries to grasp all these decisions that must be made quickly. 'Oh. Don't dare scatter her ashes. You save them for when I'm home.'

'Of course!' Her mum now. 'How about we buy a rose bush? You know how she loved—'

'Yes.' She nods. 'Perfect.'

Dad is speaking to Mum: 'Choose a hardy sort and remember to water it. Don't want her dying all over again!'

She winces. *Too soon to joke.* Mum's vegetable garden is stocked with seasonal basics, but her green fingers don't extend to flowering plants. Again, she talks about flying out, and again, her parents insist she should not. 'But don't leave it too long to visit,' Dad says. 'It will be good to see you.'

'Okay... Okay... Love you.' She doesn't say this to her parents very often.

'And love to you too.' Mum isn't one to over-use the 'love' word. She'd once memorably said, 'We're your parents, you can take our love for granted.' But sometimes, like now, it is nice to hear it.

Seeing her pocket her phone, Liam hails her then hands over her jacket and bag. 'Go home,' he says.

'I've so much to do!'

He shakes his head. 'Go. I'll close down your computer when I head back.'

He pats her shoulder, and it comforts her to know Liam is looking out for her. She acknowledges, to herself, how drained she feels. She watches Liam tuck in a shirt tail, and head back inside. No doubt he and Mike will use this time together to discuss preparations for the big unveil. While meandering down to the quayside, she phones Rachel.

'Poor lamb. You'll be feeling bereft. Here's what I want you to do. Book yourself a massage, right now if you can, one of those hot stone thingies, all oily warmth on your back.'

'I don't know.' The idea of even looking up what is available seems too much effort.

'I'm ordering it. On me. Go and sit in St Stephen's Green – it's not raining?'

'No, it's fine here. But I'm at the other site.'

'Whatever, find a café then. I'm on to it. I'll call you back shortly and you'll do as you're told. Bye… Bye.'

Rachel is as good as her word – naturally – and Carrie finds herself booked in for a full treatment. And it is wonderful. Ambient music plinks through the speakers quietening her mind. Sweet-smelling oil anoints her body, and strong warm hands stroke and knead knotted muscles in her shoulders and thighs and her twitching legs begin to settle. Ninety minutes pass before she is ready. Afterwards, she sits in the reception area, wrung out, drinking glasses of water, in no rush to leave.

Finn's daily message arrives: How's it going?

Nan's died and I'm feeling shit, she messages back.

Finn phones immediately, voice firm. 'Where are you? I'll meet you.'

Finn's face is paler than usual, his eyes dark pools of concern. He pushes back his hair. 'All right?' His arms wrap around her in a quick hug. 'Up for walking?'

'Sure.'

They are north of the Liffey, and Finn steers her away from busy thoroughfares along quieter streets he knows better than she does. He listens to fresh stories about Nan and says she is lucky. His Italian grandmother died some years back and he'd barely known her, and as for his Irish grandmother: 'She likes being a widow more than she ever enjoyed being married. I rarely see her, even on high days on holidays, she's sure to be off on cruises enjoying her latest fancy man.'

A laugh rises from her belly. Being with Finn feels good. They are in his part of the city, Mountjoy giving way to Phibsborough, and restaurants are opening. She has not eaten since breakfast and finds the tight knot in her stomach has loosened.

'Shall we get something?' she asks, hoping Finn doesn't have the rest of his evening arranged.

'I've a favourite pizzeria, even my dad agrees is pretty authentic. Shall we go there?'

It is a no-fuss kind of place, busy, but they can still hear each other talk. She hasn't lost all the weight she's gained these past months, but tonight isn't the time to hold back. 'Go for it,' Finn encourages her as she eyes the create-your-own pizza option. Soon there is a bottle of house red on the table. She watches the ruby liquid flow into her glass then raises it. 'To Nan.'

'To Nan's journey onward.' Finn chinks her glass.

The pizza is magnificent, wine smooth and fruity. They have fun pretending to identify its bouquet. 'A load of bollocks,' Finn says. 'As long as it goes down well, I haven't a clue about the rest.' Neither does she. She tells Finn about her presentation for the IAI conference, research proposals she is working up, updates him on preparation for the big unveiling event and, yes, the continuing barrage of ongoing trolling and abuse.

'Another?' she asks, holding up the empty bottle.

'Best not. Work tomorrow… but dessert?'

They share a gelato, reminding her of the many ice-creams Nan had indulged her with as a child. Life felt so safe then… Her stomach clenches, and she flinches.

'What is it?' he asks.

'Maybe I'm being neurotic, but last night I got freaked thinking there was someone outside my flat, and another night I thought I was being followed.' She gives an uneasy laugh. 'I know. I know.'

But Finn is not laughing. 'And there was that leaflet, yeah? You think someone knows where you live? That this is connected with Ballybere Man?'

'Yes!' A cry for help. That is *exactly* what she thinks but doesn't want to say out loud, because, well, it is too weird.

Finn is leaning forward. 'If you don't want to go home this evening, you can stay with me. I'll sleep on the sofa, and you can have my bed. Sofia won't mind. Chances are she's over with her boyfriend.' Sofia is his housemate, a woman from Spain, working at Trinity College. 'How about it?'

She doesn't want to be alone, thinking of her parents, thinking of Nan, thinking it would be nice to go to the funeral. And yes, thinking about a possible stalker.

'I'd like that. Thanks.'

Outside Finn's flat, she notices a motorbike parked. 'Yours?'

'Yeah.'

'I don't see you as a biker. You said you didn't drive.'

'Told you I didn't have a *car*. Even did some advanced training. Good fun.' Finn is looking fondly at his Yamaha. 'Rarely use it, to be honest. Mainly for going back to Cork for the weekend… Come in.'

His upstairs flat is modern and sparse, and thankfully Sofia is out for the evening. They leave shoes and jackets by the door then he points to the leather sofa and excuses himself. She checks her messages. Another from Dad, telling her which funeral director is dealing with things. She will order flowers to be delivered. Roses, perhaps. Nan loved her roses. Finn reappears clutching a balled-up patterned duvet cover and pillowslips then dumps them in the washing machine under a kitchen unit. 'Thought I'd better change the bedding.' He grins, looking embarrassed. 'Music?'

Together they scroll through his laptop, dismissing the edgier, harsher-toned bands, after telling him the one he favoured set her teeth on edge. They settle for Kawala, a band Finn follows but she barely knows. It suits her mood. 'And what can I get you?' he asks. 'I've beer, vodka, more wine, and…' a slight hesitation, 'I've some dope if you fancy. Sofia doesn't approve.'

Funny, Finn has talked about his teenage years hanging out and experimenting with 'a fair few illicit substances', as he had cheerfully admitted. 'It got me through those years and I'm still intact.' But they'd not really talked about adult habits.

She nods.

Glasses and a vodka bottle appear. She helps herself to a shot as Finn rolls a spliff, lights it and hands it to her. Carrie leans back and inhales. Back and forth they share it. 'Heavy in the Morning' plays.

'Love this one,' Finn says.

Tears trickle down her cheeks. What's this about? Nan? Work? The joint making her morose? She tucks her legs up under her and draws near Finn, and his arm instinctively wraps around her. Nice. Her sense of smell has become acute, her nose on his chest near an armpit. She is conscious of his hand on her upper arm squeezing a little tighter. Without reflecting, she turns her face. Finn turns. He is inches from her, his face a blur. Their lips collide and in a milli-second they are locked in what as a teenager she had called a snog: all colliding teeth, tongues, and saliva. *Wow! Really?* She hasn't planned this, and is sure he hasn't either, but somehow they are into it. Without thinking, she finds herself astride Finn grinding away and realises, without shame, she is like a bitch on heat. 'Wait. Wait.' She pulls back, takes a breath. Supporting a friend in need only goes so far. 'Far out! You okay with this?'

Finn is nodding. 'Sure... but I need to get, you know...'

In his bedroom now, clothes abandoned, vanities abandoned, she wraps her legs around her friend who has – at least for tonight – become her lover. Every bit of tension she has been harbouring for God only knows how long is released. She is so relieved Sofia is not around to hear her. Even in her alcohol- and dope-addled brain she knows she is letting go. Being loud. On top of Finn now. God, he's *so* skinny. His face close. Far away. Close... Far...

'Carrie... Carrie!' She is being shaken. Opening her eyes just a crack, she orientates. Morning. Not her bed. 'Shit!' Her eyes are wide as she sits up and focuses on Finn, already showered judging by his wet hair, and dressed for work. He grins sheepishly. 'Friends with benefits, heh. You okay?'

With one hand she gathers his duvet around her naked body and covers her mouth with the other. Foul breath. Everything floods back. Everything!

'I enjoyed last night. Hope you did too.' Finn's smile is broader. 'You were pretty enthusiastic.'

She feels herself colouring. 'God! I needed that, but... but...' How to say, she doesn't want to spoil their friendship, that she hopes he doesn't really fancy her *that* way, that – probably – they aren't best suited to a romantic relationship. She blurts out: 'We can still be friends, can't we? I don't want to lose that.'

'Me neither. We're good. Listen, I've got to go. Let yourself out and we'll touch base later, yeah?' He looks a little anxious too: new territory for them both.

'Shit!' She realises the time, allows Finn a quick hug turning her stinking mouth away, and asks him to phone a taxi. 'Got to get home before I go to work, Channel 4 are coming.' She waves him away as she picks up her discarded clothes.

Back at her own flat, after showering and changing, Carrie picks up the mail from inside the door and her heart contracts: a letter with a New Zealand stamp and Nan's spidery handwriting. Bless her. She'd managed to write a final letter from hospital. Carrie doesn't look at the other envelope but stuffs both in her bag and heads out.

Once on the tram she doesn't trust herself to open Nan's letter as she's bound to burst into tears. That must wait. She pulls out the other white envelope. No stamp. Few people write *actual* letters these days, but she remembers one of her netball friends has an engagement party coming up and must have popped it through the letterbox. She rips it open and unfolds the single sheet to find herself staring at the same sign that had been sprayed on the museum, but this one neatly printed: a reversed five-pointed star, the upside-down cross forming the T of SATAN. Underneath, written by hand in capitals: YOU ARE WARNED. DESTROY THE BODY OR ELSE.

All the good of the previous night evaporates.

28

The Director

Mike Curtis looks up to see Carrie hovering at his office door so beckons her in, appraising her. 'Well done!' He doesn't mean to sound patronising, or God forbid, sexist. Her hair is bouncy and shiny, face carefully made up, an exquisite greenstone pendant at her throat matched with dangling earrings. A wraparound dress and high chunky-heeled shoes finishes the look. His suit is Brioni. Whatever else, the two of them will look polished.

'Where are they?' She gestures to the otherwise-empty office, camera gear already set up.

'Roaming around the galleries, some random footage. They'll be back shortly.' Mike glances at his watch, wanting to get on with the interview.

'They've already filmed the Kingship and Sacrifice Gallery?' Carrie wants to know.

'Yes, they had access before opening time, then headed over here.'

Carrie indicates an envelope in her hand. 'I need to talk with you about something.'

'After the interview? I hoped we could do some last-minute prep.'

'Sure.' She places the envelope on his desk, and they rehearse the interview traps they will *not* fall into, and the points they are *determined* to get across. At the sound of approaching voices Mike checks the knot in his tie is straight, again, and resists the urge to reach for his comb.

It is Channel 4 all the way from London with one of their well-known presenters. Here she is, looking efficient, sharp, thrusting out a hand, with a jangling bracelet, introducing herself and giving a firm shake.

He introduces Carrie, and suddenly his office is in the hands of the crew, adjusting lights and sound, a make-up person dusting his face with powder, someone organising the chairs, fixing a mic to his lapel, then one to Carrie's dress. The presenter and producer are chatting. Such a palaver. He understands he will be asked broad-brush questions, and Carrie more specific technical ones. He nods compliantly.

The interview is proceeding like clockwork with his and Carrie's responses well oiled. They cover the excitement of the find and comparisons with other bodies in their possession, then he talks effusively about how they are approaching the curation with enormous sensitivity and what it will mean to the museum. He deftly sidesteps the interviewer's assertion: 'I understand the body is destined for Ballybere.'

'For the time being,' he smiles smoothly, '*we* have the pleasure of presenting Ballybere Man.'

Carrie explains the difference between ante-mortem, peri-mortem and post-mortem injury.

'Let's not beat around the bush,' the interviewer interrupts. 'The elephant in the room is whether this body you are about to display to the world is, or at least could be, Jesus.'

Carrie is shaking her head. 'The focus of our team is to establish facts and learn all we can. We know a lot—'

'Yes, yes. You've described this – the injuries, the dating of samples – which you say point to the possibility this might actually be Jesus.'

'That's *not* what I've said!' Carrie is standing firm, Mike is pleased to see.

'But come on,' the interviewer is frowning, leaning forward, 'I've read the reports and hear what you're telling me today.'

'Beyond *facts*, that few can dispute, there are enquiries we're making,' Carrie asserts. 'We're scientists, we're not judging, we're—'

'You're being disingenuous, surely.' That famous left eyebrow cocks.

'I can tell you about some of the research projects we're planning.' Mike's assistant keeper grins and begins talking animatedly about a collaborative project she is working up, looking at the contextual conjunction of science and history.

The interviewer cuts in. 'So you are saying you haven't ruled out that this might be Jesus?'

'Excuse me,' Mike interrupts, keen to save his member of staff from harassment. 'We would *never* say one way or the other—'

The interviewer's head snaps around. 'Why would you never say one way or the other?'

Mike realises he has fallen into one of those when-did-you-stop-beating-your-wife questions. He hesitates and Carrie steps in.

'Look. There is a massive amount of interest in our body – the body we are about to reveal to the public as thoughtfully as we can. It's not about what I think personally, it's—'

'Ah, so tell me what *do* you think personally, or is it that your institution does not allow you to say?' The interviewer's steely eyes move from Carrie to Mike: 'An official gag?'

Carrie laughs and glances at him, brushing off the suggestion.

An hour goes by in no time at all, giving the TV channel masses of material to work with. They say their goodbyes, the crew dismantle and pack their equipment, then Carrie hurries to an appointment.

It is when he has his office to himself that Mike remembers Carrie wanted to talk with him about something. He eyes the envelope on his desk, wondering if he should open it. It seems a little presumptuous as it is to her home address. All the same… He slips the paper out.

That sign. Those words: YOU ARE WARNED. DESTROY THE BODY OR ELSE.

This is appalling. A member of his staff has received such a revolting threat. And a person or persons, not in their right mind, *knows* where she lives. He glances at the envelope. Worse. This has been delivered by hand, meaning someone has actually *been* there. Surely no one at work would divulge this information. He shivers, imagining that someone might have followed her home.

He is about to pick up the phone and ask Carrie to return to his office when he recalls she has gone straight to another meeting. Liam then. He needs to talk to someone before he contacts the police. Is Liam doing enough to shield his co-worker? No. That is a mean thought. What on earth could Liam do about this?

Momentarily Mike recalls the comparative ease of his last job. Egos of artists to placate, sponsors to schmooze. And who wouldn't want an art gallery wing named after them, or their organisations sponsoring a high-profile exhibition? Who wouldn't want to be a 'friend' of the gallery with access to openings with celebrities attending, and discreet meet-the-artist shindigs? This Ballybere Man project is stretching his leadership skills beyond anything he is accustomed to. Among other things, he finds himself batting away those he considers the 'fashionably offended' who question whether human remains should be displayed at all. *This* had never arisen at the art gallery. Over and over, he stresses how respectful they will be when curating Ballybere Man. And Ireland itself is stretching his cultural affinities. He had not expected things to be any different from in England. Yet they are, in ways he had failed to anticipate.

Before talking with Liam, he had best speak with Fiona. Poor woman. That tumble she had taken – a push, more to the point – cracked her kneecap, and she is on crutches. Thinking of Fiona reminds him that she wants to debrief him about an encounter with Senator Ryan. 'It was unusual,' was all she had offered.

Fiona, Liam, Carrie and he gather in his office. Branding them Team Museum was an upbeat, fun, corporate kind of thing. Now it seems crass, and the team is not winning. Fiona sits leg outstretched, strapped in a sturdy knee brace; Carrie has cleaned her face of the make-up she had applied for the TV interview and looks exhausted. And frightened? How has he not spotted this? And Liam looks completely out of his depth, owl-eyed and portly, repeating, 'I'm so sorry,' to Carrie. It isn't his fault. He is not *her* personal keeper, for heaven's sake.

'I'm putting in a call.' Fiona looks determined. 'Going to the top.'

The upshot is that the police scale up their vigilance. They take Carrie's letter for evidence, will increase patrols around the museum and where Carrie lives, are investigating the more extreme groups 'known to have affiliations with the far right', give Carrie a stalking advice leaflet and a helpline number. She shrugs, folds it, and stuffs it in her bag.

Mike gets on with overseeing the museum's work, Ballybere Man's upcoming exhibition most particularly. He is lovingly crafting the details. Aesthetics matter. On seeing the 3D digital recreation of the head, the idea had come to him that they should commission a short piece of music to accompany the video. This is in progress. And a glossy publication is being prepared, a huge task drawing together numerous elements. It will be sold in the museum shop, along with bone china mugs, and various other (tasteful) souvenirs. It's all go.

Comms are dealing with invites and a reception for the grand reveal, with Marketing leading on the media campaign. For weeks now huge posters have hung in all museum sites advertising the upcoming event. He is impatient to get this body secured in his especially designed display case where it cannot be touched, safe from probing fingers. And from lunatics who want it destroyed. Safe, for the time being – or if he has his way, *forever* – from those heathens in County Clare. Hah!

Those bloody westies have a website for their proposed new museum, and he finds himself surreptitiously opening it every day or so, like looking at porn. It is the graph that draws him: donations and target. Steadily the figure is creeping upward. When Fiona told him of her encounter with Senator Ryan, he laughed, imagining the scene with the Senator leading a prayer. Fiona just looked irritated. 'I don't go in for this unmediated prayer business.' The man has deep pockets, and contacts with those with deeper ones, and contributions from the States are flowing to that back-of-beyond project.

A week later, Mike settles to watch the Channel 4 documentary. He's seen the trailer and was not impressed by the jump-cuts and edgy style of editing. In the entire hour he features for no more than a minute and Carrie for perhaps three, with everything cut and juxtaposed to place them on the back foot. He sounds defensive, and Carrie is caught glancing at him, sounding secretive, and it hadn't been like that. The documentary spends an inordinate amount of time focused on those who, in his opinion, have axes to grind: Councillor Mullens from out west sounding belligerent; those two women who frequent the Archaeological Museum entrance, placards in hand, coy about having anything to do with the graffiti. He is alarmed to hear one of them self-assuredly state: 'But never mind about that. Whoever painted the message – and we're not saying we had anything to do with it – this battle is far from over. We might've been pushed away from the museum steps. That was nothing.' She's scoffing. 'You watch this space. The world can't stand by and see the Antichrist being worshipped.'

Oh, my Lord, Mike thinks. Are they the loony fringe? Or is he so out of touch with what average people think? Whatever the case, he has his point of contact with the police. 'Call this number,' they said. 'Any fresh lead or concern, let us know.' Well, he will be doing that. He is rattled. *Watch this space*, indeed. An empty threat by a marginalised group, or something that should concern him?

Fiona's response is to request that he drafts a letter to Channel 4 for her to sign on behalf of the board, objecting to the distorted presentation. She also urges him to follow up with the police and he assures her he has already done so. 'And Carrie? She's safe?' Fiona asks.

'We are keeping a close eye out,' he assures her.

He knows that Carrie is working on her presentation for the upcoming conference. This gathering of archaeologists is heaven-sent. They can't control the message of a TV channel playing for audience ratings, but they can present themselves professionally to eminent academics from around the globe. He speaks to Liam.

'How's Carrie?'

'Fine. Why do you ask?'

'No more harassment?'

'Oh, that. Thankfully not. No, no.' Liam sounds relieved. 'I thought something fresh had taken place I wasn't aware of.'

'You're her line manager. Keep her close.'

'Yes. Yes.' The keeper doesn't need reminding of his duties. 'Carrie's robust. By the way, Mike, I invited her to stay with us if she didn't fancy being by herself at night, but she declined.'

'That's kind of you, Liam, very kind.'

Mike eases back into his chair and takes a moment to reflect. Team Museum are on top of things. He can't think of a thing he is overlooking.

Next morning, Mike is called into work early. Very early. In fact, pre-dawn. He drives up to the red-brick conservation block and parks near a private security firm's car with the company brand in bold letters across the door. The night-shift guard waits, leaning on the bonnet, while his anxious-looking facilities manager stands huddled next to him. Little time is wasted on pleasantries so early in the day, and he walks up the concrete-slab steps and inspects the glass door. A spider's-web of cracks covers both panes. It's been repeatedly attacked with a mallet or some such, but the glass has held.

'They timed it to just after I'd done my round,' the security guard says. 'I do a circle, and I always vary my routine.'

'Good job the alarm went off. *That* didn't let us down.' The facilities manager blows out his cheeks. 'CCTV shows they tried this one first then had a go at that one over there.' The grey-panelled door to their right stands askew, a crowbar on the ground.

'Thank heavens they didn't manage to break in.' Mike is beyond relief.

'They persisted, even after the alarm sounded,' the facilities manager continues. 'Probably figured no one would follow up, that it would be ignored, as is so often—'

'Excuse me! I did. Follow up, that is.' The security guard is defensive. 'Immediately.'

Mike mollifies the man. 'Of course, of course. We mean generally speaking, yes?' The facilities manager has the good sense to agree. 'So often one hears of alarms going *unattended*.' He pats the man's shoulder. 'Good work.'

'My headlights caught two men trying to jimmy open that panelled door. Chased them. Disappeared around the corner.'

Mike's gaze follows the security guard's raised hands as he indicates the direction the would-be burglars ran. No doubt a vehicle was ready to whisk them away.

'The thing I don't understand,' the security guard puzzles, 'is why anyone would want to break in here? There's nothing precious inside we've been told to be aware of.'

Something *very* precious, Mike wants to say.

The security guard gestures to Collins Barracks. 'I've been led to believe all your valuable collections are inside there, and that this building is just, well, an ordinary work block.' He shoots a pass-the-buck look at the facilities manager, who returns the favour by daring to give *him* the same don't-blame-me look. Mike sighs. The buck inevitably stops at the top. He addresses both men. 'For the time being we had best step up night-time security at all our sites. Particularly here.'

He looks at the damaged doors. So fragile. Not built to withstand a determined onslaught. Fixing metal doors is an idea. *Strong* metal barriers.

He knows *exactly* what those men, whoever they were, were after.

29

The Kingship and Sacrifice Theory

CARRIE O'NEILL IS AS READY AS SHE CAN HOPE TO BE. She is about to present her paper *Kingship and Sacrifice: Ballybere Man* before her peers, outlining, cautiously but confidently, where they have got to and avenues they are exploring. This is a big deal. An archaeological conference like this doesn't usually warrant much attention, but the media will be covering it, and yesterday Finn had profiled her, saying, 'Least I can do, and I'll be in the audience hoping you'll deliver the scoop of the century.' At her puzzled look he said, 'Kingship and Sacrifice: King of the Jews.' She punched his arm, laughing, but not really. He admitted he hadn't thought of it, and scrolled through memes and riffs doing the rounds on social media: photoshopped versions of the museum's publicity poster for the big unveiling: a close-up of Ballybere Man's face looking serene. 'Here's a "Kingdom of Heaven" one, and I kind of like this "Jesus sacrificed for all us sinners" one.'

The Christian angle would not go away.

So Finn will be in the audience, and Liam is heading over to the conference hotel for a catch-up with colleagues and to hear her deliver her paper. Rachel phoned to wish her good luck, and even Mum and Dad messaged, understanding how much this meant for her career. 'Nan would've been proud,' Dad added, and her heart contracted.

A car is fetching her, and she is ridiculously chuffed. She's never had a chauffeur pick her up when she's attended conferences abroad. Now the IAI is giving her the full treatment. Do all their speakers get this laid on? It feels like being a Nobel Prize winner.

She has chosen a bluey-grey slim-fit trouser suit with a new white T-shirt still with visible fold marks. Around her neck she wears her double-twist pounamu pendant that Nan gave her for her twenty-first. 'It's a bond,' Nan said, reading the description on a card tucked in the box under the pendant. 'To keep us connected, always.' Next, she loops her hair behind an ear, hooks the silver wire through her earlobe and fingers the jade twist, and reaches for the second earring. Appraising herself in the mirror, she is satisfied with the image staring back. It must be grieving for Nan that has shed the excess kilos, and she has made an extra effort not to chew her fingernails these past weeks. The dark plum-colour nail polish matches her lipstick.

The doorbell jangles. Wow! Not a toot of the horn or a text. Service to the door. She grabs the bag containing her laptop and hurries out. A shiny new dark blue Toyota saloon waits. Through the tinted window she glimpses a female driver already back behind the wheel. 'Thanks,' Carrie offers, settling behind her.

'Our pleasure,' comes the reply as the car shoots forward. There's no need to give directions, so Carrie opens her phone to check her messages.

Before long, they slow for traffic lights. Her eyes flicker up… Not lights. They are pulling to the side of a street. Which street? The opposite back passenger door opens. They must be picking up another speaker. Foolish to think this car is just for her. She sees legs clad in old jeans. Hah! He hasn't made any effort to look smart! Her lips form a smile in anticipation of welcoming a visiting colleague, curious as to who this is. She isn't aware of a guesthouse here, nor of other academics living locally who are due to present papers today. A man is bending, ducking his head, holding his peaked cap in place. The car starts off before he has closed the door.

'Ma'am. Pleased to see you again.'

Again? Carrie's brain whirls as she stares at the stranger settling next to her. He looks rough, weathered, the smell of cigarettes permeating his clothes. One of those archaeologists who hate being in the office, resenting any weeks spent away from fieldwork. Plenty of those. Has she met him? He is looking at her, a slight smile on his face.

Time slides and shifts. Fragments of recollections form then disintegrate. Hazy memories. Clouds. That shadow. That accent…

'Stop the car, driver.' Her voice is calm as she unbuckles her seat belt, one hand reaching for the door handle. A click of the central door lock, the man's staying hand on her arm: 'Take it easy. It's okay.' But this is far from okay.

'Stop!' Carrie lurches forward, fingers grasping a bunch of hair. 'Ouch.' The driver tries to duck. 'Fuck off!'

'Woah now!' Strong hands haul her back. 'Take it easy. We're not goin' to hurt ya.'

Hurt me? Her stomach clenches. There had been times, after yet another horrible story hit the news of a young woman abducted, raped and murdered, that Carrie thought, what if this were me? How might it feel? *Like this.* Dry mouth, heart knocking, brain foggy, trying to figure a way out. This is no random snatch: some woman walking home in the dark. This is a Dublin morning. And this isn't a bitter ex-partner or celebrity-obsessed stalker... Carrie catches her breath. *Stalker. Someone who knows where I live.*

Recollections begin to form only to dissolve. 'All part of God's creation,' this guy had told her when admiring the flowers in St Stephen's Green. Has he been stalking her?

'Stay calm, and ya won't get hurt. For the best.'

One strong hand pushes her head down as the other yanks her arms behind her. She's screaming, legs thrashing, begging, as his body weight pins her down. Metal cuffs click around her wrists. She twists to find stale-smelling crumpled fabric touching her face. For a moment she thinks she's to be gagged then a pillowcase is tugged over her head. 'No... No!'

'Keep her out of sight!' The driver's yelling.

'Not goin' to hurt ya,' the man repeats, puffing a little.

She greedily sucks in air, fearful she might suffocate, but the navy-blue musty fabric is thin and falls loosely about her shoulders. She gasps, 'What do you want?', barely recognising her own voice.

'For you to do the right thing,' the driver answers. An Irish accent. Carrie can't say more than that, doesn't recognise regional variations.

'That's about it,' the man says. 'Sorry it's come to this...'

Come to what?

'...but the Lord's will must be done. And shit, you've had a bunch of time to think on what you're doing, but ya just wouldn't listen. Now, roll down.' He nudges her onto the floor squeezed between the seats. 'There we go now.' One of his shod feet rests on her left hip.

The driver's speaking, voice jubilant: 'We have her! Yep... Yep, no prob... see you soon.'

Carrie shuts her eyes, willing her thudding heart to settle. 'Where're you taking me? Who are you?'

'Sorry, ma'am. Should've said. Ya can call me Nate. Pleased to finally meet ya.' One of her clammy cuffed hands is gripped by a hard, dry-skinned one. *A handshake?* What is she to make of this?

Nate. She repeats his name silently, needing to keep track, then becomes aware he's still talking. 'Sorry? What?' Is this how people behave when they are in danger? Remain polite so as not to antagonise the person who has power over them?

'I was saying, Cora here and some of her buddies have been real helpful.'

'We've met loads of times,' the driver is saying. 'And you know what we want.'

Time slides and shifts again. That voice. One of the placard-bearing protestors with the devil sign at the museum who had spouted off on that Channel 4 documentary. Of course!

Cora and Nate are expecting the rapture, and the presence of Ballybere Man is preventing this happening. Her own determination to preserve this body is getting in the way of their narrative.

'You'd think a lady like you would be smart.' Nate chuckles. 'A doctor, heh? Doctor O'Neill. Never met one before, apart from getting fixed up for a broken bone or stuff. You got family connections in the States? You got a Colleen O'Neill way back in your family?'

'What?'

'Never mind. Anyways, you've had tons of messages, ain't ya? Friendly, mostly – I've been told.'

No, those messages were not friendly. Should she say? Would that rile him? She says nothing. Compliant.

Her phone rings from within her jacket pocket. Nate's hand pats her side, feeling for it before drawing it out. 'Don't want them tracking us,' he says as he switches it off.

Them. The police?

'Where are you taking me?' There's a quaver in her voice, and she has an urge to pee. She is more scared than she'd ever imagined possible.

'Somewhere. While we negotiate,' Nate says. 'One sweet lady'll be returned safe 'n' sound once we're sure the other body's been taken care of. We got it all arranged.'

'That's about it,' Cora adds. 'One body in exchange for another.'

'Plan to keep you alive, though,' Nate clarifies.

'They'll be missing me,' she manages to whisper. 'I'm expected.'

'We know that, stupid,' Cora scoffs. 'But not for a while yet.'

How true! Her presentation isn't till after lunch. She had not thought to question why a car was coming so early. Why a car was coming for her at all. Who on earth had this service in the world of academia? Had she been blind? Too busy? Her ego stroked? But we don't go through life looking for inconsistencies and she'd assumed there was a formal get-together in the morning, maybe some photos or media event. Her brain races. When realistically might she be missed? There is an official lunch she is expected for, but even then no one will wonder. Perhaps they'll think she's giving her talk a last-minute polish. As these thoughts race through her head, she becomes aware of Nan's pounamu resting against her throat, the stone reflecting her body's heat. It comforts her.

As the car continues, Carrie gives up trying to figure out where they are but suspects they are still in Dublin. Perhaps on the ring road? They are travelling at speed. Before long they slow a little, and she loses track of right and left turns and how often they stop at traffic lights. Now the surface under the tyres is potholed and she can't hear any traffic. Cora is driving slowly. Stops. There is a metallic rattling sound. The car moves again then the engine is switched off. Nate is hoisting her into a sitting position, 'There we go now, wasn't so bad,' dragging the pillowcase off her head.

They are in an empty warehouse. Shafts of light from the open garage door catch a figure moving: a man, wearing an unbuttoned check shirt over a T-shirt, jeans and lace-up boots. She's never seen him before. A clanking sound as the up-and-over garage door closes. Suddenly she is in no hurry to leave the car.

The man reaches in, drags her out, holds her at arm's length, looking at his prize. 'Shit-hot!'

Another American! She stares at this scrawny tight-faced man and her heart sinks.

As her three abductors whoop and congratulate themselves she steals glances, exploring her surroundings. A half-opened door at the rear reveals a toilet booth, and a neon strip light shines through a cobwebbed window and the open door of a room. Cora pushes her in the small of her back in this direction.

She scans the stale-smelling room – an old office. They are well prepared. On a table smeared with oily-looking stains is a laptop she judges to be mid-range. It's certainly not old. There's a plate being used as an ashtray, overflowing with butts. Bottles of Coke and water, packets of biscuits and crisps. And apples. Somehow the fruit seems out of place. Four plastic chairs surround the table. The floor is concrete, one end covered with old carpet tiles in what might once have been a sitting area. Her eyes dart around. Sleeping bags are heaped in a corner. Have they been camping here? She catches sight of a pile of discarded sandwich wrappers, apple cores and scrunched-up crisp packets, and takes a steadying breath. How long might she be here? Her chest constricts.

Nate unlocks the cuffs, and she rubs her wrists. 'Hot work,' he says, and removes his sweater. She notices sweat stains on his T-shirt armpits, a strong male smell emanating from him. Her eyes rest on the shield and Warrior for Christ tattoos.

He follows her gaze. 'Best thing in my life being in the Lord's army, really sorted me out. And ya know, I was chosen for this job.'

Job? Her fingers reach to caress her pendant, the stone warm and sitting snug against her throat.

'Sit,' Cora orders. Carrie perches on the edge of a dirt-ingrained chair. She had dressed so carefully, but her outfit is all wrong and her shoes not ones she can sprint in. If she gets the chance. She is beginning to feel calmer.

'Look. I don't know what you're hoping—'

'Hush up,' Nate says. 'You listen.'

'Sure. Sure.' Her head bobs in agreement.

'We've come all the way over here to sort this out.' The other American jerks his chin towards Nate. 'We're fixin' to make it right. What's happened has upset a lot of folks where I'm from—'

'I know. Understand. But if only you'd let me—'

'Shut up!' Cora thumps the table. 'Where's that body?'

'At the museum, conservation department.'

'Still there, heh?' Nate asks. 'Didn't move it?'

That attempted break-in. 'No.'

'Locked up?'

Carrie nods.

'Who's allowed in, sweetheart?' Nate's piercing eyes are on her.

'Different people. Conservators... and Liam.'

'Liam?' Nate cocks his head.

'My boss: Doctor Harte.'

Cora's eyes gleam. 'He helped clean it up, remember?'

'Oh yeah.' Nate looks satisfied. 'Now he's going to get it all mussed up again. Let's hope Liam's a good boss and he likes you.'

Cora switches on a cheap-looking red phone, the kind that functions to make calls or text but no more. 'Know his mobile?' Carrie nods. 'Tell him he's got an important job to do.'

'Yep. His part in history so we can wreck that body,' Nate says.

The other American's face is granite as he gestures to the laptop. 'And it's gonna be witnessed.'

'Wreck it?' Carrie feels weak. 'But... but how? How do you imagine...?'

'Gonna well and truly destroy it. We got it figured. All set to go.' Again, a glance at the laptop.

'And you tell him.' Cora grabs Carrie's arm. 'No mucking about. He needs to do it. Fast.'

Three pairs of eyes are on her. *Crazy!* This is impossible. Anyway, what if Liam won't? *Can't?* Her voice quavers: 'Ballybere Man's in the hands of conservators. Liam can't just go in and, well...' She wonders what they are planning.

The other American speaks. 'I reckon he will.' There's a clunk. Carrie looks at what he has placed on the table. Hand shears. Shop-new. The stainless-steel double blades have been nowhere near a sheep's fleece.

'Hey, they're somethin', Ray.' Nate picks them up, admires them, positions his hand and squeezes. Her eyes are on his black inky tattoo – shield and cross – swelling as his biceps bulge.

Cora thrusts her phone into Carrie's hand. 'Phone him. You'll be on speaker. Don't make him panic. If he's with people, tell him to go somewhere quiet, then Nate'll talk.'

She dials. It rings and rings then silence. Liam has cancelled the call. 'He doesn't recognise the number. He'll think it's spam.'

Whispers. Curses. 'Here.' Nate hands back her own phone and she switches it on. From the contact list she selects Liam's number. Again, the ringtone. *Please pick up…*

'Carrie, I'm about to head over. You're there already, I sup—'

'Liam! Where are you?'

'In my office. Why?'

'By yourself?'

'Yes. Why?'

A wail. She can barely speak. 'Liam. Help me!'

'Carrie?'

Nate snatches her phone. 'You're her boss, right?' He is trying to disguise his voice, speaking in a lower register.

'Who's that? Where's Carrie? Carrie!'

'Right here. Liam, I've been—' A hand is over her mouth, and she knows Liam will only hear her muffled cry, will hear the sounds of chairs scraping the floor as she struggles.

'Carrie! Carrie!' Liam is shouting.

Nate again. 'You listen. Carrie's fine with us and—'

'Us?'

'Here's what you're goin' to do.'

'I want to see Carrie. Carrie? Where are you?'

'Aw, shit.' Nate switches on the video, thrusts her tear-splodged face close so Liam won't see anyone else or the surroundings. Nate is talking again. 'It's that body—'

'Ballybere Man,' Carrie sobs. 'They want him destroyed.'

'Who wants…? I don't understand. Carrie, who are they? Where are you?'

Nate flicks off the visuals. 'Shuddup 'n' listen. If you want her back safely, you're gonna destroy that evil thing.'

'But it's not—'

'Shuddup! Here's whatcha gonna to do. You're gonna start by cutting off one his fingers to show good faith.'

'But... but... you have to understand.' She hears Liam is trying to sound reasonable. 'I can't walk into the lab, turf out our conservation staff. Can't—'

'Sure you can. You're the boss, ain't ya?' Nate's goading him.

The small American picks up the sheep clippers while Nate fumbles with the phone video, bringing it close to her face. Her head is yanked back, and she sucks in air, fearing she might faint, seeing those vicious steel tips jabbing close to her throat, touching her skin. Liam is screaming, 'Stop! Stop!'

Nate's companion – *Ray! Ray!* What's wrong with her memory? – says quietly: 'Let's see how these things work.' He grasps a handful of hair close to her ear. Her hands shoot up to protect herself. She hears steel edge against steel edge, cutting through a hank of hair, flinches at stinging pain when sharp tips catch her knuckle. Moments later strands of honey-blonde hair are flying, landing in her lap.

'Christ!' Liam is moaning. 'Please... please!'

How often she has watched shearers at work, deftly shearing ewe after ewe, their electric cutters close to the skin, keeping the staple long. And at summer agricultural fairs as a child, she recalls hand shearers swearing by these old-fashioned clippers, saying they kept the sheep calm. And those ewes she had watched on their sides, a shearer bending over them, did look calm. There was no such concern for her wellbeing. Her head is thrust forward, and her scalp stings as another hank of hair is tugged back and twisted. Steel meets steel.

With hair falling around her, she sucks her bloodied knuckle where skin has been sliced away, leaving an oval-shaped wound.

In the background Liam's voice: 'Stop... Oh, God, stop... Don't hurt her!'

'First a finger,' Nate says to Liam; Nate's hand closes around her wrist, holding her bleeding hand to the screen. 'You have fifteen minutes to show us *your* severed finger—'

Carrie begs, 'It will take him fifteen minutes to drive over.'

'Twenty minutes then, otherwise you get to see *our* severed finger. And if we hear any cops arrive, well, this pretty hand of hers—'

'Wait! I—' Whatever Liam is about to say she doesn't learn.

'Sorry, sweetheart.' Nate's hand is on her head, moving to caress the back of her neck. She flinches at his touch. 'It'll grow. It's only hair.'

Cora inspects Carrie's cut knuckle. 'We got any sticky tape here? Oh, well, too bad. Got a tissue, anyone? Least you still have your finger.'

'For now,' the smaller American says matter-of-factly.

Nate is saying, 'Want me to even you up?' His hand strokes the right side of her head where her hair hangs loosely to her shoulder. She manages to shake her head. What a stupid question. Who cares? Nate fingers an earring. 'Pretty.' Then his hand slides to the pendant at her throat. 'No!' She can't bear him touching it. The chain digs into her neck as she thrusts him away. It snaps, and her pendant flies off. She's on the ground scrabbling for it. As her hand closes around the pounamu, she thinks, this was meant to keep me safe.

Kneeling on old greasy brown carpet tiles, Carrie bends her unevenly shorn head to her chest, clasping Nan's precious pendant with both hands. Sobs rack her body. This journey with Ballybere Man is taking her to a place of darkness.

30

The Keeper

LIAM HARTE QUAKES. UNCONTROLLED TREMBLING like this is a thing he has never experienced. Even his teeth are clacking, filling his ears with noise he doesn't need to be distracted by. He massages his jaw, tugs his beard, and tries to still his tumbling thoughts.

Twenty minutes! This is irrational, but he is dealing with crazed people who are holding his assistant keeper. Carrie is in danger. This much has sunk in. She looked terrified, and, oh God, the brutality with which her beautiful hair had been chopped. And had they chopped the tip of a finger off? He wasn't sure. What are these people capable of? In fact, who are they? How many? He hadn't seen anyone's face. He'd only spoken with one man; he was muffling his voice, but he sounded American. Images of fundamentalist Islamists and beheadings fill his brain. Are Christian extremists capable of anything like this?

A minute must have passed. His fingers hover over the phone he still grips in one hand. Dial emergency services?

Request the call-taker puts him through to the Gardaí? But trying to *explain* what is happening will take time – time he doesn't have.

'Let's go!' He speaks loudly to gee himself up. His small-stepped waddling walk, toes slightly pointed out, is not that of heroes in films striding determinedly to save a damsel in distress. Down the stairs, where he increases his pace, ignoring greetings and others wanting to distract him. He longs to jog but that will only draw attention. Walking faster, he is out the back door to the car park. Pray to God the lunchtime traffic will be kind. How is he going to do this thing required of him? First a finger? Then what? How on earth do they expect him to destroy Ballybere Man? – he shivers at the thought of such wanton destructiveness – and will they let Carrie go?

In a daze, he speeds to Collins Barracks and parks by the red-brick conservation building. At the lab now, saying hello to staff in a voice he hopes sounds normal. Explains he needs to view the body. Mumbles something about Carrie wanting a close-up shot of an ear for her presentation. An ear! How pathetic that sounds. 'I can do that for you, Liam,' someone offers.

He brushes that aside. 'Quicker if I do it, I know what she's after. 'Oh,' Liam says, as if as an afterthought, 'hand me a scalpel, will you? While I'm there, I'll take another hair sample.'

'Is that necessary?' A lab assistant frowns.

'Yes!' Perspiration beads his brow. His lips twitch, refusing to stretch into a normal-looking smile. The female lab assistant opens a drawer, takes out a newly wrapped scalpel, a fresh whirl-pack bag and disposable gloves but hesitates before handing them over.

'You sure you're okay? I can help you.'

'No. No.' Liam waves her aside, hurries away, glancing at his watch. God. Where has the time gone?

Fingers fumble with the bunch of keys as he selects the correct one and unlocks the door. This is where Ballybere Man is kept safe and secure. *Safe?* Hah! Here he is, the museum's Antiquities Keeper, about to do a terrible thing. At a flick of a switch a strong neon light illuminates the small room. The lab assistant is hovering. He waves her away, shuts and locks the door behind him, and makes his way to where the body is stored. He opens the locker, pulls out the trolley, and draws aside the bubble plastic cover. He gasps a ragged, 'Oh!'

Liam sags. He can't do this. He dithers. The police? No time. He takes a steadying breath. He must… He must… But he is about to commit an act of sacrilege, wilfully damaging – oh, he must not think of it – this magnificent specimen. He isn't sure he has it in him. But he must keep Carrie safe. Oh God! His heart is hammering. Is there even reception in this back room? Panic rises and he tastes again that bacon he'd had for breakfast. Quickly he punches his home number icon on his phone, waits to hear the ringtone, then hangs up. *Yes.* Any moment now…

A shrill ring: undisclosed number. He taps the green sign. 'I'm here! I'm here!'

'You done it yet?'

'Just arrived. Give me a minute,' he begs.

'No cops, right?'

'Promise. Haven't called.'

The phone goes dead.

Tearing the protective wrapper off the new scalpel he tenderly touches a leathery hand. 'Sorry. So sorry,' he whispers. Then swiftly, so as not to lose his resolve, he slices off an index finger. *Done!* Gasping, he drops the scalpel, and hears he is tittering. Horror? Victory?

Shivers convulse him as he slides to the floor, back to the wall. In one hand he clutches his phone, in the other Ballybere Man's finger.

He jerks at an unexpected sound. Not his phone. The door is opening; an angry voice:

'Liam! What the hell's going on!' Mike is bearing down. He has been summoned from his office across the car park in the main building. 'Get up, man.' A look of horror crosses his face. 'What's that in your hand?'

Liam scrambles to his feet. 'They've got Carrie. Hurting her—'

'Carrie's at the conference. Calm down.'

'No. No! Need proof I'll destroy the body...' He holds up the severed digit. 'Otherwise one of hers. Cut off, I mean.' His words trip over themselves. 'Any second. Any second now, they'll tell me what to do.'

'Liam, please.' Mike eyes the scalpel then kicks it further away, reaches for him, smiling encouragingly as you would to a child. 'Let's sit in my office, it's more comfortable.'

Loud ringtones fill the room: maximum volume in case he missed hearing it. Behind Mike the lab assistant is approaching. Liam screams: 'Out! Get out!' and the woman shoots back. He's feeling dizzy, needs Mike to understand. 'Keep out of sight. Be quiet. Switch your phone to silent. NOW!'

Mike nods, holding his hand up in front of him. Appeasing. 'All right, fine, Liam. Whatever you say.'

'I've done it!' Liam tells the listener on the phone as he presses the loudspeaker icon. 'Done it!'

'Let's see.' The same man's voice 'You're alone?'

'Yes,' he answers firmly.

In the background Carrie is calling his name, saying she is okay. And next to him Mike whispers, 'What in God's name?' *Too loud!* Liam waves him back, clutches the phone tighter, switches the visuals on, then turns the camera to his own right hand so Ballybere Man's sliced-off finger fills the screen. He imagines they must have a phone with a webcam.

'Oh, Liam!' The howl is Carrie's. 'I'm so sorry.'

'Shut her up! We wanna see the body.' The same man is speaking. A slight drawl.

Liam angles the phone to show Ballybere Man, drawing the bubble plastic back further.

'That's it? That ol' swamp thing ain't worth keepin'. One heap of trouble.'

Got to be Southern American. Texas, maybe?

'See... You can see where I've cut the finger off.' Liam helpfully goes closer, holds one of Ballybere Man's leathery hands in his own palm. Strange. He is no longer shaking or sweaty.

There is a chuckle down the line. 'That's a start. The rest is gonna be easy. Wait.'

The phone call ends.

Mike is staring, voice cautious: 'Do I understand fanatics are holding Carrie?'

Liam is calmer now. 'She's been taken hostage.' He gestures to their prize possession. 'This Antichrist must be destroyed. The finger was a gesture of goodwill. Proof I had begun. Would you have them cut off one of Carrie's fingers?'

He hears Mike suck in a sharp breath.

His phone rings again: undisclosed number. *'Nobody* called the cops, right?' *Same man speaking. Always the same man.*

'Promise.'

'And just so you know, we've a bunch of phones, burner phones... Now you listen. Get that thing packed up, ready to carry out, then show us. Once you're out of the building we've got you covered.'

Covered? Guns? Cameras?

'Listen,' Liam is told. 'You'll see a blue Fiat parked some ways behind a white van.'

Blue Fiat. White van.

'You head to that van. You're gonna slide that thing in the back, *real easy*.'

'Yes!' *White van. Body in back.*

'Then get the hell out of the way. Fast. We're taking it out. Understand?'

He nods. 'Yes!' *Get out fast. Taking it away.*

He feels he is losing track, but one thing he is sure of. 'I'll do anything to keep Carrie safe. I'm her boss. Her friend.'

'Her keeper, right?' The American chuckles.

'That's right,' Liam says. 'Her keeper. She's much more important than this bog body, for all that he is unique, and we would love to—'

'Five minutes to get that thing ready to go or else—'

'No. No. You'll get the body. Promise me Carrie will be released.'

'Deal.'

'Deal,' he agrees, 'but I need longer—'

The phone goes dead.

Mike supports himself against the wall. 'The police? We must, Liam. We must.' His hand is in his pocket reaching for his phone.

'No! Wait!'

His own phone is ringing. Not them. The IAI conference organiser's name appears. They'll be following up, expecting Carrie by now. He dismisses the call.

Body. Out to waiting van.

'Liam?' Mike's voice is faint.

And beyond him cautious knocking and voices: 'Mike? Everything okay in there? Can we assist you with something?' The conservators are getting anxious, sensing not all is well with their charge.

'No. No. Thank you,' Mike answers. 'We'll be with you shortly. Sorry, Liam, I *must* inform the police. It's my duty.'

'I can't stop you.' Liam's mind whirls. For some reason they want to take the body away. Must have a driver waiting. Maybe the police can tail it... *Focus. Focus.* He peers closely at labelled crates, dismissing first one, then another. *Where is it?* He must work fast.

31

The Journalist

FINN DURANTE TAPS THE KEYPAD OF HIS PHONE:
Where are you?

He expected Carrie to be here by now.

He's listening to a presentation about modes of transport in coastal areas with the sea as both border and highway, how remote communities can be isolated yet linked to the wider world. The screen shows a stony outcrop on a ridge above an estuary; the speaker uses his electronic pointer to draw attention to specific features. Finn twists around to see if Carrie has sneaked into the conference hall, then checks his phone to see if she has replied to his text. She said she'd be here for the morning's presentations on the off chance she might cross-reference something in her own presentation, and what he is listening to *is* relevant to Ballybere's location on the Shannon Estuary.

This conference has attracted international speakers and delegates. His ear has picked up Italian, Dutch, Spanish, French, but the Scandinavian languages have him guessing.

And there are Gaelic speakers amongst them. He did not sit that language exam in his final school year, a matter of some regret.

Perhaps he should phone Carrie. He chose to sit at the end of a row of chairs, but latecomers glared at him, so he has moved into the centre.

He stands. 'Excuse me.' He squeezes past knees, bags and jackets, half listening to the speaker talking about cultural transformation of these coastal communities. In the foyer he phones Carrie but finds her phone is switched off. Very unlike her. He scrolls through his contact list of museum staff. Though he barely knows Liam Harte, he guesses he won't mind being contacted. He dials the direct landline office number and voicemail kicks in. Finn hangs up, hesitates then looks for Liam's personal mobile number; Carrie shared it one evening, telling him, 'Don't you dare bother him unless absolutely necessary. He'd kill me for giving it to you.' He promised, and this wasn't an emergency, but time is ticking, and Carrie is due to speak after lunch. He taps the icon for Liam's mobile.

'What now!' Liam's harassed voice. 'We're working on it!'

'Doctor Harte? Finn Durante. *Irish Times.* I—'

'Who? Ah, yes. I thought... Never mind. Can't talk.' The line goes dead. Rude or what! He calls again and within a second Liam gabbles, 'Need the line clear. Leave me alone!' Again, the call ends. *What is going on?* Maybe Liam isn't at work. Maybe there is a home emergency. Finn flinches, feeling bad about disturbing him. Carrie has mentioned he has a child with some sort of learning difficulty; maybe that is it. Finn is about to phone the Archaeological Museum reception, then decides to head over himself. It will only take a few minutes. He has his bike with him today. After work he is heading to Cork for a rare weekend home visit.

The woman at the Archaeological Museum reception desk smiles, recognising him. 'Morning, or afternoon, I should say. I thought you would be at the hotel for Doctor O'Neill's talk.' She eyes his black leather jacket, small backpack resting over one shoulder and black helmet clutched under an arm.

'Wouldn't miss it.' Finn smiles back. 'Is she busy? She hasn't left yet, I take it.'

'You're the second person to ask.' The woman frowns. 'A conference organiser phoned us earlier in a bit of a flap. She's not been in today. I've been told she's heading straight there from home.'

Finn is uneasy. Since that stalking scare and everything else, Carrie has given him a spare key to her flat. He had best go over and check nothing has happened. 'Thanks.'

He is about to go when the woman says, 'Mr Harte might have an update.'

'He's here?' Finn is surprised. 'Can you reach him for me?'

'I'll check.' She dials, then shrugs. 'Voicemail, I'm afraid.' She tries another member of staff. 'Hi, front desk. Trying to track down Carrie... Any idea... Or Liam...? Uh-huh... Okay... Okay. Thanks anyway.' She ends the call and raises her shoulders. 'Seems Liam was here... I'll try Mr Curtis's assistant, on the off chance they're over there.'

As he calculates how long it will take to get to Carrie's flat, Finn is aware of the brief conversation taking place with Mike's PA. The call ends. 'I think Mr Curtis might be with Mr Harte. He just had an urgent call from someone in the conservation department.'

Urgent. Yes. That sums up the tone of Liam's voice. Finn's instincts to hunt down a good story kick in. Damn Carrie! She is holding back on something. All his senses tell him this concerns Ballybere Man. Carrie only ever reaches out to him as a last resort, either professionally or personally. Yet again, he is pissed off with her. He leans on the desk, giving the woman the most charming smile he can summon. 'Might I pop over?'

'I suppose. If that's where they are. Sorry, I've not been much help.'

Finn hurries through a group of visitors fingering souvenirs in the shop. Why must people dawdle? Or buy shite? As he heads through the wide door, a group of tourists pushes through. French. 'Excuse me… Excuse me.' He runs down the steps and around the building to where he has parked his bike.

Within five minutes he is on the south side of the river riding along Wellington Quay towards Heuston Station. He crosses the river, retracing a short stretch of the Liffey's one-way system, then turns into the National Museum's Collins Barracks site. He parks near the archway, planning to head through to reception. As he removes his helmet, he looks away from the grand stone military building. Across the car park, by a red-brick building, he sees Liam with another man who is wearing a brown dust coat, pushing a trolley holding a crate. *What?* Finn walks slowly in their direction. Good grief! The man with Liam is the museum's director, Mike Curtis. Why is he doing menial work, and dressed like a janitor?

Finn quickens his pace. The Antiquities Keeper will remember him. 'Mr Harte!'

Liam's head jerks up. Then he ducks down, ignores him, and picks up his pace. It is Mike Curtis, normally so sleek and silky, who hastens towards him looking extremely out of sorts. *There is a story here.* Something is going on. 'Finn Durante. *Irish Times.* Can you—'

'Not now!' Mike pushes him. Physically lays hands on his chest and bloody well pushes him!

'Excuse me! I'm looking for Carrie.'

'Leave. You must go.' Mike looks strained as he swivels away.

'Wait!' Finn grabs his shoulder. 'Can you just... Is that the body in there?' He stares to where Liam is trying to push the trolley with one hand, holding his phone to his ear with the other.

Mike licks his lips, mumbles something about giving permission for Carrie to use it in her presentation. Barks, 'Go! Go!' Again, a strong push to Finn's chest, before hurrying back to assist Liam.

Confused, Finn withdraws around a corner of the building.

No way would they take Ballybere Man out of a controlled environment unless it was to an institution for further analysis. That might happen, but not like this. He tries calling Carrie, but her phone is still switched off. He is in two minds: should he go to her flat, or hang around?

Liam and Mike have paused, peering at a blue car. They're pushing the trolley again, towards a trades van by the looks of it. He can't see who's in the driver's seat... Ah! Okay. Maybe Carrie is inside. So, this *might* be Ballybere Man in there. Liam is fumbling with the crate lock, opening it, holding his camera out. They don't bother closing it again. *What?*

He is determined to make Mike give him the time of day. He starts towards them.

Still at some distance he watches as they open the back of the van, slide the crate inside before shutting the doors. Mike wheels the empty trolley away while Liam double checks the doors are secure, then he repeatedly thumps the van door, shouting, 'Done it!'

Done what?

Finn catches Mike's eye. 'Mr—'

WHOOMPH.

The shock of the explosion stops him short.

The van's back doors shoot through the air. Windows shatter. Pieces of metal fly and clouds of light grey smoke billow upwards. A man, Liam, is hurled off his feet.

'Carrie!' Finn can't hear for the ringing in his ears. His feet are propelling him towards the destroyed van. *Carrie!* Dimly he is aware that Mike is running, shouting Liam's name. Others have appeared, all zeroing in on this calamity.

Finn grabs Mike Curtis's brown coat, screaming: 'Is Carrie…?' Glancing at the destroyed van.

Mike shrugs him off. 'Not here! Not here!'

Relief floods through him then he momentarily spares a thought for whoever was about to drive away.

'Help me!' Mike appeals, gesturing towards Liam's prone body. Mike takes hold of one leg and Finn grabs the other. They drag Liam, leaving a trail of red on the grey tarmac. Smashed glasses are askew, there is a gash on Liam's cheek and his trousers are torn and bloodied.

Finn glances at the burning van; dark grey smoke is billowing now, and flames licking. Someone dashes forward and peers in the cab, shouts, 'Empty!' before retreating at speed.

Others have arrived – museum staff, he figures. They're kneeling, tending to Liam. A panicking woman has an ear to his nose: 'Is he breathing? Can't tell.'

Finn feels himself being tugged, a voice urging him back. He steadies himself, and a fresh burst of flames shoots skyward as the van's fuel tank explodes.

It dawns on him. This wasn't accidental. This was deliberate, a remote-control bomb, and he is a *witness*. A journalist. Hurriedly he takes out his phone and films. Short videos. Images. Over and over, his hands becoming steadier each time he captures the scene.

Distant sirens.

'Where's Carrie?' He shakes the dazed museum director, who pushes him aside, all his attention on Liam. A woman adjusts Liam's prone position, places palms one on top of the other on Liam's sternum, commences deep rhythmic compressions.

The sirens are closer, somewhere down near the river. Again, Finn shakes Mike, insisting on an answer. 'Tell me. Where's Carrie?' But Mike's attention is torn between Liam and listening to the police sirens. One is heading their way, the sound coming closer, but at least two others continue. He sees Mike momentarily squeeze his eyes shut, and catches a whispered, 'Thank God!'

What the hell is happening?

'Mike!' he bellows, but the museum director is not the slightest bit interested in him, and is hurrying to the police car that is skidding to a halt. Other vehicles – he still hears sirens – are heading away from the city centre.

Spinning on his heels he races back to where his motorbike is parked, thinking that for a guy not yet thirty he is massively unfit. Hurriedly he fixes his earbud in place, cursing himself once again for being too cheap to buy a decent Bluetooth setup. He mounts, thrusts on his helmet, flicks the kickstand back, turns the ignition key, presses start.

He roars around the side street then pauses at the junction by the Liffey. The police cars aren't in sight, of course, but he hears distant sirens. Lunchtime traffic clogs the street along Wolfe Tone Quay. He finds a gap and sets off westward. At the junction with Phoenix Park, he stops at a red light and scans the traffic. Did they turn into the park? Can't tell, so he decides to stay on Conyngham Road.

At the green light he takes steadying feet off the ground and shoots forward, filtering past slower traffic. Oh man, this is nuts. He wonders if he has lost the plot and seen too many Hollywood chases. Carrie is most likely fine and already at the conference. He should turn back and cover that exploding van. Check if Liam is all right. And yet. All his journalistic instincts tell him to stick with it. The worst that can happen is he ends up following the police to a traffic accident.

His phone is ringing. Shit. He has no time for this, but the damn phone keeps on ringing. Stopped at the side of the street he tugs a leather glove off his hand with his teeth and takes his phone from his pocket. Work. The news editor.

'Finn. Just heard what's happened. You're there, right?'

'Was. Not now!'

'Why not? Get back there. Mike Curtis, you know, the museum director, phoned. Needs to talk, says it's urgent…'

He strains to hear the sirens but can't. They'll be running all the red lights.

'…insisted you call him immediately.'

He punches in Mike's number then drops his phone into his breast pocket – still connected to his earpiece – opens the throttle, and sets off, not knowing where he is heading. No sirens to be heard.

'Finn? Thank God.' Mike is gasping. 'If you're following the police. Are you? ARE YOU?'

'Trying to.'

'STOP! DON'T!'

Finn's heart is thumping, and he isn't inclined to follow Mike's command. He overtakes a grey Renault, a black Honda. 'Why?'

'BECAUSE CARRIE'S IN DANGER!'

The words strike him. *Carrie. Danger.* Has Mike really said that? 'Where is she? Where's Carrie?' His eyes scan the traffic ahead. He knows he must try and tail the Gardaí.

'Pull over, Finn. Trust me. I beg you! Don't get in the way of the police operation. We don't know where they're holding her, so pl—'

'Holding her?' Sparks are shooting through his brain, behind his eyes.

'They are holding her captive till they've evidence the bog body is destroyed.'

That bomb!

'But, but…' Mike is breathless.

They? He wants to ask Mike.

Sirens behind him now. Two more police cars hurtle past, top lights spinning.

He knows Mike will be able to hear the roar of his engine above the sound of wind on the mic. 'Finn. Leave it to the police!'

'The Guards! When have they taken on something like this?'

'Finn, I beg—'

Finn fumbles with the button through his gloved hand and abruptly ends the call. He needs to focus entirely on following the police.

Here he'd been childishly sulking, thinking Carrie was ignoring him when all the while she needed him. The police vehicles are well ahead. He doesn't want them knowing he is trailing them; they may send another vehicle to head him off. He figures he can play cat and mouse and remain out of sight, but if they head into the country he's stuffed, as they'd be sure to spot him. Thank goodness nothing about him stands out. No flashes on his bike nor helmet. Straight out black. A dark rider. Imagining where she might be held and what might be happening makes him shiver. He remembers all those trolling messages she'd received, and he knows whoever has her in their grasp will not stop until what they see as the devil's work is destroyed. But Ballybere Man *has* been destroyed. They must have proof of that blast. If they harm a hair on her body…

He pulls out to pass a slow driver in a Clio, looks right, left, then well ahead he catches a glimpse of a flashing police light before more vehicles get in the way. He'll not be stopping for any red lights.

32

The Body

THE BODY! THEY'VE DONE IT! MISSION ACCOMPLISHED!
The Antichrist is blown to smithereens, and he, li'l old Nate
Porter, has taken him out. Pity about collateral damage. None
of them are too sure if that man Liam survived.

'One moment!' Ray clasps his hands, closing his eyes. Nate
joins his own hands and bows his head.

'Lord, we warriors are here to serve you.' Ray speaks at
a clip. 'Serve your higher purpose. By ridding the world of
this beast of Lucifer we have cleared the way for your return.
Amen.'

'Amen,' Nate repeats.

Nate thanks the sweet Lord his buddy is at his side. Ray
became tired of his 'friggin' inability to get the job done', as
he'd berated him more than once. 'Seems to me this task is
too much for ya shoulders. I'm comin' over.' And within days,
Dublin city had found itself hosting two Kentucky Men for
Christ. Yep, it was good to have Ray here. He'd always been
the leader of the pack.

Nate shoots a look at Carrie with her shorn hair. He knows how precious ladies are about their crowning glory, but a salon will fix things. He feels bad seeing her sitting pale and shivering, staring at the computer screen. The remote camera set up in the Fiat was still operating.

Carrie is crying all over again. When she saw her boss thrown back by the blast, she screamed and hollered, 'Murderers!' Not so. Wasn't their fault!

Why on earth did the museum man go back, anyway? Hadn't he made it clear they'd detonate the van? He frowns, thinking back to the words he'd actually used.

Cora is grabbing her bits and pieces ready to leave.

'Wait up a minute.' Ray's eyes are fixed on the computer screen. Cops are there. Yeah, they figured that would happen; now they need to shift their butts. He can't wait to get home to big skies and wide horizons, where a man can breathe.

'Come on, let's go!' Cora urges.

Ray's hand stays her. 'Wait!' He's looking at his phone, flicking between two video clips: the body, just before the case was closed and wheeled out, and the other when Liam opened the crate before loading it into the van. Nate peers again at the outdoor image of the mummified corpse. It looks different somehow. Or perhaps it's the light. He squints. Uhh…

'Shit!' Ray's thinking what he's thinking. His buddy grabs Carrie, his face turning purple, voice uncertain: 'You have more of those things?' Gripping the back of her neck with one hand, with the other he thrusts the phone close to her face.

'Oh!' She draws a sharp breath. 'In st-st-storage. Not on display.'

With a howl of rage Ray tosses his phone aside then turns cold eyes on Carrie, who's clutching the edge of the table. Nate watched a snarl lift the corner of Ray's mouth: 'You rigged this. Gave him a signal.' Carrie is denying it, shaking her head, backing away from Ray, who has yanked her clear, kicking away the table, both hands gripping her neck. 'Devil's whore!'

Nate's own anger matches his buddy's. *How dare she muck up God's plan!* He yanks her out of Ray's clasp and her head snaps forward, making her yelp. With a mighty shove he thrusts. She stumbles into a chair but retains her balance. Still not satisfied, he swings at her, fist connecting with her chin. 'Bitch!' Her head snaps sideways and she drops. He hears the thwack of her head connecting with concrete.

Ray is spitting rich curses and Cora is shrieking, 'We've been fuckin' conned!' She backs away towards the door. 'I'm outta here. Helped you this far. That's it.'

'Uh-huh. We're in this together.' Ray reaches behind under his shirt and pulls out a pistol tucked into his jeans held snugly by a broad leather belt. Ray knew people who knew people, so getting hold of two old Berettas was something Nate *had* managed to get done before Ray flew in and got the bomb organised.

'We've a situation here,' Ray says.

'Yeah.' Nate's eyes dart to Carrie, flat on her back, one leg cocked, face white, not stirring.

'You dumb fucks!' Cora flies across the short distance and pummels his chest, then swings around to face Ray. 'How didn't you notice?'

'Sure, I checked. Saw the leathery thing.' Ray sounds defensive. 'How did I know there were more of those things kicking around!'

Nate thinks of the short, tubby man who's made fools of them! What's his job? Keeper. That's it. An old-fashioned kind of job like something from a *Harry Potter* movie. The Keeper of Secrets or some such. Who'd have thought that guy would have the balls to do what he did!

'When the mission's accomplished we're outta there,' Ray said when he arrived. 'Leastways, that's Plan A.' Nate pats his pants pocket where his Plan A airplane ticket sits snug. He and Ray are flying out later. 'Plan B,' Ray was clear, 'we face some years inside. Gotta prepare for that.'

Up until now his path has been laid out. As Warriors of Xist they are prepared to kill – door-to-door clearances if required – to pave the way for the resurrection, but… For the first time a flicker of doubt passes through Nate's mind.

There's Cora having a go at Ray, shrieking: 'You gobdaw! You come over here, all talk. Can't get your shit togeth—' She staggers back as Ray slaps her real hard.

'Feckin' eejit!' Cora is flying at *him* now, calling him all manner of names. He catches her wrist. Nate balls his right hand into a fist and gives the Irish woman a punch under her ribs that leaves her doubled over and gasping.

He can't think with all this going on.

Ray yells at Cora, 'If you don't want your own damned head busted like this one' – he prods Carrie – 'then you're goin' ta fix things.'

'Oh yeah?' Cora's wheezing, laughing in his face. 'Fix it, how?'

He's distracted by the sound of Carrie groaning and sees her stir. Least she's not dead. One less problem to deal with. Anyhow, she's nice.

A vein in Ray's forehead sticks out and his eyes narrow to slits. He's stuck his Beretta in his jeans waistband again, but Nate knows that look. Ray won't stand for any shit – hates it when things don't go according to plan. He's seen that often enough. Even at home when, say, Ray wanted to watch films in a certain order, but someone had another idea, Ray couldn't handle it. This is a whole different thing. And this was Cora's idea. She'd said Carrie's boss was a soft touch.

'Fix it!' Cora's laughing hysterically, waving her arms around. 'You dumb—'

BAM!

A massive explosion rips through the air; his ears take a pounding. Smoke billows. The small door next to the up-and-over bursts its hinges and falls inward.

'Aw, shit!' Nate's Beretta is in his hand as he covers the distance to Ray's side. He sees figures: armed, helmeted, shielded. Hears yelling: 'Police! Get down! Weapons down!' Other voices: Cora, Ray. These things happen fast – he's played enough video games to know that – so his reactions are sharp. He doesn't much like using soft bodies as shields – this is a sucker's way of doing things. But now there's no choice. He and Ray hunker down behind Carrie, pistols trained at the cops. 'Keep back!'

The Irish woman, somewhere to the side, yells, 'Don't shoot!' and inches far away, while four cops are down on one knee, guns pointing. A stand-off.

Ray's pistol is trained on Carrie. 'Understand', he yells to the cops, 'we don't want to hurt her. We've been friggin' conned. Ain't taking it.'

The cops are saying something: harsh words in a sweet sing-song accent. If this had been back home, he and Ray would've been blasted to kingdom come. Shoot first, questions later. Still, this isn't looking good. He doesn't aim to be a martyr for Christ unless he absolutely has to.

Ray, shouting all the while, eyes those cops creeping forward, his pistol to Carrie's temple now. Nate's eyes dance over the cops, Cora, Ray, and Carrie, whose terrified eyes are fixed on Ray. Ray's shrieking, 'I'll friggin' do it!' That vein is pulsing in Ray's forehead and Nate knows Ray *will* do it. He hears the click as Ray cocks the pistol.

The cops are yelling. 'Weapons down. A man is dead. Don't make it worse. Drop your weapons.' Carrie is shrieking and calling Liam's name.

Dead then, huh? For all his clumsy, interfering ways, that man did not deserve to die. The only creatures Nate has shot are deer and wild hogs, killed to be eaten. He has never been responsible for the death of a man, a creature in God's own image.

Game over.

He drops his pistol and raises his arms. Ray's pistol is trained on *him* now, his buddy spitting all the curses he knows and then some. Nate's arms are yanked behind him, wrists cuffed. A resigned smile stretches across his lips. He – and Ray, he won't let him off the hook – have screwed up, big time. They won't be making that flight out tonight. One thing is sure, there's no death penalty in this country – he researched that before stepping on the airplane at Cincinnati. He's not that dumb.

Things are moving fast. The warehouse overhead roller door is rattling up. Light floods in. Marked police vehicles have moved into place, lights flashing... they would've parked further back, he guesses. There is someone else in the warehouse now. A young guy in black leathers scoots past, yelling Carrie's name over and over. Who the hell's he? Nate shrugs. He has other things to think about. Even though the man who is Carrie's keeper hadn't meant to get blown up, he admires him for trying to protect her. Yes, sir. That man will be welcomed by Our Lord.

Nate shakes his head. The Lord will not be rewarding *him* for this mess, and he fears what the future holds beyond his life on earth. He shudders, and momentarily squeezes his eyes closed. He's heard enough about hell from brother Jake's preaching, and from his own Bible studies. He will have to man up to face whatever that is. Some wasted opportunity to do good with this bog body. Come to think of it, some wasted life.

Ray is putting on a show, struggling and yelling, 'This thing ain't finished. Ya just wait 'n' see.' His buddy looks like a scrawny rooster. One of those cocks scratching in the back yard, who make up for lack of size by ruffling feathers, taking every opportunity to crow. No point. He and Cora allow themselves to be led out, meek as lambs heading to slaughter.

33

The Archaeologist

CARRIE O'NEILL DISCOVERS HER SKELETON REFUSES to define her shape. She tries to stand but her limbs buckle. Instead, she crawls, a soggy creature inching along a grey seabed of concrete floor trying to reach daylight. Liam is dead. The police said so.

'It's okay! I've got you.' Finn helps her to her feet, wraps his arm around her, leads her outside, holds her steady as she doubles over and dry retches.

'Easy now.' Finn is helping her to the ground. From where she rests against the concrete block wall of the warehouse, she is dimly aware of a raucous chorus of voices and flashing lights.

Once she had been a strong woman, striding forward, navigating life with just a few hiccups here and there. But now... She closes her eyes and focuses on the warmth of her greenstone pendant still clutched in a hand.

More police arrive. An ambulance. Are people questioning her? Hazy. Foggy.

Later, at the hospital, it is Finn who phones her parents; explains, assuring them: 'Please... Please, Mrs O'Neill, honestly, she wasn't harmed, beyond concussion...Yes, Mr O'Neill, of course...' He hands her the phone, her propped up in a hospital bed, him perched at the end, feet drawn up, sitting cross-legged, gaze intense. He only intervenes to tell her things she doesn't know, or things her parents need to know. 'And tell them I'm here for you,' he says softly.

Aside from being the first journalist on the scene, Finn is, a TV reporter states, 'as Doctor Carrie O'Neill's boyfriend, well placed to get the inside narrative.'

So Finn has the scoop of his career. And Carrie is delighted for him.

Fifteen days pass and she is at Rachel's, recuperating, wrapping herself in the warmth of her adopted Irish family.

'This is still fresh,' Rachel reminds her. 'Traumas mark the body and the mind. Give it time.'

Guilt lies heavy.

At night she jerks awake, seeing that van blast on screen, and at random times during the day flashes of memory make her dizzy: the overpowering odour of sweat and some potent aftershave from Nate making her silently heave.

Liam!

She relives that moment when she had watched the screen, willing Liam to move out of the way. Knowing that any moment... What hadn't he understood?

Oh, Liam!

Rachel is here for her. When she sobs uncontrollably, she finds another mug of tea at her side, a reassuring arm around her shoulders, feels a hand ruffling her restyled hair. Or Buster might settle near her, resting his head on her feet. Or she is left alone.

'Even Cillian won't be pestering you,' Rachel has reassured her. And that was a tough call. Instead, the Limerick journalist focuses on whether this tragedy might cause a rethink at local level. But no, the local council is even more determined to press on with their museum and get Ballybere Man safely 'out west'.

Time and again she wonders would it have been better if that digger's metal claw had ripped the body to shreds? If he had never been discovered? If that shopping centre had already been built. If...

Liam! What might she have done differently? Is she to blame?

Each morning Carrie sees Rachel's family off, and she walks Buster, enjoying the simple pleasure of being a woman walking a dog in the countryside. If anyone recognises her they don't say, and the only exchanges she has are brief acknowledgements from other dog walkers. She talks with Finn at least two or three times a day. 'What are you up to?' he asks.

'Did some baking,' she might reply, forwarding a photo of oaty ANZAC biscuits that Nan used to toss off without reference to a recipe.

'Enjoy!' he might say. 'Speak later.' Step by step, little things are grounding her in ordinary life.

Initially, media attention is all about her abduction and Liam's murder. And the Americans. She grapples with the mindset that could do such a thing. While she has no religious belief, Christian or otherwise, she likes to believe she is open-minded about others' beliefs and cultures. But *this?* This toxic pick-and-mix dogma, and call to arms that must, surely, suck in vulnerable people. She witnessed how Nate and Ray interacted, Nate's longing to shape up to be the warrior expected of him. The two of them had been terrifying while they were in control. When they drew their guns, widening their stance, eyes bulging, mouths spitting venom – she expected to die. Seeing them being cuffed and led away she'd realised what a runty man Ray was with his slicked-back hair. And Nate? She senses his life took a wrong turn but dismisses any tinge of pity.

The evangelical church in Ireland that Cora belonged to is horrified, issuing a formal statement declaring they condemned her actions, stressing, 'Cora Walsh was not acting for us. We have no connection whatsoever with Warriors for Xist or radical evangelical churches anywhere in the world.' When interviewed on TV, a sweet-looking woman with permed grey hair speaks earnestly. 'This is a terrible thing to have happened on our doorstep. But you know, this has nothing to do with our message of God's love and grace. We offer unconditional love.' And Carrie thinks she looks like she would do just that.

Soon media focus shifts from the event itself to broader issues, and one day Carrie listens to a radio interview with the Roman Catholic bishop she had visited.

'Oh no! I'm not in favour of this bog body being destroyed. It would serve no purpose. Without entering debates about who, why or what, I do believe that this man's body deserves respect.'

'In a museum display case, Your Grace?' the interviewer asks.

'As you know, the Vatican has suggested a spiritual location might be more appropriate.'

'But in saying this, you seem to hint that the Vatican is not ruling out the body *might* be Christ?'

Carrie notes a moment's silence.

'It is not our place to speculate. But again, a body that has suffered during life, and has been preserved in death for whatever reason, allows us to reflect on what it is to be human: to be in this world for a short time, and to reflect on the world to come.'

The Church of Ireland says one or two things in the same vein.

One evening, while the TV news is giving the latest police update, Rachel says, 'Enough of this,' and reaches for the remote control. 'What's it to be? *Grease? Back to the Future? What We Do in the Shadows?*'

'*Shadows!*' Sam yells, deciding for them all. The corny jokes, familiar accents, and low-budget special effects ease a tight band around Carrie's ribs and she finds she can laugh.

But she can't stay with Rachel and Dan for ever, can't block out the real world. She needs to get back to work. The presentation she prepared for the conference will be shared with delegates, and aspects of that paper are to feature in a public-friendly narrative for exhibition displays in the museum. Those display panels need to get to the printers. Mike has assured her, 'Not to worry, we've time enough.' Then he cautiously asked, 'Might others of your team deal with this?' No! She will oversee it. *With Liam*, she longs to add.

One more breakfast with Rachel, Dan and the kids then she packs her bag and drives home.

That evening she goes to Finn's. He greets her at the door, and as she wrinkles her nose and inhales he says, 'Paella. Veggie option and seafood. Sofia's cooking – wants to make amends.' Carrie smiles. The Spanish woman had torn a strip off Finn for leaving the sitting room a mess that long-ago drunken night. Finn takes her bag – she is staying over – and draws her inside. 'All right?' he asks, kissing her lightly.

She wraps her arms around him and holds him tight. Then his arms are around her, one hand encircling her waist, the other holding the back of her head. They stand body to body, cheek to cheek, swaying in an intimate dance. No need to talk. It feels *so* good, she doesn't want to move.

Later, lying in bed next to Finn, he asks if she would like to visit his parents one weekend. 'They'd love to meet you. Think I've been hiding you too long.'

Finn's parents. Getting serious.

Carrie grins. 'My car, or your bike?'

'Weather dependent.'

'And Ballybere Man dependent,' she reminds him.

'Goes without saying. I know how that man has you wrapped around his little finger.' He grimaces. 'Sorry. All the same, after the grand opening, things will be calmer. And there's no date for the Americans' trial yet so you'll not be needed for some time.'

'Yes,' she agrees. 'After the opening, things will settle down.'

She fingers Nan's pendant. In the past she has only worn it for special occasions but has come to realise that every day is special, and life is precarious. Every day her smooth poumamu reminds her of those who are dear to her, alive and dead. It is a touchstone. She wraps her legs around Finn, drawing him close.

Huge banners proclaiming Ballybere Man's opening exhibition confront Carrie when she arrives for work at the Archaeological Museum. As if she could possibly forget the big unveil is only ten days away. She receives sympathetic smiles and greetings from colleagues, along with cautious 'How are you?'s, and turns aside from a visitor's whispered, 'That's her!' before hurrying to the stairs. First, a meeting with Mike and Fiona, in what was Liam's office.

'Carrie! How are you?' Fiona rises, long since free from crutches, and wraps her arms around her. Mike steps forward to offer a hug of his own.

'Fine. I'm fine.' Lightly, she pushes them away. 'Don't start me off!' Too much touchy-feely sympathy will make her blub.

'May I offer you a tea, or coffee?' Mike gestures and she smiles to see Liam's collection put to good purpose. A sturdy mug with a picture of a helmeted Viking warrior; an intricately patterned Celtic design on bone china, which Fiona has claimed (perhaps the cleanest?); another of his Down's Syndrome charity mugs. *Ah, Liam.* She bites her lip.

They talk about temporary arrangements in her department: who is covering which aspects of Liam's work and what can wait. Fiona says diplomatically, 'We're leaving it a while before we advertise his post.' Carrie nods, grateful she won't be required to adjust to a new boss before she is ready, grateful Liam's office has not been cleared yet. She grasps her mug firmly with both hands.

'This is where we're at,' Mike says. 'We thought long and hard about whether to delay the opening in light of what's happened, but we thought that would only fuel the flames.'

What had already been a big attraction is even more of a hot ticket after the way the tabloids piled it on. The event has everything: a controversial bog body, abduction, death. 'And we're having to issue timed entrance gallery tickets for the coming months,' Mike adds.

'Booked four months solid.' Fiona can't hide her pride. 'This will make our case, as nothing will.'

The ongoing tug-of-war between the museum and County Clare has not eased, Carrie finds. In the past week, their government minister said publicly that the body will be permanently housed at the new Ballybere museum: designs are signed off, grant approved, money raised. He added it was only fair that, of course, the National Museum will have its slice of the pie.

'Slice of the pie!' Fiona looks indignant. 'Any day I'm expecting the minister to invite me and Councillor Mullen to her office for a Judgement of Solomon re-enactment.'

'Sorry?'

'The Old Testament story. You must know it. Two women present themselves to him, each claiming to be the mother of a baby. And wise man that he was, he offered—'

'To slice the baby in two and give each a part. I remember now. The real mother begged him to give it to the other woman to save her baby.'

'Exactly so. And you know, perhaps it mightn't be a bad plan.' Fiona smiles at her. 'I'd have to practise my weeping and wailing and wringing of hands.'

'Please, no talk about slicing up of bodies.' Mike glances at her, then at his watch. His time is pressing, and the countdown to the grand reveal is closing. Fresh anxiety presses Carrie. There remains a lot to be done.

Together, they go to the large room that is being prepared for Ballybere Man. The Kildare gallery, off the Treasury gallery, is all his. By a wall, touch-screen display cases are already operational, so Carrie flicks through educational stories visitors will be invited to engage with. Other screens, currently blank, are attached to walls at eye level. A film production company is putting the finishing touches to micro-documentaries: the process of conservation and analysis, modelling of the head. 'Just the credits to finalise,' Mike tells her.

'Yes.' She nods, trying to stay in the moment.

She looks at a display board with a close-up of Ballybere Man's wrist wound, remembering their initial debate: caused before, during or after death? Accidental trauma or act of violence? *Liam!* There was no doubt the trauma that arrested Liam's generous heart was a violent *peri-mortem* injury.

Her own heart needs to get back into this project.

Fiona is outlining the running order: '...then after the minister's speech, I'll be saying a few words before handing to Mike for the unveiling.'

'Yes.' She nods again.

The unveiling is to be a dramatic moment, with a specially commissioned cloth covering the display, slowly drawn away to reveal Ballybere Man lying at rest in his new, perhaps temporary, home. A display case in the centre is ready to receive the body. For the invitation-only opening this will be easily viewed, then the gallery will be closed for a few days while a discreet pod is erected around it, similar to those in the downstairs Kingship and Sacrifice gallery.

There was endless debate about this drapery. Did the deep maroon cloth with gold stitching look too much like an altar covering? Fiona was particularly unsure about that when consulted, before firmly stating, 'If we try and avoid all liturgical colours, we're on a hiding to nothing. Or someone, somewhere will take offence at something else. Go ahead, Mike, you have my blessing.'

The fun has gone from being part of Team Museum, but Carrie is determined to delve deep within herself and make sure her man is presented to the world to the best of her ability. She means him to look magnificent. He is to be displayed appropriately and sympathetically, as are all their human exhibits, but he will be receiving special attention.

Ballybere Man is nearly ready. His severed finger is back in place with some judicious stitch marks to tell their own story.

While with the conservators Carrie delicately strokes the restored hand. She weeps, and her colleagues discreetly withdraw. Through her tears she gazes at the bronzed, serene face, wanting to communicate to him the trauma and loss they are experiencing. Apart from being a scientific and historical journey into the past there is something more, though exactly what, she cannot describe nor fully comprehend. With one hand she clasps the warm pounamu nestled at her throat, while her other strokes Ballybere Man's cool, leathery cheek. *Because of you, Liam was willing to risk his life for me.*

34

The Reveal

Joe Cassidy is wriggling the knot of his tie.
Next Carrie watches him fidget with the invitation in his
hand. Poor Joe. She makes her way through the throng of
guests to where he stands with his wife

'Mr Cassidy. Joe. Good to see you. So glad you could both
make it.'

'Ah, Doctor O'Neill—'

'Carrie, please—'

'Ah, sure, sure. You've not met my wife, Breda. She knows
all about you.'

Carrie shakes hands with Joe's wife, who is wearing a silky
floral dress with matching jacket; it looks as if it might have
been purchased for a family wedding. Carrie insisted they
were invited, but she senses their discomfort at not knowing
anyone here except her and Rachel.

Next, she makes her way to Professor Byrne seated in his
wheelchair positioned close to Ballybere Man's display case.
She last saw him at Liam's funeral, when he had stated, 'This

is the wrong way round: it should be Liam seeing me off.' On that occasion Professor Byrne took her hand, drawing her down, and she found her forehead being kissed by thin lips. 'I'm sorry,' he whispered. 'His fate was a cruel one.'

Today, Professor Byrne's bony fingers pick at the draped fabric completely covering the glass cabinet.

'No peeking, Professor. Won't be long now.'

'Would I do such a thing?

Yes, you might! 'We placed him here two days ago. The gallery's been closed, and we stepped up night-time security. Two guards.'

Professor Byrne nods approvingly. 'Best avoid any last-minute attempt to disrupt things or dislodge our find.'

Our find? 'I'll catch up with you later.'

She heads over to Dan and Rachel and pecks their cheeks. Dan appraises her. 'You've scrubbed up well. Look great.'

'Thanks.' She is wearing a new milky-jade linen trouser suit: loose double-breasted jacket, short wide trousers. Her hair, short and spiky, shows Nan's earrings to good effect and, of course, at her throat her pounamu. Nan is with her in spirit to share her big day.

Everyone who is anyone is here. She catches herself: except Liam. His wife is not here; Carrie understands legal action against the museum is being considered. The minister – the government minister – stands chatting with Mike and Fiona. Elsewhere she spots senior church ministers, Catholic and Church of Ireland, dignified in their long cassocks. It is fitting they have been invited. The Archbishop of Dublin catches her eye, steps towards her and takes both her hands in his. 'This has been so shocking for you. I hope you received my message.'

'Thank you, Your Grace, I appreciated it.' She had been touched when he had reached out with kind words after those 'misguided souls' had taken her hostage and she was still raw from grief over the loss of Liam.'Good, good. I won't hold you up.' The grey-haired man smiles kindly, his long black cassock swishing as he strides away.

Guests from major institutions, universities and museums in Ireland and Europe, chat noisily. These specialists who know each other from countless conferences are here to share their big moment. *Her* big moment. They've all voiced condolences:'Liam will be missed.''Tragic.''So happy you were not harmed…'

Journalists are here and TV crews positioned. Finn circulates, notepad in hand, attaching himself to various worthy folk for a quote here and there.

They are crowded into the gallery, waiting, expectant, like an audience on opening night of a musical anticipating being dazzled by a famous leading lady: in this case, leading man. There are three reveals: the lifelike bust; the 3D digital reconstruction morphing from leathery distorted face to smiling man; and Ballybere Man himself, snug in his glass case.

The invitation design is classy. **REVEAL** is printed in bold black letters on thick white matte paper, edges tucked in. Unfolded, it reveals an embossed image of Ballybere Man's head in profile, as he would have been in life. She has watched guests' fingertips trace the soft rise and fall of the contours on the paper.

'Ladies and gentlemen, may we have your attention.' Fiona is at a microphone on a raised platform positioned in front of the soon-to-be unveiled bust. Mike and the government minister stand next to her. Guests shuffle into a horseshoe shape for a better view.

Finn sidles up and reaches for her hand. She is happy he is at her side to share this moment. 'Over there,' he whispers. 'Councillor Mullen.' She sees the barrel-chested besuited man Finn indicates. Who invited him?

Carrie gives her attention to Fiona, who acknowledges key guests, thanking everyone for attending. 'This is a special day for us. We are marking the end of a cycle, a ritual, if you like, from discovery to display. It is not far-fetched to say that tragedy has stalked us, and I am immensely proud of my staff.' She pauses, looking first at Mike before scanning the room. Carrie takes a breath. Heads turn in her direction, with murmurs of, 'Hear, hear,' and muted clapping. She ducks her head and Finn squeezes her hand. Fiona continues. 'As the *National* Museum of Ireland, we are conscious of the role we play within our country and internationally, leading the way in our research and how we display *our* collections. Nothing has challenged us more than taking *possession* of Ballybere Man.'

Is Fiona emphasising certain words, Carrie wonders, or is she imagining this? Her eyes flicker towards Councillor Mullen, who is scrunching his invitation in one hand.

The National Museum chair continues, 'It is with pleasure I invite the Minister for Tourism, Arts, Gaeltacht, Sport and Media to unveil Ballybere Man's bust. You have a hint of him in your invitation card; now we will meet him face to face.'

Fiona steps aside and the minister takes her place, greeting everyone in Gaelic and in English. 'Thank you, Mrs McCormac. This grand institution you lead has been severely tested.' She smiles compassionately at Fiona. 'But before too long – perhaps within a year? – the weight will be lifted from your shoulders, when Ballybere Man will be *re*housed in the place he was found.' A mottled pink blush appears on Fiona's neck. The minister continues, 'I've been longing to meet him.' She reaches out and, with Mike the other side, gently lifts the dark cloth off a small eye-level glass case.

A collective gasp. A collective step forward, the need to be closer too strong to resist.

'Wow, he's magnificent,' Finn whispers. 'Don't let him get away. He's a keeper.'

The modellers have given Ballybere Man a slight smile, the edges of his mouth lifting, small creases defining his cheeks. With his head tilted a little off centre, he seems to meet the gaze of the museum's guests with a slightly bemused look: *I'm a long-dead man. What's all this fuss about?*

But there *is* a fuss. Finn joins others from the media to get a better view. Cameras click. Film crews draw nearer. They can't get enough of him, and curious guests press forward to view him from front and sides. 'Love his nose!' a man says. 'Very *Jewish*, don't you think?'

'Please. Please.' Mike has moved the microphone stand out of the way. 'You'll have plenty of opportunity to view him later... Michael Curtis, museum director. It's an honour to be overseeing this fabulous addition to our world-renowned collection.' He gestures to the soon-to-be-unveiled glass cabinet. 'And we look forward to welcoming visitors to view Ballybere Man as part of our *permanent, extended,* Kingship and Sacrifice exhibition.'

Finn is at her side again, soft voice at her ear: 'If I were a betting man, I'd say it might be more than a year – if ever – before your bosses relinquish him.'

The tug-of-war is still to be played out, and Carrie fights the urge to grip an imaginary rope on Team Museum's side.

Mike continues, 'Before we come face to face with the actual body, one more reminder of how we are bringing the past to life.'

A large screen lights up, and for three minutes they watch the magic of Ballybere Man's leathery face morphing into a digital reconstruction. There are slight differences between this interpretation and the sculptured head, but not many. A newly commissioned tune plays over, reminding Carrie of songs that have enabled Ireland to win the Eurovision Song Contest again and again. Hearts are being tugged and Carrie watches rapt faces. Mike was right, she realises, to introduce visitors first to these reconstructions. They will get a sense of a living real man. The music fades and the screen blanks.

Mike resumes, 'That was stunning, don't you agree?' He beams around the room, ringmaster of his circus. 'Now the moment we've all been waiting for. We're delighted that Professor Colm Byrne is here to help unveil Ballybere Man. He, along with Liam Harte, was instrumental in developing the Kingship and Sacrifice exhibition.'

A wave of bodies parts, making way for Fiona, Mike and the government minister to join Professor Byrne at the elaborately covered glass cabinet. Soon her old professor will have his moment. He is at one corner of the cabinet with the others stationed at the other three.

More photos. More filming.

The elaborate drape over the glass display case has its edges neatly folded, like a national flag might cover a casket of a fallen military hero. A thick cord encircles the entire case, secured with a wax seal. Mike loves his dramatic touches. With large dressmaking scissors the minister slices, and the golden silky cord falls to the floor.

'Professor Byrne, will you do the honours with me?' Mike asks.

Carrie angles the professor's wheelchair nearer. He holds out both liver-spotted white hands, shaking fingers seeking to grip his corner of the fabric. 'Wait… Wait…' He looks up. 'Doctor O'Neill. Come!' His quavering voice can still command.

She bends at his side, placing her hands next to his. Together they take a firm grip. At the other end, as the minister and Fiona fold the cloth upward, reaching high, she, the professor and Mike slide the heavy drape towards them.

Bodies press in behind her, everyone wanting to be the first to view. She concentrates on controlling her corner to ensure Professor Byrne isn't swamped by the heavy cloth. Those at Fiona and the minister's end can see first.

Again, a collective gasp, this time louder than elicited by the sculptured bust or the digital reconstruction. Yes, Carrie thinks, you might well react like this. He looks magnificent and I love him to bits.

Then Fiona wails. 'It's gone!'

The minister's brisk tones: 'If this is a joke, Mrs McCormac, it's in extremely bad taste.'

Momentarily Carrie thinks this is a setup, a prearranged jest between these two women who have become adversaries, at loggerheads over who will claim this body.

The cover slides off, and the veil that had been preventing her from seeing is removed.

Gone. Empty. The glass base, without a hint that anything has lain here. Not a thread of red hair.

Her head whips up to see Mike's wide-eyed stare, his slack jaw. 'Oh, bugger me!' His perfect enunciation is loud enough to be picked up by broadcast microphones.

Carrie finds she has slid to the floor, half sitting on the bunched-up cover, a hand gripping Professor Byrne's. Someone pushes down on her shoulder as that person presses forward for a better view. A heavily shod foot treads on her ankle. A high-pitched whining fills her ears. She blinks. Stares.

Still nothing. A vacuum.

Two days earlier, she and the conservators transported Ballybere Man from secure storage at their other site and carefully laid him to rest on this glass base. *Right here.* She was the last person, the *final* person, in their team to touch him. She rearranged a lock of matted hair till it sat just so, then she stood back as specialists moved in with their equipment to lower heavy rectangular glass casing – four sides and top – and secure the cabinet to the base.

Professor Byrne is patting her hand. He is saying something that sounds Latin, something like, 'Credo ut intelligam.'

'What?' she asks, trying to focus, twisting to look at his astonished face.

'Carrie... Carrie? What's going on?' Finn is tugging her to her feet.

'I... I...' She pulls away, pushes aside visitors getting in her way, until she has space to spread her hands on the glass, touch her nose to it and *really* see. Her eyes travel from the top to each corner, then down each side to the base. Tremors ripple through her body.

Fingers clutch her shoulders, and she stumbles back into Rachel and Dan's orbit.

'Carrie. What the hell?' Rachel's eyes pierce hers.

'He's not there!' Stating the obvious, but she needs to say it, needs others to confirm it.

Dan gives a nervous laugh. 'More of those hardcase nutters from the States been visiting?'

Breathing is difficult. She swallows. 'Not possible. High security.'

'Or that lot?' Dan jerks his head to where Councillor Mullen and his cohorts huddle, fingers jabbing as they talk. 'Carrie, do you think they've got the wherewithal to have done the dirty on you?'

Rachel prods him. 'Dan!' But to be fair, he is only trying to lighten the mood.

Carrie's eyes sweep the room. What had been a polite, orderly gathering of guests in best clothes and on best behaviour is rapidly disintegrating. The archbishops are standing hands laced, heads bowed... *Praying?* Do they suppose the body might have evaporated into thin air? Gone to Heaven? Anger rises. There will be a logical explanation, and she will not rest until the culprits are found.

Fiona is back at the microphone, calling for calm but sounding far from serene. 'Let's collect ourselves. We don't know what's going on here... PLEASE! STEP BACK FROM THE GLASS! Don't touch it. There may be fingerprints. Something. I don't know...' Fiona, always so organised and on top of things, is unravelling.

Mike takes over. 'We have an incident. Shocking... Shocking. I assure you this is not some hoax – as if we ever would – and at this moment we are at a loss to explain.' And he does look at a loss. He rakes his fingers through his hair and takes a steadying breath. 'Someone has already notified the Garda, and I assure you we will get to the bottom of this. Ballybere Man will be recovered. Will be returned.'

Carrie walks stiff-legged to where Finn is sitting in a corner hunched over his tablet, furious fingers already filing something for his publication. This story will be on the *Irish Times* internet news within minutes. They share a look.

She brushes aside questions from colleagues who have travelled from aboard. 'Scam!' accusing eyes seem to say. But some of them have visited and viewed the body with her while discussing projects they might collaborate on. They know the body *was* here. It exists. At a persistent tap on her shoulder, she turns to Joe Cassidy's puzzled face.

'Doctor O'Neill, er, Carrie. Is this yer man, Mike Curtis's idea? My wife reminded me that he went for gimmicky arty performance stuff for his gallery exhibition openings. Is this what's going on? Are we supposed to hang around?'

'No, Joe, no. I'm afraid...' She spreads her hands, backing away. Eyes averted, and pulling her jacket tight to her ribs, Carrie makes her way to the bust and looks at it afresh. Blocking out the commotion around her, she gazes on this man she had found and lost. Yes, this reconstructed face has got the expression spot on: *I'm just a dead man. What's all the fuss about?*

'Help me,' she whispers.

?

The only question that applies:
WHAT IS GOING ON?

Has the glass case been raised from the base, and the body slid out? But how? This structure, and the weight of it, is massive.

The Garda are thorough as they investigate while the media carry out their own lines of enquiry, looking to outdo each other.

The tabloid that was the first to splash the Jesus story shouts, OI! GIVE OUR BODY BACK! Other tabloids write in the same vein. They are all having a field day. Speculation is rife.

Wildfire news spreads around the world: mainstream and right-wing media, religious media, social media, academic institutions. All... want... answers.

But no traces of fingerprints are found on the glass cabinet other than those of invited guests and museum staff.

The two security guards working minding the gallery are adamant they did not take unauthorised breaks. They stayed alert. Saw nothing. Were not doped – the very idea! And, definitely, did not sleep! Specialists pore over internal and external CCTV and conclude it has not been tampered with.

A witness – a waitress – reports that Mr Curtis and Mrs McCormac were overheard saying, 'Let's hide him away, till the county council backs down.'

Councillor Mullen's rant at that council meeting is on record: 'We'll bloody well steal him from that lot over there if we have to!'

Garda who arrested the Americans report Ray threatening, 'This thing ain't finished. Ya just wait 'n' see.' But border controls at airports in the Republic and Northern Ireland have no record of arrivals with suspect profiles, and ferries from Spain, France, Scotland, and Wales have been checked.

Might Senator Ryan be involved? 'Maybe,' someone speculates, 'that politician wants Ballybere Man and will stop at nothing to get him to the States.'

The senator denies it, scoffing at such accusations, but is of the opinion that, 'This must be a second resurrection. I am only sorry I didn't get to see the body. That would have been the dream of a lifetime.'

Is the government behind this? The Republic is a modern nation, wanting no part in this throwback to superstitious times. Who better to have contact with undercover agents? Were Mossad involved? The minister quashes such talk, with a firm, 'This is arrant nonsense!' Yet in America especially, talk of the deep state intensifies.

At the Ballybere Seekers camp, believers are filmed praying, standing at their makeshift cross, all of them jubilant. 'This absolutely proves it was Christ.' 'How can you not see that?' 'For sure, a miracle has taken place.' Further miracles are reported, and the camp continues to flourish.

From pulpits around the world, preachers and priests make their points. 'This proves we are not ready, not yet worthy. It is not yet the time for Our Lord to return to earth. He has, once again, risen.'

Another maintains, 'Lucifer has claimed his own, just as I said must happen. The Lord has banished that creature of the dark!' Elsewhere worshippers are filmed sobbing, keening filling the air. Their loss is real. In Kentucky, at Jake Porter's church, the mood is sombre. Two of their own, Nate and Ray, have been led astray and the pastor is bereft. Even the scriptures cannot ease his pain. Is it something he said that fuelled his brother's madness? That is on *his* mind. He weeps and seeks guidance from above.

And more. Much more from religious media and outlets, all with their angles, from cries of unworthiness to 'we told you so's. Highly placed church leaders and theologians weigh in, the Archbishop of Dublin offering, 'I may still be pondering this till the day I die. Truly fascinating.' Within Religious Studies departments at august colleges, professors hurriedly consider new research projects and amend course content.

The state-run media do their best to provide balanced coverage but find it impossible. There was a body. Now there is no body.

A month later, the police have no leads. Two months pass. The media frenzy dies down.

The museum unobtrusively removes promotional banners and their website exhibition booking facility disappears. All material relating to Ballybere Man exhibition goes into storage, 'just for the time being,' Mike Curtis assures his sorrowful staff.

Three months pass. Ballybere Man is not, *yet*, to be found.

Professor Byrne writes to Carrie. She opens the envelope to find a floral notelet – the kind Nan had favoured – allowing enough to be written, but no more. His writing is faint and spidery, as Nan's had been towards the end.

My dear Carrie,

We have all suffered a tremendous shock. I do wonder whether your find would ever have measured up to people's expectations: a tall order from whichever viewpoint. I have turned to my old friend Plato to be my companion in my closing weeks (I am told it will not be longer). He shows us that his old teacher Socrates still has much to offer. One of his supposed sayings, which you must be aware of, is worth repeating. 'True knowledge exists in knowing that you know nothing.' I do recommend these early philosophers to you.

With warmest wishes,

Colm Byrne

P.S. I would appreciate a visit. Soon.

Carrie manages a final meeting with her old professor, and he jests, half in earnest, that before long he expects to find out if the body has ascended.

She continues to function on a day-to-day basis. But through all this she feels herself to be a woman apart, occupying a liminal space between understanding and not understanding, straddling the past and present, finding breath in the gap between dying and living.

She does her best to learn how to rebalance.

35

The Bog

THE BOG, THE DESTROYED LOWER SECTION, IS TO BE rewetted and replanted. It is agreed unanimously with Councillor Mullen, who admits: 'Let's be honest, we never really had the resources to support the ongoing costs associated with a museum. All that security for starters.' Someone drums the table in support while another ventures: 'Should we revert to the shopping centre idea?' Male eyes turn on a woman councillor. She thinks about it for a moment, before saying, 'I enjoy shopping as much as the next woman, but I'd far rather pop over to Limerick.' There is a collective sigh. What has happened, they decide, is a blessing in disguise. While those campers, who called themselves Seekers, have more or less disbanded, it is imagined people will continue to visit what has become a special place. And the council welcomes this. So, a wetland again, and councillors discuss commissioning a *stylish* statue of Ballybere Man. 'All those in favour?' A united reply: 'Aye!'

Ballybere is changing. All those Seekers with different dietary requests have left their mark on the town. The local baker has learnt a thing or two about sourdough. 'Who would've thought?' Joe Cassidy's wife shakes her head in amazement. The caff – café – now possesses a barista coffee machine and has trained the staff. Demand for smoothies with all manner of exotic ingredients has dropped to zero, but fruit and green teas stay on the menu, packets of teabags being cheap and easy to store. Although the younger generation is turning away from tea, builder's tea in particular – the café's widely advertised 'bog-standard' tea remains a favourite: a basic brand teabag dropped in a mug of boiling water resulting in a brick-red beverage that can be topped with milk, and/or sugar. They had the foresight to buy a stack of Ballybere Man mugs from the campsite stall.

The council hires a landscape designer. Cassidy Construction is contracted to dump tons of peat, truckload after truckload, back where the same firm had scraped it away. Joe doesn't grumble. It pays the bills. Over time what had been a levelled surface once again takes on a pleasing rise from the coastal road, leading up to the stone wall with the protected bog beyond. The architectural firm that designed the sure-to-be-a-prizewinner museum is not happy. 'But,' Councillor Mullen shrugs, 'what can you do?'

?

One Saturday in late summer Carrie and Finn visit Ballybere. After lunch at the café, they make their way to sit by the crumbling harbour walls. A small fishing vessel chugs back to shore, screeching gulls circle above. Rachel is due.

In the last months Carrie has struggled and failed to make sense of things. How can a rational person accept that Ballybere Man can simply disappear? Daily she requested police updates from Mike, until he shook his head, sighing, 'Carrie, we must move on.' And the museum did move on. The Keeper's post was advertised and Rachael – Cork Rachael – has been appointed. The archaeologist who applied for Carrie's job has leapfrogged her and will now be her boss. Rachael will take up her post in a month but has visited to say hello. Carrie fixed a professional smile on her face and offered the newly appointed Keeper her best wishes. She found her hand grasped in Rachael's right hand and the other supporting her elbow. Rachael's face leaned in, with words of sympathy, condolence, professional support. Carrie was not ready for this intensity, certainly not ready for someone to sit in Liam's chair. Liam was the Keeper. Her keeper. Mike and Fiona urged her to take time out, and from the far side of the world she was urged by her parents: 'Come home.'

A repetitive tooting announces Rachel's arrival. *Her* Rachel. Carrie is on her feet, greeting her friend as she bounds from a badly parked car.

'Carrie!' Rachel's arms are around her. 'And Finn! How're you doing?'

Hugs. Kisses. Later she and Finn will stay over at Rachel and Dan's place – somehow room will be found – but they have agreed to meet first at Ballybere.

Rachel looks at her. 'When are you off?'

'Next Saturday. Open return.'

'Good woman.' Rachel nods approvingly. 'And good man!'

Finn grins. 'But I'll be back in a month. Carrie's going to give me what she calls a tiki tour, taking in the scenic routes.'

'I'm getting him kitted out with walking boots.' Carrie knuckles Finn's arm. 'And we might go skiing – all the resorts are reporting good snow.' She plans to wash some of the city boy out of her friend.

'Yeah.' A slight flinch in Finn's voice.

She talks some more about what she expects to do in New

Zealand: the friends she wants to introduce Finn to, the rose bush she intends buy to commemorate Nan, to be planted in just the right spot in her parents' garden. 'Peace, it's called, one of her favourites. It's a creamy colour with a lovely scent.'

'I know it.' Rachel nods. 'Good choice.'

'I haven't fixed a date to start work again, but I will be back.'

'Maybe,' Rachel says softly. 'Stay open to what comes next.'

Finn looks away. Carrie knows he is discomfited by the thought of losing her. He's said as much. This was why she said, 'Come too. Spend a few weeks with me.'

'I'd like that,' he said. 'Let's see if I can arrange it.'

And it was arranged. The *Irish Times* management is mindful it isn't only Carrie who has had a tough time. Finn grinned. 'They decided their star reporter has earned a break.'

They sit at the harbour a while longer, then Rachel stands and brushes her hands. 'Come on!'

Carrie and Finn follow Rachel's car. They pass the chippy, the laundrette, the small grocery store to where the town peters out. Ahead she sees a digger, grader and dump truck standing idle. This is the weekend, and Joe's men aren't working.

As they walk around the denuded site, Carrie takes in the changes. Rewetting and replanting the site is a perfect solution and she tries imagining how it might look next time she visits. New contours are shaping the land, rising gently to the nature reservation. She understands water run-off will feed a wildlife pond where the body had been found. A well-known artist has been commissioned to create a bronze statue of Ballybere Man as he might have looked, and the museum will assist by supplying 3D images. There might even be a small café and visitor centre. No one is too sure.

'You know,' Rachel says, 'if people want to contemplate what lies beyond, being in nature is a great way to reflect, don't you think?'

Together they head up the slope, cross the stone stile and walk through the gorse and heathers, the wind picking up the higher they rise. Carrie stoops to pick some springy sphagnum moss, rubbing it between her fingers. This is the stuff that conserved Ballybere Man, allowing him to be found, retrieved and cleaned, allowing her to ponder his origin. Yet she was not able to keep hold of him. No one was. She tosses the moss away.

At the top of the ridge Carrie looks south over the stretch of water towards County Kerry. Turning westward she imagines a sailing boat hugging the Atlantic shore, slowly progressing up the estuary, carrying the honey-embalmed body. Down the slope, somewhere near the parked grader, was the place those long-ago travellers laid their charge to rest in a shallow lake. Then it was different: a liminal place between sea and land, possibly a sacred place between the known and unknown worlds.

And Carrie herself is suspended in a liminal state, not yet accepting there might never be conclusive answers to the questions crowding her mind, not yet settling for uncertainty. It makes her uncomfortable to consider there may be something beyond what can be explained. In the ebb and flow of her life to come she might yet learn to let go of what she thought she possessed, and might learn to embrace not-knowing. *Might.* She is far from that time. This is too fresh. Deep inside herself she hopes that Ballybere Man will be found. Or, failing that, a plausible explanation found.

As if sensing her thoughts, Finn takes one hand, squeezing it gently, and Rachel reaches for the other. 'Give it time, heh?'

She listens to the sounds around her. The trill of a plain brown bird – 'A sedge warbler,' Rachel says – that is clinging to a clump of bracken beginning to lose its summer greenery. Overhead are swallows and swifts – these she knows by sight

– and house martins which Rachel identifies, 'Just passing through for summer.'

Carrie tightens her hold on both friends. Yes, she thinks, we are all just passing through.

So be it.

Author's Note and Acknowledgements

The idea for *The Find* did not stem from my imagination. My partner, Hubert, was ill in bed when he told me a story that was forming in his feverish brain. 'Great idea,' I said, and later brought his laptop to him. From those few paragraphs I germinated the seed, encouraging it to grow.

Early on I decided to make my main character a New Zealander – where I am from. Carrie planted me in the unfamiliar world I set about building.

I knew nothing of bog body science so delved into YouTube films and academic papers. I am indebted to Dr Emma Tollefsen, a real-life bog body specialist, for her advice and assistance. Any scientific errors are my own or deliberately overlooked in favour of keeping the story moving.

I am intrigued by myths and philosophies we create to explain the world and understand our place in it. As a student, studying for an undergraduate degree, I changed universities so I could major in comparative Religious Studies alongside English. Researching for *The Find* took me down some interesting rabbit holes.

The Find is a fiction, and I am sure the National Museum of Ireland has not had to contend with anything of this nature. Thanks to beta readers who provided critical feedback, checked Irish cultural and dialogue authenticity, assured me my story would not offend religious believers. Thanks to Vivienne Hamblin and Jane Scroxton, trusted 'go-to' friendly early readers. Fellow writers Gavin Tangen and Patrick ten Brink. Liam Conroy, Teresa McElroy, June Gould, Luther Kwisthout. Thanks to Lynne Patrick for her light-touch line editing. And finally, thanks to my number-one fan, Hubert Kwisthout, for his enthusiasm in sharing research, many suggestions, reading and responding to multiple drafts. We've both enjoyed considering 'what if…?'

Anna M Holmes

www.annamholmes.com

WAYWARD VOYAGE

Anna M Holmes

Historical Fiction. The Golden Age of Piracy is a period when frontiers are being explored and boundaries pushed. **Wayward Voyage**, following Anne Bonny's journey into piracy, creates a vivid and gritty picture of colonial life in the Americas and at sea.

*

Anna is a natural storyteller and a gifted writer with colourful language that makes the reader so absorbed that they feel they are part of the adventure. The Bahamas Historical Society

Holmes's depiction of the rough lingo and harsh conditions on tall ships at sea and dimly lit establishments ashore demonstrates both historical fidelity and rich imagination. A Woman's Write

Both at sea and on land, the reality and precariousness of life, whether pirate or reformed character, are wonderfully captured and brought to life. Historical Fiction with Spirit, blogger

Intense and powerful, it is a description of life and death at the extremes. Holmes has recreated a world of uncertainty and danger, excitement and adventure. Northern Reader, blogger

I recommend it to fans of adventure stories, and to those who like female historical characters who break the mould of their time period. Historical Novel Society

BLIND EYE

Anna M Holmes

Environmental Thriller. Set in the Indonesian rainforest, **Blind Eye** explores moral predicaments and choices. Will Ben Fletcher, a pragmatic economist, open his eyes to what others turn away from?

*

A compelling environmental thriller that underscores the challenge of combating environmental degradation in the face of powerful interests. Lord Jonny Oates, Liberal Democrat Lords Spokesperson on Energy and Climate Change

If the end result of reading this book is not just an enjoyable ride through some thrilling pages but also beginning to open our eyes a little wider, then we can be grateful for this story on multiple levels. Scintilla, blogger

I have found it difficult to put this one down... I love a thriller and this one is unlike anything I've come across before. Little Miss Book Lover, blogger

This action-driven suspenseful novel is a great start for anyone curious about such topics but also keen on well-written stories. Wildwritinglife, blogger

Bold and interesting, this is quite a read! Varietats, blogger